Cold Sacrifice

Waltham Forest Public Libraries

Cold Sacrifice

The First DS Ian Peterson Murder Investigation

Leigh Russell

W F HOWES LTD

This large print edition published in 2014 by
W F Howes Ltd
Unit 4, Rearsby Business Park, Gaddesby Lane,
Rearsby, Leicester LE7 4YH

1 3 5 7 9 10 8 6 4 2

First published in the United Kingdom in 2013
by No Exit Press

A CIP catalogue record for this book is available
from the British Library

ISBN 978 1 47126 740 6

Typeset by Palimpsest Book Production Limited,
Falkirk, Stirlingshire
Printed and bound by
www.printondemand-worldwide.com of Peterborough, England

Dedicated to
Michael, Jo, Phillipa and Phil

GLOSSARY OF ACRONYMS

DCI   – Detective Chief Inspector (senior officer on case)

DI   – Detective Inspector

DS   – Detective Sergeant

SOCO – Scene of Crime Officer (collects forensic evidence at scene)

PM   – Post Mortem or Autopsy (examination of dead body to establish cause of death)

CCTV – Closed Circuit Television (security cameras)

CHAPTER 1

A flash of moonlight touched her hair with silver as she scurried along the street into town. It wasn't safe to go back yet. She had to allow time for his temper to subside. Another half hour should do it. After walking fast for about fifteen minutes, she was more than a mile from home. The night air was chilly on her face, the side streets peaceful. There was no one around to see that she had been crying. Once, she thought she heard footsteps behind her. Fearful he had followed her she looked round, but the street was deserted. Shoving her hands into the pockets of her woolly jacket, she hurried on.

'What are you saying?' he had asked, so softly she had failed to notice the warning signs.

Too late, she had registered the heightened colour of his face. Apologies were no use once rage took hold of him. She had stared, mesmerised by the spittle on his lips as he shouted obscenities at her.

'It's only a hoover,' she had whispered when he quietened down. 'We can get another one—'

As soon as the words left her mouth she had

realised her mistake, but his anger made her panic so she couldn't think clearly.

'Only a hoover? So I'll just go and buy another one, shall I?' He had leaned forward until he was so close she could feel the soft spray of his saliva on her face. 'Do you think we're made of money?'

'No. No.'

This had nothing to do with money.

It was pointless to protest once he lost control like that. All she could do was protect herself until she was able to escape. Reaching the deserted Memorial Park she stumbled along the path towards the pond. In the darkness she found a bench, and sat down facing the water. It was still February, too cold to stay there for long. She was about to stand up when something struck her on the back of her head. Soundlessly she slumped forward and keeled over sideways on the hard seat. For a moment she lay quite still, stunned. Whimpering quietly she twisted her head round until she was looking straight up, blinking, struggling to make sense of her situation. She remembered her husband's fury, his eyes bulging with the effort of shouting at her. Now she was lying on a hard surface in darkness with a pounding headache, and the sour taste of vomit in her throat. She had no idea where she was.

In the darkness a blurred moon hovered far away, while close up a face shifted in and out of focus. Her terror slipped away.

'Thank God you've come.'

She reached out to touch him, but his features dissolved like a reflection in water.

'Help me.'

As he raised his arm, moonlight glittered on the blade he was clutching.

CHAPTER 2

Ian Peterson tidied up his desk, checked the time, and set off for the car park at a trot. He had hoped that Bev would be more relaxed about his work relationships now they were married, but two months had passed since the wedding and she had become, if anything, more carping and suspicious than before. If he was home late, she was bound to kick off. It was driving him nuts. A detective sergeant in his mid-thirties, successful in a career he loved, he was reduced to an apologetic coward by one sharp word from his wife. They had been together, on and off, since they had met at school. He hadn't been alone in his infatuation. All the boys in his year had fancied her. His teenage crush had developed into a serious attachment when they started dating. After they left school he had driven long distances to spend time with her whenever he could. It was thanks to his determination that they had stayed together.

The first time he had asked her to live with him, Bev had refused outright to move away from Kent.

'All my family are here, and my friends. And there's my job. I know you think your work is so important, but I happen to value my job too.'

When he had joined the Kent constabulary and she had finally agreed to move in with him, he had been blissfully happy. For a few years they had lived together harmoniously but somehow, since the wedding, Bev had changed. She complained more and more about the long hours he worked.

'You knew about my job when you agreed to marry me,' he had protested more than once. 'Working on murder investigations isn't a nine-to-five job. If I'm on a case, I can't drop everything just because you're expecting me home.'

'So I'm supposed to wait here by myself while you hang around in the pub until all hours—'

'What are you talking about? When I'm not here, I'm working. Whatever gave you the idea I was out drinking to all hours?'

'I don't know *what* you're doing. You don't tell me anything. I never know where you are, or who you're with, do I?'

'Don't be stupid.'

'So now I'm stupid.'

It baffled Ian that someone as beautiful as Bev could be so insecure. He did his best to reassure her, but it was wearing.

'You know I love you.'

'So you say.'

'I married you, didn't I?'

'Well, thanks for doing me a favour. How kind of you, taking pity on me—'

'Now you're being ridiculous.'

'So I'm ridiculous as well as stupid.'

He just couldn't win. Sometimes he wondered if he'd made a mistake. 'Marry the girl,' his father had advised him. It had worked well for the previous generation, but the world had been a different place when his parents were young. He had hoped to encounter a security like his parents enjoyed in marriage, but now he wondered if Bev would ever really feel settled with him. Looking back, he wondered if they had ever been happy, after the initial excitement of the relationship had worn off. He felt as though he had always been hanging on, waiting for the good times to come.

Before the wedding they had lived about two miles away from the police station. Bev had insisted on moving. The property they were buying was a stretch, even on their joint salaries, although the area was certainly pleasant.

'I want to feel safe coming home after dark on my own,' she had told him. 'It's not as if you're always around in the evenings. I never know when you're going to be called away unexpectedly, and I can't rely on knowing when you'll be home. You know I don't like being on my own in the house at night.'

Ian had caved in, even though the move meant he spent at least an hour a day driving in to work and back.

This evening the traffic was light and he was home relatively early. Even so, Bev's car was already in the drive and lights were on in the house. He hoped she would be in a good mood with him. Constantly worrying about his wife's moods wasn't how he had envisaged married life. Sometimes he arrived home to find her in tears, for no apparent reason. He tried to find out if she was depressed or just unhappy. Either way, he was prepared to do anything in his power to help her, but she clammed up when he asked her about it. He hated the fact that she wouldn't confide in him, but he couldn't force her to talk. When he pressed her, she would snap at him.

'You're not at work now. I'm not one of your suspects.'

Steeling himself, he went inside and found her busy in the kitchen. Her short blonde hair looked shiny and neat, and she was wearing make-up. She turned to him with a welcoming smile. With a pang, he recalled how loving she had been in the early days in their relationship. Always an optimist, he dared to hope they had come through a rocky patch. Moving house and organising a wedding, not to mention making a lifelong commitment to another person, was bound to be stressful. She had probably needed time to adjust to her new life as the wife of a detective.

'Dinner's nearly ready,' she smiled.

'It smells great,' he said, wary of upsetting her. 'You look tired.'

'I'm knackered.'

'Go and sit down and I'll pour you a drink. There's some beers in the fridge.'

Ian went into the lounge and pulled off his tie. He leaned back in an armchair, stretched out his long legs, and ran a hand over his light brown hair in an attempt to smooth it down.

When they had finished eating, Bev came and sat beside him on the sofa to finish her glass of wine before clearing up in the kitchen. She often complained that he never talked to her about his work, so he decided to try and explain his passion for his job, although he hardly understood it himself.

'I've never told anyone this before, but when I was a kid I wanted to be Superman.'

'You wanted to be Superman?' she repeated, laughing, 'so you could fly around in a cape with your underpants over your trousers?'

'No. I'm being serious. He was my hero because he was always fighting injustice, and that's what I wanted to do. What I still want to do. I know one person can't really make a difference, but there are so many wrongs in the world, I just feel I have to do what I can.'

He didn't go on to say he had dedicated his life to the pursuit of justice, for fear she would sulk. She would have liked him to dedicate his life to her alone.

Instead, he launched into a description of his new detective inspector. Tall, thin and grey-haired, Rob Wellbeck looked older than his forty years.

'He acts it too. I mean, he's a decent enough bloke, but he's so serious, all the time. If he's got a sense of humour, he hides it up his arse crack when he comes into work. I know you think I'm obsessed with my job but he's far worse than me, honestly.'

Bev chuckled, but there was an edge to her voice. 'Worse than you? You're pulling my leg! Please tell me he's not married.'

'He is.'

'His poor wife!'

Uneasily, Ian joined in her laughter.

CHAPTER 3

The front door slammed behind him and Mark ran into the living room. His long dark fringe flopped over eyes that flicked rapidly round the room. His father was lying stretched out on the sofa.

'Where's mum?'

His father merely grunted without raising his head.

The young man dropped his jacket on the floor and flung himself down on an armchair. Long and loose-limbed, he took after his father. The chair was well padded, with a matching footstool, but he fidgeted uncomfortably.

'What are you watching?'

Henry stared at the television without answering.

'What did you have for supper?'

Mark glared at his father sprawled along the length of the sofa, eyes fixed on the screen. He paid no attention to his son's petulant expression, if he even noticed it.

'Dad, where's mum?'

'I don't know.'

★　★　★

Mark scowled at the screen. Holding onto the remote control, his father was watching a gardening programme he had recorded earlier in the week. It was too much hassle to try and persuade him to change channel. Mark was stuck watching some dreary old bloke drivelling on about compost. It was so unfair. He was eighteen. It wasn't as though his parents didn't have enough money to help him to buy a place of his own. His father might not earn very much, but his mother was a seriously wealthy woman. Yet however much Mark had nagged her to cough up for a deposit, she had flatly refused.

'Why would you want to go and live all by yourself? You're only just out of school. You might want to go to university next year—'

'I'm not going to university. I'll get a job – when I have my own bills to pay. There's no point in my hanging around, living here with you forever.'

'Well, you're too young to live on your own, and in any case, the house is big enough for us all.'

'Far too big. What do you need such a massive house for? You could sell it and have enough to get yourselves a really nice modern place.' And have enough money left over to buy him a flat of his own.

'Are you hungry?' he asked.

His father didn't stir. He looked half asleep. Mark swore under his breath. He knew perfectly well what had happened. He couldn't help overhearing their constant arguments. It was just one of the reasons he was so desperate to get a place of his own. They were at it all the time, his father yelling, his mother crying. Afterwards he would see his mother creeping around the house, her head turned to one side in a pointless attempt to hide her inflamed red eyes. Over the years he had become hardened to the sounds of their fighting, and the frustration of being powerless to intervene. Although his father was the aggressor, his mother wasn't blameless. In its own way her passivity was provocative. There were times when he wanted to slap some sense into her himself. He had given up trying to understand why she put up with it.

When he was thirteen he had challenged her about it.

'Why don't you stand up to him?' he had demanded.

At first she had pretended not to understand what he meant. It was impossible to believe she was stupid enough to think he didn't know what was happening right under his nose.

'You don't have to put on a show with me. I know dad shouts at you all the time.'

'What are you talking about? That's a wicked thing to say. Your father is a kind and considerate man, and you should treat him with more respect.'

'For God's sake, mum, the whole bloody street can hear him.'

If he hadn't felt so sad about it he would have

been tempted to laugh at her for defending his father's tantrums. It was ridiculous.

'He doesn't mean to upset anyone,' she had insisted. 'You don't understand. He can't help himself. Now, I don't want to talk about it again.'

In spite of her rebuff, he had tried again a couple of weeks later, in the aftermath of another fight. He not only came up against the same blank refusal to acknowledge the truth, but this time she had been angry with him which was grossly unfair. He had only wanted to help her. She had threatened to send him to his room if he brought the subject up again, and something inside him had just given up. He wondered if she actually liked being abused. After that he had resolved to ignore it when his father raised his voice against her – and sometimes his hand. If his mother was prepared to put up with it, then it served her right. There was nothing Mark could do about it however desperate he was to help her. He had tried.

He hadn't raised the subject again until he was seventeen, when he had asked her directly why she didn't leave his father.

'Leave him?' she had repeated, as though he had been speaking to her in a foreign language. 'He's my husband.'

'He'll kill you if you let him carry on treating you the way he does.'

'Don't speak to me like that.'

13

'But you can't be happy with him. Why don't you get a divorce? You've certainly got grounds—'

She had been genuinely shocked.

'Just because I don't go to church regularly doesn't mean I don't know right from wrong.'

When he was small, he used to accompany her to church every week. Confession had been important to her, but he hadn't minded when his father had arbitrarily put a stop to the weekly outing.

'No son of mine is going to be indoctrinated with all that claptrap.'

And that was that. She hadn't protested, even though he had heard her crying a lot. That was when he had begun to despise her, although he felt sorry for her at the same time. As a child he had found it very confusing. Now he was eighteen, and an adult, he still couldn't understand why she stayed with his father.

It was growing late and his mother still hadn't come home. His father was glued to another anodyne television programme.

'Where did mum go?'

No answer.

'When's she coming home?'

'How the hell should I know?'

Mark was starving. He couldn't go all night without anything to eat.

'I'm going out to get something before the take-away closes,' he announced, leaping to his feet. 'Do you want anything?'

Half an hour later he was back home, scoffing sausage and chips in front of the television with his father.

'I said no vinegar,' Henry grumbled.

Mark took no notice. Instead he asked again where his mother was.

'Do you think she's all right?'

'What?'

'Do you think something's happened to her?'

'Stop yapping, will you? I'm trying to listen.'

'But—'

'She'll come home when she's ready. Now shut up about your bloody mother, will you, I'm trying to listen to the news.'

CHAPTER 4

When Ben's mother sent him out for chips, it placed him in a quandary. He could make up an excuse to get out of it, only then she might drop the idea altogether. If she decided to go out herself, she was unlikely to bring anything back for him, and he was starving. But it was risky, going out alone in the dark. He might be mugged before he even reached the chippy, if he was spotted by a gang from one of the other blocks of flats. Then he would have to tell his mother he'd lost the money and Eddy would thrash him.

'Do you think we're made of money, you little shit?' Eddy would shout as he thumped him.

Eddy's readiness with his fists was just one of many reasons why Ben hated him. His mother had been off her trolley when she had agreed to let him move in. As soon as Ben was sixteen, he was out of there. He was going to make a life for himself, and he would never see either of them again. Meanwhile, his mother was standing in front of him holding out a fiver. He took it.

★　★　★

16

More often than not he was lucky and didn't see the other kids. When they were hanging around the estate, he could still get away if he kept his ears and eyes open. He had given up trying to fight back. He was wiry and light, and his fists were quick, but there was no weight behind his punches. Besides, there were three of them, sometimes four, and they were older than him. Once they set on him there was nothing to do but protect himself as best he could, and run like hell at the first opportunity. This evening, he made it to the chip shop without any bother and was soon on his way home, clutching a hot newspaper parcel. He swore and yanked up his hood as a fine rain began to fall. He considered making a dash for it but preferred to take his time. That way he could stuff himself with more than his fair share on the way. Steam from the chips mixed with a sharp smell of vinegar as he fumbled inside the newspaper.

With his hood up, rustling the paper and munching, he didn't hear them coming. The first he knew of their arrival was when one of them snatched at his chips. Desperately he grabbed for the package which landed on the ground with a soft thud. A few chips spilled out over the glistening pavement. Dismay at losing his dinner was overshadowed by fear of what Eddy would do. He could feel his muscles tensing at the prospect. But the immediate problem was right in his face. A gang that had mugged him before was blocking his way, taunting him and elbowing one another in their eagerness to terrorise him. The ringleader demanded he hand over his money.

Avoiding looking directly at them, he tried to keep his voice steady as he explained that he didn't have any cash on him, only chips. He pointed to the newspaper packet at his feet.

'That's all I got. My mum only gave me a fiver. I haven't got any more.'

He hated himself for sounding as though he was going to cry.

'My mummy gave it to me,' one of them sneered and the other three laughed.

A boy stooped down and picked up the packet. In the dim light from the street lamp his mates gathered round, shoving and grasping. Ben seized his chance and fled. He turned off the road along a path between a car showroom and forecourt. With any luck his tormentors would be content to stuff themselves, and wouldn't bother pursuing him.

Heart thumping, he dashed across the road and into the park where he crouched down behind a low hedge, listening. There was no sound of footsteps or voices in pursuit. They had lost interest in him. Warily he straightened up, eyes straining to see through the thick darkness of the night. It was almost pitch black in the park, only the faint glow from the moon falling on trees and grass. He shivered, alone in the cold, wondering whether he should make his way home and own up to Eddy that he'd been mugged. He wished he had let the gang rough him up a bit. That way, Eddy might have left him alone. The other kids liked to kick out a bit, but with Eddy the beating was systematic while his mother just looked away, stony faced, probably relieved she wasn't on the receiving end of Eddy's fists. He was sorry he had taken her money in the first place. He had only managed to scoff a couple of the chips before they had been knocked out of his hand, and he had lost his appetite now anyway. He would have been better off staying at home, waiting for the hunger to pass.

Right now he was in no hurry to leave the safety of his hiding place. No one would notice if he didn't go home until the morning, by which time his mother would have forgotten all about her rotten chips. Meanwhile, the gang hadn't followed him round the block. He decided to make himself comfortable and stay there for a while. Sitting down on the soft earth he leaned back against the trunk of a tree which afforded him some shelter from the rain, pulled his knees up to his chin, and waited. When he was sure he had been there long enough for the other kids to have moved on, he scrambled to his feet. Standing upright, he stretched and yawned. He ought to go home but he was starving again. There had been several portions of chips wrapped in the newspaper he'd dropped. There was a slim chance the gang hadn't found them all. Instead of going the long way round the block back home, he retraced his footsteps warily to see if they had left any of the packets lying on the ground. Cold soggy chips would be better than nothing.

Trotting back to the road, he listened out and glanced around every few steps to make sure he was alone. There was no sign of the other kids, and no newspaper parcel lying on the pavement. At last his vigilance was rewarded when he caught sight of something lying in the kerb. He scrambled over to it, but his groping fingers didn't close on squishy greasy paper. Instead he felt something cold and hard. He dropped it in surprise. As he stood up, his foot kicked the object that had clattered onto the pavement in front of him. He stooped to pick it up, weighing it in his hand, and a grin spread slowly across his face. With a quick glance around, he squatted down once more. Paying no attention to the rain that was now falling heavily, he admired the knife. It had a chunky black handle, and the blade was bent as though it had been bashed out of shape. He wiped the dirty blade on his jeans before slipping it inside his T-shirt where he could feel it jolting against his body as he strode away. If the gang came after him now, he was ready. He almost hoped they would come round the corner and try to mug him. They wouldn't know what had hit them.

CHAPTER 5

Ian switched the television on, while Bev clattered about in the kitchen clearing up. Comfortably full after a good dinner, he felt a surge of optimism about the future.

'Have you had a good day?' he asked her, muting the television when she came into the lounge.

She launched into a litany of irritations she had endured that day in her job at a recruitment agency. Ian half-listened, nodding and mumbling at appropriate intervals.

'He knows I'm only supposed to work till five, but he kept me there until nearly half past.'

'What a cheek.'

'It's not as if it was urgent. It could easily have waited until tomorrow, but he had it in his head that he wanted the letters to go out today, and he didn't even ask if that was all right. I had better things to do with my time. Do you think I should refuse to work after five if it happens again? Or shall I ask if I'm getting paid overtime? Ian? Ian?'

Ian must have dozed off because he woke to the sound of his wife bleating his name.

21

'I'm not sure –' he equivocated. 'What do *you* think?'

Bev resumed her tirade, unaware that he had lost the thread of her rant. Reprieved, he sat forward and paid careful attention as she carried on.

'The thing is, if I ask about overtime and he refuses, I'm no worse off, am I? And either way, it makes the point, doesn't it?'

'Yes, it does.'

'But if I carry on doing the extra hours without raising it as an issue, he's just going to carry on taking advantage, isn't he?'

'Yes, he probably will.'

'So you think I should ask him?'

'It does no harm to ask, as long as you're diplomatic.'

'Diplomatic?'

'I know he's not the best of bosses, but it's best not to put his back up. You still have to work for him.'

'Do you think I'm tactless, then?'

Ian sighed. He should have known her good mood wouldn't last. Stifling another sigh, he tried to persuade her that she had misinterpreted his comment.

'So this is my fault, is it?'

'What are you talking about? It's nobody's fault. No one's done anything wrong. We're just talking about your boss, that's all. Come here.'

He held out his arms to her and she came and sank down on the sofa beside him.

22

'I'm sorry,' she whispered. 'It's just that you never seem to care about what I do. I know it's only recruitment, and you're out solving your important murders, but we get people into jobs. That matters too.'

He leaned down and kissed her gently on the lips. She put her arms round him as she kissed him back, stroking his neck. Their kiss grew more passionate.

His work phone couldn't have rung at a more frustrating time. Reluctantly he extricated himself from her embrace.

'Sorry, love, I've got to get it.'

'Of course you have.' He tried to ignore the animosity in her tone, but she wouldn't let it drop. 'Don't mind me. Just answer your bloody phone. You know you can't wait to get back to work.'

She jumped up and ran out of the room. He was half out of his seat ready to follow her when the phone started ringing again. Whoever was calling wasn't going to give up until he answered. It must be important.

'Just give me a minute,' he shouted after her. 'I won't be long.'

They both knew that was a lie.

Even though there wasn't much traffic, it took Ian just over half an hour to drive to work. He drew into the car park and ran along the corridor to the Major Incident Room. The rest of the team were already there, waiting for the detective chief inspector. Ian breathed a silent sigh of relief. The detective inspector threw him an icy glare which Ian ignored. He had arrived in time. The briefing hadn't started yet. Detective Constable Polly Mortimer smiled at him.

'You haven't missed anything,' she muttered, as she flicked her dark brown hair back from her face.

Ian nodded gratefully. He wasn't even late. But it had been a close thing.

Seconds later the detective chief inspector strode into the room. Poker-faced, he brought the assembled officers up to speed, speaking in a rapid monotone. Ian had to listen carefully so as not to miss anything. Glancing around, he saw his colleagues all leaning forwards, intent on the senior investigating officer's words. The body of a woman aged mid-to-late fifties had been discovered in a park, stabbed to death.

'There's no question we're dealing with an unlawful killing,' the detective chief inspector concluded. 'So what we need to do now is establish the identity of the victim and nail whoever did this. Any questions?'

'Wasn't there anything on the victim to identify her?' someone asked.

The chief inspector shook his head.

'She had no keys, no purse, nothing on her at all, which suggests it could have been a mugging

24

that went wrong. Scene of crime officers are busy right now, so check with the duty sergeant, and let's get started.'

There was a sudden air of bustle. Everyone knew it was important to gather information promptly, before the trail went cold.

CHAPTER 6

Ian stared morosely at the back of the detective inspector's head as they crossed the car park. Remembering his wife's unfounded suspicions about his relationship with his attractive former detective inspector, he supposed he should be relieved his new inspector was a dour-faced middle-aged man. He wondered what Bev would say if he ended up working with a young female constable, like Polly. She would certainly be a more attractive partner than Rob. It wasn't that Ian fancied her, but he appreciated her cheerful nature and wicked sense of humour.

Rob sat in silence as Ian drove to the site where a woman's body had been discovered earlier that evening. 'Park' was a rather grandiose name for a scrubby area of grass beside a lake. An overgrown copse of trees and reeds grew in unattractive disorder on an artificial island in the centre of the water. Empty bottles and cans floated on the surface of the scummy water, beside which a sign warned the public to: 'Keep children and pets away from the water. The Environment Agency has advised that there may be blue-green algae present'. A white forensic tent stood on the path at the water's edge, another blight on the scene. Even in the fresh night air, the breeze carried a foul stench.

'It stinks here,' Rob muttered, wrinkling his nose, as they pulled on their white protective suits and blue shoes before entering the tent. Ian shivered and wished he had thought to put on a coat before rushing out of the house. He shrugged and turned his attention to the job.

Inside the tent, white-clad scene of crime officers had gathered in a huddle. Between their hunched backs Ian could see a woman lying on a bench. She could have been asleep were it not for a large blood stain on her T-shirt.

'It looks like she was stabbed through the heart,' one of the SOCOs said. 'A doctor's been and gone but he just stopped long enough to certify she's dead. He said there was no point in his hanging around as there'll be an autopsy.'

Ian frowned impatiently. He wished he had been given a chance to speak to the doctor then and there.

'Can we move the body yet?' another SOCO asked. 'The mortuary van's waiting.'

'Give us a minute,' Rob said. 'Was she killed here, do you think?'

'There's no sign she was moved after she was

stabbed, but it's difficult to say with any degree of certainty because there was a heavy downpour earlier on. The path in front of the bench slopes towards the lake, so it's impossible to say how much blood could have been washed into the water.'

'Surely there'll be traces?'

'Yes, we'll find traces but it might not be possible to ascertain how much blood there was. If we find enough evidence to establish she was killed here, all well and good, but it could be inconclusive if we don't.'

Ian shivered again and thrust his hands into the sleeves of his protective suit. Despite the cold, he didn't object to a few moments' delay. Even though they couldn't tell much before seeing a full post mortem report, it was useful to study the body at the site of the murder, to help them build an impression of what had happened there. He tried to focus on the victim. As far as he could tell, the dead woman had been slender and short. Her dark grey hair was streaked with chestnut brown that glimmered in the bright lights. Pulled back off her face, it gave her a severe appearance. Ian guessed her eyes were also brown but they were closed, as though she was sleeping peacefully. She had small neat features, well-proportioned, and must have been quite attractive when she was younger. In death her face looked ghastly, grey and somehow shrunken, as though her cheeks had collapsed

28

inwards. Dressed in muddy white trainers, a navy track suit and white T-shirt drenched in blood, she was wearing a plain gold wedding ring. No other jewellery was visible, not even a watch.

'Have we found a murder weapon?' Rob's voice broke his concentration.

'Not yet,' a SOCO replied. 'We're still looking.'

'Have you come across anything that might point us in the right direction?'

The SOCO shook his head. The body had been reported by a group of teenagers who had gone to the park to 'hang out'. Several officers had queried what the youngsters had been doing, out on the streets so late at night. It was unfortunate there had been eight or nine of them, trampling around the area, destroying or contaminating any potential evidence. In addition, they needed a statement from a man who claimed to have arrived first on the scene, shortly before the gang of kids turned up. It was going to be a long night.

Ian was still staring at the woman.

'Was she lying on her back like that when she was found?' he asked.

'Yes, but she wasn't killed in that position,' a SOCO replied. 'The pattern of blood on her shirt and trousers suggests she was stabbed in the chest while she was in an upright position. It looks as though she was stabbed from directly in front, and then she fell onto her side. You can see the indentations from the bench on her face. She must have been moved onto her back some time after she died.'

'So someone turned her over onto her back after she was dead?' Ian repeated. 'It's quite possible whoever did that wasn't the killer. Do we know for certain those teenagers didn't disturb the body?' He turned to the SOCO. 'Or is it possible someone else turned her over?'

The SOCO shrugged.

'I can't say if someone else came along.'

'But why would they have turned her over and then just left her?' Rob asked.

'To see who she was, or maybe to get at her pockets,' Ian mused aloud. 'She could have been robbed after she was dead, by someone other than the killer.'

'Or maybe her pockets were emptied to stop her being identified,' Rob suggested.

They discussed possible scenarios for a few minutes, but at this stage they could only speculate.

There was nothing else the SOCO team could tell them. After staring helplessly at the dead woman for a few minutes longer, Ian followed the inspector out of the tent. They couldn't walk around the park area, which was being searched for footprints or any other evidence the killer might have left behind. The group of teenagers who had stumbled on the body were standing together just outside the park, under the watchful eye of a female constable. Ian suspected the youngsters might have shifted the dead woman's position in order to comb through her pockets, although they all strenuously denied having gone anywhere near the corpse. Ian and Rob took their details and questioned them briefly on the pavement.

One of the girls shuddered, while another squealed in horror.

'I ain't going nowhere near that old stiff. Catch me!'

'He ain't telling you to go near it, bitch,' one of the boys said. 'The pig wants to know if she was like that before or what.'

'Before what?'

'Before we was there.'

'Well, if we wasn't there, how are we supposed to know what she was like? Them pigs is well thick.'

'That's why they're pigs, innit?'

'Hey, you,' Rob interrupted sternly, 'watch your mouth or you'll be spending the night in a cell.'

'Are you threatening me?' The boy turned to his mates. 'Is he threatening me? That's police harassment, innit? You all heard it.'

No one bothered to answer.

They dismissed the group of teenagers. Now it was time to leave, Ian was unaccountably reluctant to go. He stood by the entrance to the park area, gazing around.

'What are you looking at?' Rob asked.

Ian shook his head. He wasn't looking for anything specific. If there was any evidence to be found, the search team would discover it. He just wanted to get a feel of the place, to give the murder scene some kind of existence in his mind. But although the victim was real enough, it was impossible to visualise her killer without knowing anything more. They didn't even know if she had been stabbed to death by a man or a woman.

'Come on,' Rob said, after Ian had been standing silently observing the sparse grass and withered bushes. 'Let's make a move. See if we can get some sleep tonight. We don't want to be done in before we even get started.'

But the investigation had already started, and so far it wasn't going well.

'An anonymous victim, no sign of the killer, no witnesses, and no murder weapon,' Rob said grimly before he walked off with a constable who was driving him back to the police station.

CHAPTER 7

Rob set off back to the station to write up his report, leaving Ian to question the old man who had been in the park when the teenagers had found the victim. Ian sympathised with the witness. It was difficult enough for Ian to view bodies at a crime scene or in the mortuary with his colleagues, when he knew what to expect. It must be traumatic to see a body without any warning, when you were out by yourself. Ian thought back to the first corpse he had seen, spreadeagled on a table in the morgue. Horribly white, its chest neatly slit open, the body had barely looked human. The clinical approach adopted by his colleagues ought to have made the situation easier for Ian to deal with, but he had struggled to reach the toilet before he threw up. He had managed to get his reactions under control since that first embarrassing incident, and was fairly confident he had succeeded in keeping his nausea a secret from his colleagues. But he had to resign himself to his predicament. He would never feel comfortable in the presence of death, and he came up against it regularly in the course of his work.

The streets around the park area had been cordoned off. The witness was standing just outside the park, beside a uniformed constable. Neither of them was talking. Old and frail, Frank Whittaker's distress was evident. He was unnaturally pale and was smoking feverishly, exhaling out of one side of his mouth to avoid blowing smoke in the constable's face. In his youth Whittaker must have been a hefty bloke, but his frame was bowed, as though aged by a serious illness. He looked up apprehensively when Ian went over and addressed him by name. The cigarette trembled in his hand, and he looked cowed, as though he had been caught out doing something wrong, although there was no reason to suspect he was implicated in the stabbing. Ian reassured Whittaker that he only wanted to ask him a few questions about what he had seen.

Despite his nervous manner, Whittaker's account was straightforward.

'I go out every evening, unless it's really raining hard, and sometimes even then. My wife insists I need to get out of the house more, since I retired. She isn't happy unless I go out for a brisk walk, twice a day, morning and evening. Doctor's orders. But the truth is I don't go as far as she thinks.' He gave an apologetic shrug. 'I only walk as far as the park where I can sit on a bench and have a quiet smoke. The wife doesn't approve, you see. So I have a smoke in peace, she thinks I'm getting my daily exercise, and we're both happy.'

After taking a long drag on his cigarette, he chucked it on the ground, crushing it beneath his shoe.

Although Ian hadn't asked what he was doing there, he seemed to think he ought to account for his presence.

'I come here because it isn't far, and it's usually quiet. There's sometimes kids hanging around but they usually turn up later on. Apart from that there's never anyone here in the evening, and there's a bench to sit on, if it's not wet. So I came here this evening, like I often do, and blow me if there wasn't someone sitting on the bench in the rain. There's never anyone there.' He paused.

'What do you remember next?'

'I remember I was surprised, because I never saw anyone sitting there before, not in the evening. And who would want to sit on a park bench in the rain? So I took a look as I was walking by—'

He hesitated.

Ian looked up from his notebook and saw that the witness was looking down at his hands as he fumbled with his cigarette packet.

'What did you see?'

He waited for him to finish fidgeting with his

lighter. The end of the cigarette made glowing patterns in the night air as Whittaker gesticulated while he spoke.

'I was looking straight at her as I walked past, because, like I said, I was curious. I looked her straight in the eye as I went past. She didn't even blink and I couldn't help noticing she wasn't moving. Then I saw a dark stain on the front of her jacket and went closer to see if she was all right. I think I already knew she was dead, really. She was so still. I mean, it's not natural for a woman not to react in any way when a strange man approaches and stares at her, is it?'

Concerned and curious, he had craned his neck forward for a closer look. As he did so, a cloud had drifted away from the moon, throwing a shaft of light down on the inert figure on the bench. When she didn't respond to his calling out, he had taken a step nearer and tapped her gingerly on the shoulder. Still she didn't react. As he dithered, he had heard voices and shouts of laughter from a gang of teenagers loitering nearby. There was no way back to the street without risk of being spotted, so he hid behind a tree trunk and waited for an opportunity to get away.

'Why did you hide?'

'I was scared of being mugged. And seeing that dead woman had me all shook up.'

He had little else to tell. The kids had started jeering at the woman on the bench, then one of the girls started screaming and that set them all off. Next thing Whittaker knew, they were all on their phones, summoning the police.

'Why didn't you call us?'

'I haven't got my phone on me. Don't tell my wife, will you? She'll kill me if she knows I've come out without it.'

CHAPTER 8

From the outside it was a perfectly normal detached house in Canterbury Road, an ordinary residential street. Even now, when he opened the gate, he felt a tremor of apprehension in case he had come to the wrong address. It was hard to believe that behind its closed curtains this place was sacred. The property was reasonably well maintained, although behind a tall hedge the garden had been left to run wild. Grasses and brambles grew to waist height with here and there a flowering weed providing a bright splash of colour against an urban wilderness of foliage. The path, cracked and uneven, was barely visible between the encroaching plants. He approached the front door with a familiar sense of awe, knocked three times, paused, then knocked again. It was opened by a tall man dressed in black who gazed at him with a stern expression.

'What do you want?'

'I've come to see the leader.'

'Everyone wants to see the leader.'

★   ★   ★

As the door swung closed behind them, a girl came running down the stairs. She had long fair hair and looked very young.

'What do you want?' she asked in her turn.

'I've come to see the leader.'

'Everyone wants to see the leader.'

He had hoped to be taken to the leader straight away, but he wasn't going to complain about being greeted by a female disciple. It was better than waiting alone. Without a word he followed the girl upstairs to a small bedroom where she slipped out of her robe and welcomed him to the house. The bed was narrow and had a musty smell but the girl was sweetly perfumed and lithe.

When she was getting dressed again, he repeated his request to see the leader.

'Everyone wants to see the leader,' she replied with a dreamy smile.

'You don't understand,' he protested. 'I've waited long enough. Tell him I've earned the right to see him. I've done what he asked.'

'Wait here.'

The girl skipped away leaving him to pace impatiently up and down the narrow space between the small bed and a grey plastic chair in what was more of a box room than a bedroom. The walls were bare, apart from a picture of the leader who stared down at him with huge dark eyes. His skin looked white in the picture, but there was nothing weak about his expression. He remembered the first time he had met the leader in the street, apparently by accident. Since then he had studied the leader's teachings and knew that nothing happened by chance.

After a long time, the girl returned. Smiling, she held out a white robe identical to her own.

'Put this on. The leader will see you now.'

He stood up, experiencing an unexpected flicker of fear. Everything had seemed so clear the last time the leader had spoken to him. Having sent the other disciples away, the leader had put his request very simply.

'All the gods ask of you is one simple act of devotion, one small sacrifice to prove you are worthy to accompany us on our journey into the light of salvation.'

It hadn't sounded like a small sacrifice. Shocked, he had dared to challenge the leader.

'Why her, of all people?'

'You know the answer to that,' the leader had answered gently, 'just as you know what you must do.'

Now that he was going to see him again, all at once he wasn't sure he had understood the leader's intentions correctly. He pulled the robe over his head. The fabric that appeared to fall in soft folds on the other disciples felt rough against his skin.

'I'm ready,' he croaked.

He was speaking as much for himself as for her,

but the girl was already walking away. He followed her slim figure back down the stairs and into a room off the hall where more white-robed disciples sat facing each other in two rows. On a dais at the far end of the room sat the leader himself, gazing down the rows towards the newcomer.

'You are welcome.'

The voice rang out, seeming to echo inside his head as the leader addressed him directly. He nodded, too overcome with emotion to speak. He was in the inner sanctuary. Nothing else mattered.

'Look at this man,' the leader told the others. 'Look at him carefully.'

Ten pairs of eyes turned to stare at him. He stood quite still, unable to drag his eyes away from the leader's face.

'This man wishes to join us,' the leader said, staring at him as though reading his thoughts. 'He wants to become a disciple. He is willing to make the supreme sacrifice and dedicate his life to our cause.'

Embarrassed, he wanted to explain that it wouldn't be much of a sacrifice really. His life wasn't that great. While he wondered whether he dared speak, the leader handed each of them a small portion of ambrosia, food of the gods. As if by magic, a silver goblet appeared in the leader's outstretched hand.

'Drink from the cup of salvation,' he intoned.

'Drink from the cup of salvation,' the disciples chanted in chorus.

'He is welcome here,' the leader said softly.

He thought he would faint with joy as he gazed into the leader's hypnotic eyes. The room seemed to spin until all he could see were those huge dark eyes, gazing into his mind.

'I have done what you asked.'

'Approach.' The leader smiled at him. 'We will call you Warrior.'

'Thank you,' he stammered.

His legs crumpled beneath him and he collapsed on the floor at the leader's feet.

Two disciples lifted him into a chair. The leader stared at him, his eyes glowing with kindness.

'Is anything troubling you?'

Warrior hesitated.

'Tell me what is in your mind,' the leader insisted gently.

'I want to stay here. Let me come and live with you, and be your disciple.'

The leader shook his head, his expression sad.

'You are not yet ready to live among us, but your time will come soon. Don't be afraid. One day you will perform a great service for the cause, and you will never leave us again. Now, tell me, was it done wisely?'

He nodded his head, eager to tell the leader how he had found her sitting on a park bench in the park one evening. The place had been deserted. It had been easy. But the leader raised his hand.

'We will not speak of this again. Come, sit with us until you have to leave.'

At a signal from the leader the disciples sat down.

A few motes of dust floating in the air vanished as he sat among them, relieved that he had passed the test. The room fell silent. All eyes remained fixed on the leader's beatific smile. His silent presence reassured them of the peace that passed all understanding. Nothing ever stirred in that silent room. Time itself was stilled. The disciples sat like statues, their hands folded neatly in their laps. Warrior felt his spirits soothed by their serenity. In the leader's presence all his fears faded away, and he could breathe freely for the first time in years.

The leader broke the silence. His voice was like rippling water, enveloping them in its tranquillity.

'All around us people are engaged in struggle. Here we are at peace.' He had stared directly at Warrior. 'You are a true follower. Your soul has begun its journey to the eternal light. You will be with us for all eternity. Through sacrifice you will attain salvation.'

The other disciples took up the chant, repeating it over and over again.

'Through sacrifice we will attain salvation.'

CHAPTER 9

The following morning, Ian checked to see who else was around that weekend. He hated viewing cadavers in the mortuary. It was worst when he had to go alone. Even the dour presence of his detective inspector offered some distraction from a body, but Rob had been called away to a meeting that morning. Ian's spirits lifted when he discovered that Polly was on duty. He found her in the canteen.

'Late breakfast or early morning break?' he asked as he joined her.

He nodded at her large glass of orange juice and plain buttered toast.

'You look like you've got a hangover. I mean because you're drinking orange juice,' he added quickly, seeing her face twist in exasperation.

'A date at the morgue?' she laughed, when he invited her to accompany him. 'You certainly know how to give a girl a good time.'

He smiled, pleased to see her good mood restored.

'Do you want to come? Or are you busy?'

'Sure I'll come. Why not? Anything's better than being stuck here.'

'Thanks, Polly. Only Rob's tied up and it's good to have someone else to bounce ideas off.'

He didn't tell her how much he would value the diversion of her company. She chatted happily in the car and he hardly thought about the viewing on the way to the mortuary. But as they stepped into the cold hushed building, a familiar dread took hold of him.

He led Polly along the corridor, determined not to show his feelings. It was embarrassing, and pathetic, for a detective working on murder investigations to experience a physical revulsion at the sight of a corpse at an autopsy. He could cope without difficulty at crime scenes – as long as the murder wasn't too gruesome – but seeing a victim carved up on a slab, like the carcass of a cow or a sheep being prepared for the butcher, made him heave. Sometimes he had to dash to the toilet to throw up. He wondered what Polly would think of him if that happened, and told himself fiercely that he would be fine.

'Do you always put on a mask?' she asked him and he nodded.

'It's just as well to be protected,' he replied, aware that he sounded pompous. 'And it helps with the smell.'

The truth was that with the lower part of his face covered, it was easier to conceal his revulsion.

The pathologist was leaning back against a table, chatting to one of his colleagues, mask dangling carelessly from one ear. His relaxed attitude calmed Ian, who was familiar with Dr Millard from previous cases. It was reassuring to know the post mortem was in his reliable hands. The pathologist's nickname at the station, Dr Death, was a good-natured reference to his skeletal physique, an impression heightened by his bald head. But he was friendly and helpful, as well as competent. After an exchange of greetings they stood in silence for a moment, gazing at the body displayed on the table. She looked very small, like a plastic model of a person, so that Ian felt a curious sense of detachment from her. He wondered if this was how other officers always felt when they viewed autopsies, and whether he had finally managed to master his emotional response at the sight of a cadaver.

'This is a woman in her fifties,' Millard began quietly.

Ian was taken aback by an unexpected surge of anger. He wanted to protest that the bundle of skin and bones on the table wasn't a woman at all.

The dead woman's hair had been shaved to expose a nasty bruise on the side of her head where she had fallen, or been hit. Naked, she lay flat on her back, her eyes closed, her face a white mask of displeasure with the ends of her lips curved downwards, and her eyebrows lowered in vexation. Her chest had been cut open but she was otherwise intact.

'We don't have an identity yet,' Millard went on in his low even voice. He could have been chatting about the weather. 'Her clothes are casual but they look quite new, and she seems to have looked after herself. The chances are she had a regular dentist which means we should get a match with dental records before too long, hopefully before the end of the day. Is there anything from your end to tell us who we're looking at?'

Ian shook his head. There had been no reports yet of a missing woman matching the description of the body discovered on a park bench.

'Is it safe to assume the cause of death was the stab wound in her chest?' he asked.

'Yes, death resulted from a stab wound, as you can see.'

'She was attacked from the front?' Ian continued, pressing the pathologist to reveal as much as he could about the nature of the attack.

Millard nodded, his bald pate shining under the bright lights as he lowered his head.

'Yes, although there's no sign of any defence wounds, which is a bit odd given that her killer must have been standing in front of her.'

47

Ian seized on the remark.

'Odd in what way?'

'You'd expect there to be some indication of a struggle, even if he took her by surprise. Yet there's no evidence of any attempt to escape, either before or during the attack.'

'It was night-time, and the park is poorly lit. Presumably she didn't see him coming.'

'She might have known him,' Polly said.

'True.' The pathologist inclined his head. 'It's possible she was caught completely off guard, but even so, she didn't die immediately. Why didn't she react in any way? A scraping of skin or a speck of blood under her finger nails would have made our job so much simpler.' He sighed. 'She hasn't made it easy for us.'

'Talk us through how she died,' Ian said after a brief pause.

'She died within minutes from blood loss and shock.'

The pathologist probed inside the woman's chest with a bony finger. Glancing up, Ian saw that Polly's eyes were glued to Millard's skinny hand. She didn't look at all perturbed.

'It was unfortunate for the victim that the killer managed to drive the blade right between her ribs. It was a lucky hit,' Millard went on.

'What do you mean, lucky?'

'Lucky for the killer, that is. Each rib being wider than the spaces between them, there was more

48

than a fifty per cent chance the blade would have glanced off a bone instead of penetrating directly into the heart. Although we don't yet have an identity for the victim, we can say for certain that she was in her mid-to-late fifties, five foot one in height, and slight. She was brunette, turning grey, and reasonably fit for her age. She had a child by caesarean section,' he pointed to a line that ran across the lower part of her abdomen, 'and she was married, or at least she had been.'

Ian nodded. He had already seen the dead woman's wedding ring. It had been removed, but the indentation was still visible on the ring finger of her left hand.

'What about the attack? Is there anything else you can tell us about that? What about the wound itself?'

'She was stabbed once in the chest with a blade with one sharp cutting edge. The other edge of the blade was blunt. As you can see if you come closer, the wound is sharper at one end than the other. This isn't always obvious, as the blunt edge of the knife often splits the skin, making the laceration resemble a double edged knife wound, but in this instance the nature of the blade is apparent. Look, there's a clear difference between the rounded end and the opposite angle of the wound, which has a sharp point. The blade was at least ten centimetres long, although it's impossible to be exact. The depth of the wound may be longer than the length of the knife due to indentation caused by the impact of a forceful thrust with the knife. The measurement of the long axis of the wound, from angle to angle, is seven centimetres, four millimetres wide. That gives us the width of the blade at its widest as possibly five centimetres, tapered from tip to hilt, the exact angle of the taper impossible to ascertain. The blade wasn't serrated.'

They gazed at the body for a minute.

'What can you tell us about the nature of the attack?' Ian persisted.

'It's difficult to say anything with absolute certainty.'

'OK, but off the record, what's your impression? Would it take considerable strength to inflict a wound this severe?'

'Not necessarily. There are so many other factors that might influence the outcome. Remarkably little force is required to produce a deep wound like this, especially if the stabbing action is fast. The important determinant is the sharpness of the blade. This kind of wound can be produced with minimal force. But markings on the skin around the entry site, which indicate the knife had a handle, suggest the wound was made with some force to bruise the skin like that, so the blade might not have been razor sharp. In fact, assuming I'm correct about the cause of the bruising, this was a forceful penetration effected with considerable violence. And there's something else that will interest you. The blade of the knife was misshapen.'

'What do you mean?'

'The wound track wasn't absolutely straight which means the blade had been bent before this attack took place.'

Ian considered the wound more closely, interested in spite of his revulsion.

'Can you make any estimate about the height of the attacker, from the direction of the stabbing?'

'Not really, I'm afraid. The victim of a stabbing like this is rarely static. The knife entered the upper part of the left side of the chest and travelled downwards but that doesn't necessarily mean the killer was taller than the victim who may have been crouching, or in this instance probably seated. Examination of the skin wound, and the direction the blade took through the deep tissues, is no more than an indication of the direction of the blade relative to the body. You're asking me to make a judgement about the height and strength of the killer but to draw any such conclusions from the evidence here would be no more than speculation. I wouldn't want to hazard a guess.'

Millard had provided quite a lot of information about the actual knife wound, but nothing about the killer. Having learned what he could, Ian was pleased to leave the mortuary.

'I ought to like him, but he gives me the creeps,' he said.

'I know,' Polly agreed, misunderstanding what he meant. 'He's so skinny. It can't be healthy.'

CHAPTER 10

Later that morning they learned that the dental records of the victim had provided a definite match. The detective chief inspector called the team together to make sure everyone was up to speed with the information. The dead woman's name was Martha Martin. She was a fifty-three year old former nurse who had been married to Henry Martin for thirty-two years. She had given up her career when they had married. Her husband, who was now fifty-nine, worked as a washing machine installer for a local branch of a nationwide chain that supplied white goods and other domestic electrical equipment. They lived in Herne Bay with their only son. Rob and Ian set off to deliver the news to Martha's husband – possibly her killer.

As they drove to Herne Bay, Rob speculated about why the victim hadn't been reported missing.

'It's nearly twenty-four hours since she was killed. Doesn't it strike you as odd that the alarm wasn't raised?'

'Perhaps her husband thought she'd gone away

somewhere,' Ian suggested. 'It only happened last night.'

He wondered what he would do if Bev didn't come home one night. If he was on a case, the chances were he'd be so tired by the time he arrived home he would go to bed assuming she had gone out for the evening. Fast asleep, he wouldn't even realise that she hadn't come home. In the morning, he would be surprised to discover she had gone out early without leaving a message. He would suppose she had told him she would be going out, and he had forgotten about it. Only when she failed to come home for the second night would he actually start to worry.

'Without a handbag?' Rob persisted. 'I thought women never went anywhere without their hand-bags? I know my wife doesn't.'

'But remember, she had no money, phone or keys with her. It doesn't mean she went out without them. Who goes out without a key at least?'

'True. She must have lost them, bag or no bag, or, given that she was stabbed, it's more likely she was mugged.'

Rob sat back and lapsed into his customary silence. Ian didn't mind. He had problems of his own to think about. Bev had been furious about his call-out the previous evening.

'You'd better not be home late again tomorrow,' she had warned him as he left. 'You know I hate being left alone in the house at night.'

54

He had promised to be back as soon as he could. It was a vain promise because his time wasn't his own once he was assigned to a case. His thoughts were constantly with the victims, puzzling over what had happened to them. He had been home before two the previous night only because he had driven like a maniac, cursing himself for agreeing to live so far from the station. He might as well not have bothered speeding because Bev had been asleep when he raced upstairs. She had still been asleep when he left home that morning. He had hesitated over whether to wake her up but had decided against it. There was no time for another row.

Henry Martin lived near the coast in a corner property on Beltinge Road, a street of large detached houses. Some had been divided into flats, while a few had been converted into nursing homes for the elderly. With cars parked on both sides, the road was still wide enough for two vehicles to pass. The detectives exchanged a grim look as Rob reached out and rang the bell. From the other side of the door they heard a faint clanging before the door was flung open by a middle-aged man. Tall and sturdy, white hair neatly combed above an unlined face, he carried himself with an air of confidence.

'Henry Martin?' Rob enquired.

'What of it? Who wants to know?'

If he had dyed his hair, he could have been

mistaken for a man twenty years younger than his actual age. Ian knew it was important not to be swayed by personal feelings, but the man's antagonistic tone put his back up straight away.

Rob introduced himself and his colleague, displaying his warrant card as he spoke. Ian wished the inspector would address members of the public in the same brisk tone he adopted with colleagues, but there was nothing he could say. Rob was his superior officer, and in any case he could hardly accuse the inspector to his face of sounding like a dodgy salesman with his oily, patronising tone of voice.

'What are you after?' Henry asked.

He made no move to invite them in. His eyes narrowed with unwarranted hostility. With a flash of irritation, Ian was tempted to ask the man if he had lost anything recently, 'like your wife?' But he kept quiet and let Rob ask the questions.

'Your wife's name is Martha Martin?'

'What of it?' Henry craned his head forward, suddenly alert. 'Has something happened? Has she been kicking up a fuss?'

He glared from the detective inspector to the detective sergeant and back again. Ian wanted to ask what he meant by that, but Rob pressed on, regardless. Ian did his best to study Henry's face as he heard the news. If it was news to him.

'I'm sorry to tell you your wife's dead, Mr Martin.'

56

'Dead? Martha? What are you talking about?'

'I'm afraid it's true. Now may we come in?'

Reluctantly Henry moved aside to allow them to enter the property. When he spoke, his tone was surly.

'It's not like I have any say in the matter, is it?'

He didn't invite them in beyond the hall. The three of them stood awkwardly together at the foot of a wide staircase, while Rob explained that Martha had been murdered. Henry's whole demeanour changed. He looked astonished. Then his bushy eyebrows gathered in a scowl, his lips pressed together as though he was struggling to keep his temper under control.

'What happened?' he asked heavily.

'I'm very sorry to tell you that your wife was stabbed in the chest last night. It appears she died instantaneously, because there was no sign of any struggle.'

The man shook his white head. He looked baffled.

'She was stabbed, you say?'

'Yes.'

'Stabbed in the chest, you said?'

'Yes.'

'Some bugger attacked her and she didn't fight back? Typical. Always the martyr, was Martha.'

Ian knew that shock could be expressed in different ways, but even so he was taken aback by Henry's response. He kept his feelings to himself, careful to maintain a blank expression. A crabby nature was no proof that a man had murdered his wife.

At a nod from his senior officer, Ian challenged Henry.

'Didn't you wonder what had happened to your wife when she didn't come home last night?'

'Yes . . . no. I thought she'd gone out . . . Oh my God, what am I going to say to Mark? The boy'll be devastated.'

'Unlike you,' Ian thought, while aloud he said, 'Your son?'

'Yes.'

'Would you like us to tell him?'

'No, no! I'll do it. I don't need you to speak to my own son for me. But are you sure it's her? How can you be sure it's Martha?'

Rob answered. 'The dental records are conclusive, Mr Martin. It's your wife all right. I'm very sorry.'

'Mark'll be devastated,' he repeated, glaring at them in desperation. 'Martha worshipped the boy, and he was always so protective towards her. They were very close.'

Ian wondered if Henry had been close to his wife, and how close he had been to her at the time of her death.

CHAPTER 11

Henry sat down heavily on the sofa and stared morosely at Martha's empty chair. They had given up any pretence that they were happy together years ago. It hadn't taken either of them very long to realise their marriage was a mistake, but by then Martha had been pregnant. Even when she had lost the baby she had refused to consider a divorce. Her obstinacy had infuriated him, and rightly so. It wasn't as though she was a Catholic, not any more. Even though he had pointed out that everyone got divorced these days, she had remained steadfast. In her eyes divorce was a sin, and that was the end of it. Weak-willed regarding just about everything else, on this one point she refused to budge. Now at last he was rid of her. He just hoped he had enough time left to enjoy his new freedom.

Footsteps crossed the hall. Mark was home. Henry heaved a sigh. How could he tell his son that his mother had been murdered? He hoped Mark would go out again, so he could postpone having to face him. But no such luck.

'There you are, dad.' Mark looked around. 'Still no sign of mum?'

It was always the same. Mark had never cared for his father, he had only ever been interested in Martha.

'Where's mum?' Mark repeated.

Henry shifted awkwardly in his chair. He couldn't meet his son's eye.

'Your mother's not here,' he mumbled.

'I can see that. Where is she?'

'She isn't coming home.'

'What?'

'I said she's not coming home. Ever. We're never going to see her again.'

Mark flopped down in an armchair and glanced towards the television.

'She finally left you then?'

'In a manner of speaking.'

'What's that supposed to mean?'

'Your mother's dead.'

'That's a despicable thing to say,' Mark retorted angrily. 'Are you going to tell me where she's gone, or do I have to wait for her to get in touch—'

'I can't tell you where she's gone . . . maybe to that heaven she was always banging on about.' Henry sat forward, staring in to Mark's face. 'Listen to me, son. Your mother's dead. I don't mean dead to me, I mean she's dead. I'm sorry. The police came here and told me. She was stabbed in the park last night and she's dead.'

★   ★   ★

He dropped his head in his hands. The finality of the words shocked him more than when he had first known his wife was dead. Martha hadn't died accidentally. She hadn't fallen ill, or been run over. A knife had pierced her chest and she had died, all alone, in the dark.

'She was scared of the dark,' he whispered wretchedly, 'and she had lost her faith.'

He swallowed a sob, like a hiccup, overcome with guilt. In her dying moments, Martha hadn't even had the comfort of believing she would go to heaven when she was dead. That was his fault. It must have been difficult to continue believing in a benevolent God throughout thirty-two years of marriage to a forceful atheist.

Mark was staring at his father, aghast. His eyes seemed to be bulging out of his pale face.

'What do you mean she was stabbed?' His eyes grew sharp with understanding. 'Did you say the police were here?'

'I just told you they were.'

'But who was it killed her? Who? What happened? What did they say?'

'They just told me she'd been stabbed. That was all they said.'

'Didn't you ask them who did it?'

'What difference does it make now? Don't worry, they'll catch the sick bastard who did this.'

'The sooner the better. Although I don't suppose you care much, one way or the other,' Mark muttered.

'What the hell's that supposed to mean?'

'You weren't exactly the loving husband, were you?'

'Don't say that.'

'Come on, dad, we both know how you felt. You hated her. I expect you're pleased she's dead.'

Mark was crying, virtually incoherent in his grief.

Henry started up out of his chair, agitated by his son's remark. If his own son was ready to accuse him of hating Martha enough to kill her, God only knew what the police might be thinking. They must already be aware that he stood to inherit a fortune from his wife. They hadn't questioned him yet about his movements on Friday night, but it could only be a matter of time before they started on at him. Shock at what had happened had distracted him from thinking about possible consequences. He paced the room, fighting a growing sense of panic. He had to keep a clear head but it was difficult to concentrate with Mark blubbering.

'Mark, you know we were both here at home last night?'

Mark didn't answer. He kept his face hidden in his hands.

'We need to be clear about that, just in case the police get it into their heads to ask us where we were on Friday evening, when your mother . . . when it happened.'

'Why would anyone do that to her?'

Henry cleared his throat nervously. It was a tricky

subject. He had to broach it without rousing suspicion.

'In cases like this, it's usually the husband who turns out to be responsible. But you know I had nothing to do with this terrible thing that's happened.'

'How do I know that?'

Henry scowled. He spoke slowly, emphasising every word so there could be no confusion.

'We were both here on Friday evening, when it happened.'

Mark looked thoughtful.

'I didn't come home till about ten and then I went out to get something to eat,' he said slowly. 'I was out most of the evening.'

Henry sat down, trying to control his alarm.

'It's probably best not to mention that if the police ask—'

'You want me to lie to the police?'

'Yes . . . that is, no. No, of course not. On second thoughts, perhaps you should mention it in case something shows up on some CCTV camera, somewhere. But you could say you weren't out of the house for long. Tell them you just nipped out to the chip shop.'

'I was out most of the evening.'

Mark stared at his father for a moment, before he dropped his eyes. Henry wondered what he was thinking. Whatever it was, he wasn't sure his son was going to help him.

CHAPTER 12

As they reached the car, Ian glanced back and thought he noticed a curtain twitching upstairs in the Martins' house. He couldn't be sure, but it looked as though a figure was standing by the window, watching them.

'I'm starving,' Rob announced.

Hearing the inspector's voice, Ian turned round. When he looked back at the house, the curtain was closed.

'Let's go and get some lunch,' Rob continued briskly. 'We can look into the Martins at the station and then come back here this evening to see if we can ferret out any more information on the spot, speak to neighbours and anyone else who's around. What do you say?'

'Lunch sounds good. It's very generous of you to offer, but before we take this any further, I should warn you I'm married—'

'Stop jawing and get in,' Rob answered, with a rare smile. 'It's a working lunch for us.'

'And there's me thinking you were whisking me away to the bright lights of Margate for the weekend.'

★   ★   ★

64

There wasn't anything new going on at the station. Ian grabbed a coffee and a roll in the canteen and went straight back to his desk, which was relatively quiet at lunchtime. Most of his colleagues were either working or in the canteen queuing for food, sitting around, eating and chatting. As he devoured a bacon sandwich, he scanned the background report on Martha. Originally from a small town in Southern Ireland, when she was two her mother had left Martha's violent and abusive father and moved to England with the child. Martha had grown up in Portsmouth. Shortly after her mother died, she had married Henry, who was six years older than her. She had trained as a nurse, giving up her career on the birth of her only son. Ten years later she had inherited a substantial fortune on the death of her father and had bought a large house in Herne Bay.

Henry's history was more erratic. He too had been brought up by a single mother, but he had lived in a rough high-rise block in South London. When Henry was thirteen his mother had died and he had been sent to a children's home. No one was interested in fostering a surly thirteen-year-old boy and he had spent the remainder of his formative years in a succession of children's homes. In his late twenties he had married Martha. It was his third marriage. His first wife had left him after a year, and he had married Martha when he was twenty-seven, only a few months after his second

65

divorce was finalised. His work history was stable by comparison. He had been employed by the same company all his adult life.

Ian was finishing his lunch when Rob called him. Chucking his sandwich wrapper in the bin he hurried along the corridor to the detective inspector's office, still clutching his coffee. He was pleased to see Polly was there and they all mulled over the case together, focusing on the victim's husband. A gruff man, Ian thought Henry had received the news of his wife's murder with an expression of irritation, rather than dismay. Rob agreed.

'I think he's the sort of man who doesn't express emotion,' Ian said. 'Some men see it as a sign of weakness.'

'Perhaps he was so upset, he just couldn't say anything about it,' Polly suggested.

'There is another possibility,' Rob said quietly.

'Yes, he didn't seem exactly grief stricken at the news. Do you think he wanted her dead?'

Rob considered before replying.

'I'm not sure he was surprised to hear she'd been murdered. What was your impression of him?'

'It's difficult to say. He seemed to be holding something back, but that doesn't mean he killed her.'

'He could have been feeling guilty because he didn't love his wife,' Polly said.

★   ★   ★

Rob stood up.

'Let's go and chat to some of the neighbours, see what we can pick up.'

Ian gulped down the dregs of his coffee and jumped to his feet, eager to get going. On the way they agreed to split up, and visit the properties on either side of the Martins' house simultaneously. It was important to gather as much information about Henry as they could. He was a possible suspect, partly because they felt there was something suspicious about him, but more significantly because statistically a woman's husband was the most likely person to have murdered her.

Ian dropped Rob off. As he turned into the side road next to Henry's house he glanced back and saw his colleague, intermittently lit up and vanishing into the shadows between the street lamps. Tall and thin, he looked a menacing figure in his long black coat, with his collar turned up against the chill of the evening. The inspector had disappeared by the time Ian climbed out of the car. The air was crisp and he hummed to himself as he strode along. Rob was checking the neighbours opposite, leaving Ian to try next door. He rang the neighbour's bell and a short plump woman came to the door. Ian introduced himself, holding up his warrant card. The woman's expression relaxed. Ian returned her smile, encouraged by her reaction. People weren't always pleased when the police came calling. He took a deep breath and began to question her, aware that statements from potential witnesses could be crucial. Discounting crackpots and neighbours with grievances, any piece of gossip might prove valuable.

Mrs Jamieson was eager to share her views, but it soon became apparent that she harboured a personal grudge against her neighbours. Ian kept his thoughts to himself, nodding solemnly while she told him about the shouting she had frequently heard from the house next door.

'It was worse in the summer, when they had the windows open. In the cold weather, we hardly heard anything from them.'

'What did you hear when the weather was fine?'

The neighbour hesitated. She looked embarrassed.

'I wouldn't want to give you the wrong impression. I mean, we didn't sit here listening to them all the time. It was just that sometimes we couldn't help hearing them, when we were out in the garden. It was him, mostly. I don't ever remember hearing a peep out of her, poor soul, but he hectored her constantly. I'm telling you, he was a real bully, always on at her about something.'

'What did he say?'

'I don't know, but we'd hear him shouting at her all the time, calling her stupid and things like that. He was always insulting her. It wasn't what you'd call normal. We felt so sorry for that poor boy, their son. He was such a quiet gentle boy, and devoted to his poor mother. They were very close.'

Ian nodded. Henry had used the same phrase to describe his son's relationship with his mother.

Ian refused tea and pressed her to tell him more about her neighbours.

'Anything you can remember might help us build a picture of what went on next door.'

Mrs Jamieson's eyes widened as she asked eagerly, 'Was it him then?'

'I'm sorry?'

'Him, Henry Martin. He was the one who killed her, wasn't he?' She clapped her palms to her cheeks in a gesture of mock horror. 'Oh my God, please tell me we haven't got a killer living right next door to us.'

Ian shook his head.

'I'm just here to make initial enquiries, Mrs Jamieson. There's no need for you to be alarmed.'

He could see his advice was falling on deaf ears. As soon as he left, Mrs Jamieson would be on the phone to all her friends, telling them she was living next door to a man who had murdered his wife. For all Ian knew, she was right.

CHAPTER 13

Lying in bed that night, Ian was troubled by the idea that Henry might learn about his neighbour's allegations. Mrs Jamieson didn't strike him as a particularly discreet woman. If she mentioned her suspicions to enough people, sooner or later Henry would discover she was going round telling everyone he had killed his wife. And if she was correct, and he was indeed capable of homicide, there was no knowing what provocation would prompt him to kill again. The catalyst for another murder might well be a stupid woman running around blackening his name in the neighbourhood, with perhaps the added fear that she would convince the police to investigate his whereabouts on the night of his wife's death. 'There's no need for you to be alarmed,' were the last words he had spoken to her.

What if he was wrong?

'Can't you sleep either?' Bev asked as he shifted position yet again. 'What's on your mind?'

'Nothing,' he lied. 'Go back to sleep.'

It was late. The problem was too complicated to discuss right then. In any case, he wasn't sure Bev would understand his concern. There was nothing to suggest Henry had killed his wife. He could be suspecting an innocent man, and it was never helpful to allow his judgement to be clouded by vague impressions. He had to deal with facts. In his mind he ran through his meeting with the widower again. Henry hadn't appeared upset by the news that his wife was dead. While that could be construed as suspicious, Ian would have expected some show of grief from him if he was actually guilty. At the same time, he had the distinct impression Henry was concealing something. And then there was the next-door neighbour who had quickly jumped to the conclusion that Henry was guilty. Perhaps there was more to her chatter than Ian had realised. He wished he had questioned her in more detail, and decided to speak to her again the following day. Having reached that decision, he turned to his wife.

'It's nothing,' he repeated.

Bev always knew when he was lying.

'Who is she?' she asked.

'Her name's Patricia Jamieson—'

Too late, he realised Bev had been teasing. With a childish pout, she pulled away from his embrace and sat up. Leaning forward so that her chin rested on her knees, she wrapped her arms around her shins.

71

'Who is she?' she repeated, her voice unnaturally composed.

Ian half sat up, leaning his upper body weight on one elbow, so that he was facing her and stifled a sigh. This was all he needed right now, a tantrum from his beautiful wife at two o'clock in the morning.

'She's a witness in the case, at least she might be, and I'm afraid I may have been too quick to dismiss what she was saying, and as a result, there's a chance her life might be in danger.'

It sounded foolishly melodramatic.

'Bev?'

She didn't answer.

'Bev? Come on, lie down and let's get some sleep. I'm knackered.'

Bev muttered something ominously under her breath, but she lay down and he closed his eyes gratefully.

He slept badly and woke very early, feeling as though he had a hangover. His throat was dry and slightly sore when he swallowed, and his head felt hot. A strong cup of tea and a fried egg on toast helped and he set off for work relieved that he didn't seem to be going down with a cold after all. Bev was still asleep when he left, and he didn't wake her. If she was going to be in a mood with him, he preferred not to let it ruin his day. He would deal with her later on. In the meantime, he had work to do. As the husband of the victim,

Henry was automatically under suspicion until they could eliminate him from their list of suspects. As it happened, his name was currently the only one on the list. Polly had been looking in to Henry's background. He had been employed as a washing machine fitter all his working life, and seemed to have been a hard worker, although he had never earned much. His wife, on the other hand, had been a relatively wealthy woman. An only child, she had inherited a sizeable fortune which had enabled her to move to Herne Bay and buy the large detached house where she had lived until her death. The house and a considerable portfolio of investments now belonged to Henry.

Ian wondered whether Henry might have murdered his wife for her money. If the evidence of their neighbour was reliable, the couple had not been on good terms. He bumped into Polly in the corridor and they went to his office to discuss the case. Leaning back in his chair, Ian couldn't help thinking how nice it was to have an uncomplicated friendship with an attractive woman. He had been crazy about Bev since his teens, but he now wondered if he had mistaken adolescent infatuation for what was glibly called 'the real thing', whatever that was. They were so nearly well-suited, but the truth was that Bev would have been far happier with a dependable husband in a steady nine-to-five job. Henry had been married to

Martha for over thirty years. Ian could see how that might wear a man down.

Polly looked surprised when he told her what he was thinking about the Martins.

'Even if he was unhappy with her, murder's a bit extreme, isn't it, to say the least? I mean, if every husband who was fed up with his wife decided to kill her, instead of getting divorced, there wouldn't be many married women left in the world.'

She was right, of course. Henry could have left his wife.

'They had a son,' Ian said. 'Maybe he was afraid of alienating him if he left his wife.'

'Yes,' she agreed, 'and he wouldn't have got his hands on all her money if he'd divorced her.'

'Martha was brought up as a Catholic. Perhaps she didn't believe in divorce.'

'Do you really think so? In this day and age?'

'There are still people who think marriage is sacred.'

He wondered what Bev's view on divorce would be. They had never discussed it. Some topics were best left alone. Bev might be irritatingly possessive, but he couldn't really complain about having a beautiful wife who loved him so much.

'What are you grinning about?' Polly asked.

Ian shrugged.

'I was just thinking how helpful this is, being

able to discuss the case with you. A woman's perspective being different and all that –' he faltered awkwardly, afraid she would accuse him of making sexist remarks. But Polly smiled.

CHAPTER 14

It didn't occur to Henry to be seriously frightened until he passed one of his neighbours in the street. It was a bright Sunday morning, so he decided to stroll down the road to the newsagents for some milk. He would have to stock up on food soon, but he hadn't gone shopping by himself for a long time. Martha had always accompanied him, ticking items methodically off her list as he pushed a trolley round the store. It would be strange to go shopping without her. Strange, and oddly liberating. He would be free to fill his trolley with cans of beer, frozen chips, pizza, and anything else he fancied. He could imagine her voice, whining at him about fatty foods and looking after his health, and all that claptrap. Martha had watched her diet obsessively, but her preoccupation with health hadn't saved her. Right now he didn't feel like making a special trip to the supermarket. He could go on his way home from work one evening. He virtually drove past the door. Meanwhile, he had run out of milk.

Whistling, he closed his gate and almost bumped into the woman from next door who happened to be passing. Catching sight of her expression, he remembered he had just lost his wife in tragic circumstances. Abruptly he stopped whistling and tried to look sad. His neighbour hurried away, but not before he had seen the disgust on her face. He could imagine her describing the encounter to her cronies.

'There he was, whistling like he didn't have a care in the world, and his poor murdered wife not yet cold in her grave. It's not natural. If you ask me, he did her in himself. Why else would he be looking so cheerful about it? That poor woman.'

Henry felt sick, his enjoyment of the morning ruined. As though responding to his mood, a dark cloud drifted in front of the sun and the air grew chilly. He walked faster, thinking. First his son, now his neighbour. Mark had been openly hostile to his father on hearing the news of his mother's death, as good as accusing Henry of stabbing Martha himself.

'We both know how you felt. You couldn't stand the sight of her.' He had pointedly refused to provide Henry with an alibi. 'You want me to lie to the police?'

If his son and his next-door neighbour both believed he had killed Martha, what chance did he have of convincing the police he was innocent?

His mood didn't improve when he reached the corner shop and met an acquaintance he played darts with from time to time.

'Morning, Bert,' he called out.

He was careful not to appear too cheerful. He didn't know who might be watching and judging him. The police might come snooping round the area, questioning the shopkeeper.

'Mr Martin? Yes, he was here, shopping, as though nothing had happened. I would never have guessed poor Mrs Martin had just been murdered. If anything, he looked happier than usual.'

The shop had CCTV, which the police might watch. If they saw Henry out shopping in good spirits, so soon after his wife had been brutally murdered, they were bound to think the worst of him.

Bert scowled and turned away. Henry shivered, although it wasn't cold in the shop. He wondered what Bert had heard, but didn't know him well enough to ask. In any case, he had probably misinterpreted Bert's apparent hostility. He couldn't have heard about the stabbing. Henry made an effort to stay calm, reasoning that if Bert had heard about the murder, he would have offered his condolences, not turned his back so rudely – unless he too believed that Henry was guilty. Bert went up to the counter and began talking very rapidly in an undertone to the Asian guy behind the counter. Sanjay kept his eyes fixed on Bert's face, listening intently. Henry couldn't hear what Bert was saying. He edged closer to try and listen, but Sanjay gave a warning frown. Bert fell silent,

78

and twisted his head round to look at Henry over his shoulder. For an instant Henry stood perfectly still, while the other two men stared coldly at him.

'Hello, Bert,' he repeated loudly.

This time he elicited a curt response before Bert turned back to Sanjay and made his purchase.

Henry wanted to ask Bert what he had been saying, but it would sound odd. He watched Bert leave without speaking to him again.

'Here all by yourself today,' Sanjay said pointedly as Henry held up a litre of milk.

The shopkeeper peered over the till, glaring at Henry. He might just as well have come out with it and accused him of having killed his wife. The whole world seemed to be turning against him. Even a relative stranger serving in the corner shop was behaving like some jumped-up self-appointed judge and jury. Sanjay had no idea what had happened to Martha, yet he was ready with his barbed comments. First the police, then Mark, the woman next door, and Bert, whom he hardly knew. Now even the bloody shopkeeper on the corner was at it, needling him with uncalled-for jibes. Henry felt his patience snap. He heard himself shouting, his temper out of control.

The outburst startled Sanjay. His thin black eyebrows disappeared beneath his fringe and his eyes widened stupidly as Henry slammed a bottle of milk down on the counter. He was still yelling.

'You mind your own fucking business.'

Henry stared past the shopkeeper's head.

'That,' he yelled, pointing a shaking finger at the whisky. 'Give me that large bottle.'

'Ah.'

Sanjay gave a knowing smile, reassured to discover the ostensible cause of his customer's aggression. Henry let it go. It was certainly one explanation for his volatile behaviour, if not the right one. Clutching the bottle of Scotch, he hurried home. Later on he would sort out an alibi, once he had done some serious thinking. But first he was going to get plastered. He could afford the most expensive bottle of Scotch, and there was no one to spoil his enjoyment by nagging him about wasting money.

CHAPTER 15

After an early lunch, Ian drove back to Herne Bay and parked in the street alongside Henry Martin's house. He and Rob would be returning together to speak to the widower again soon. With any luck, they would make an arrest and the investigation would be over. But before that, there was a lot of work to get through. Right now it was vital to gather as much information as possible. They not only had to make an arrest, they had to make sure their case was watertight. A prosecution that failed to get a conviction was a waste of police time and effort, as well as an opportunity for the killer to make good his escape – and possibly kill again.

For the second time in two days, Ian knocked on the Jamiesons' front door. This time it was opened by a short, stout man with greying hair. His bushy beard and moustache were white.

'Yes? What is it? What do you want?'

His brisk tone softened after he had put on steel-rimmed spectacles to peer at Ian's warrant card.

'Hmm, a detective sergeant? Well, in that case, perhaps you'd better come in.' He hesitated. 'What's this about?'

Briefly Ian explained the purpose of his call and Mr Jamieson nodded, his head turned quizzically to one side.

'Yes, Patsy told me you'd been here, asking questions.'

'Your wife?'

'Yes, yes. Come on in. I expect she'll want to see you.'

He turned and bawled his wife's name and a second later she came into the hall, wiping floury hands on a dish cloth.

'Sorry, I've got a cake in the oven.'

She led them into a large square kitchen, neat and clean apart from a floury work surface.

'You'll have to excuse the mess,' she added hurriedly.

Her husband smiled complacently at her and Ian felt a surge of optimism. Baking on a Sunday afternoon, content in her marriage, Mrs Jamieson could appear before any jury as a decent, reliable witness. He accepted the offer of a cup of tea and was disappointed when it wasn't accompanied by a slice of the cake he could smell. It couldn't have been ready yet. Bad timing, he thought. He hoped that wasn't a bad omen. Sipping his tea, he listened to Mrs Jamieson discussing her neighbours as though she had been preparing for his visit. It was hardly necessary for him to prompt her with questions.

'I always said he'd do her an injury one day,' Mrs Jamieson began, speaking very loudly.

Her husband remonstrated with her.

'There's lots of couples argue.'

'Not like that,' she replied, turning to face her husband.

There was a pause.

'Like what?' Ian asked and the Jamiesons both turned to him looking slightly surprised, as though they had forgotten he was there.

'You weren't here during the day,' she went on, speaking to her husband. She turned back to Ian. 'He wasn't here in the day. He didn't hear it all.'

'All what?'

'Now, Patsy,' her husband warned her, but she rounded on him.

'Stop interfering, Donald. I'm only saying what I heard, no more and no less. You don't know what went on.' She turned to Ian and lowered her voice. 'You wouldn't know it, because he lip-reads, but my husband's deaf.'

Ian sat down and took out his notebook. Mrs Jamieson's account of her neighbours was petty and inconsequential, but she was keen to talk about them and Ian was prepared to listen to her again. Somewhere in her ramblings she might inadvertently furnish him with a lead. It was five years since the Jamiesons had moved into their ground floor flat, next door to the Martins.

'They own the whole house,' she said, a touch sharply, as though that was something reprehensible. 'Just the two of them and that boy of theirs.'

Ian guided her gently to talk about the arguments she had overheard.

'I don't like to eavesdrop, but in the summer when I sit out on the patio, I can't help hearing them. It's not like I go out specially to hear what's going on in there.'

Ian nodded to indicate he understood.

After a few more minutes talking around the subject, Mrs Jamieson tackled the issue of her neighbours' rows.

'He screams at her, I mean really yelling. It would make a trooper blush, the way that man talks to his wife – talked to her, I suppose I should say. Well, let's hope she's gone to a better place.'

She shook her head sadly, and offered Ian another cup of tea which he declined.

'What kind of things did he say?'

'Oh, I couldn't possibly repeat what he said. Such foul language. It was shameful, really it was, for a man to speak to his wife like that.'

'Can you remember what they argued about?'

'Oh, all sorts from the sound of it. Anything and everything. He didn't like this, and he didn't like that, this wasn't right, and that wasn't right. It was endless. And then there was the divorce.'

'The divorce?'

'Yes, he wanted a divorce. He was always on at her about it.'

'And what did she say about it?'

'The honest truth is that I never heard a peep out of her. She wasn't one to raise her voice. But she can't have agreed to a divorce, because whenever it came up he used to scream and shout at her for being obstinate. Though God only knows why she refused to get divorced. It can't have been much of a life, living with a foul-mouthed man like him. She'd have done far better to have given him his divorce and got clean away. Still, she didn't, and now look what's happened. If he couldn't be shot of her one way . . .'

Ian looked up from his notebook.

'Are you suggesting Mr Martin killed his wife as a way of ending his marriage?'

'Well, he couldn't get away from her any other way, could he? Not with her refusing to get a divorce.'

'But that doesn't mean he was responsible for her death.'

'Oh doesn't it?' she asked, with a knowing smile.

Ian was irritated. He wasn't there to play guessing games.

'Mrs Jamieson, if you have any evidence to suggest that Mr Martin was implicated, directly or indirectly, in his wife's death, you must tell me. Otherwise this is all just speculation and gossip.'

★   ★   ★

Startled by his peremptory tone, she dropped her coy expression and continued gravely.

'It's only what I heard about him insisting he wanted a divorce and getting angry with her for refusing. But he did threaten to kill her, I'm sure of that. I heard him. I was out in the garden, on the patio, reading my book, or trying to with them having one of their set-tos next door. I couldn't hear what she was saying, just the faint drone of her voice in the background.'

'So you couldn't be sure it was Martha he was speaking to?'

'No, except that he was begging her for a divorce, so it must've been her, mustn't it? Anyway, he was going on and on about it, and threatening to make her sorry. She must have said something like, "over my dead body" or, "you'll have to kill me first" because he shouted out, "I bloody well will kill you, if that's what it takes to get rid of you".'

'Are you sure that's what you heard?'

'As clear as I can hear you now. He must have been standing right by the open window.'

'And you couldn't have been mistaken?'

'No. I remember it, word for word. It's not the sort of thing you forget. I was sitting quietly, minding my own business, in the garden, and I heard him shouting at her. It upset me, I can tell you.'

As Ian scribbled down the wording, Mr Jamieson leaned forward and patted his wife on her knee.

86

'What about it then?' he asked.

'What?'

'The seed cake. Is it ready yet?'

Mrs Jamieson smiled indulgently.

'Poor thing, he didn't hear a word I said, did you dear?'

CHAPTER 16

He consciously enjoyed drinking in the comfort of his own home without anyone watching him and criticising, but the pleasure soon faded. The house felt disconcertingly empty. Even the noise of the television didn't fill the silence. He flipped restlessly between channels, scowling at false laughter and seemingly endless adverts. Mark had gone out. No one else ever came round. Until now, Henry hadn't realised how much he had come to depend on Martha. For thirty years she had lingered in the house like a bad smell. It was no wonder he had lost interest in her as a woman when all she did was complain. She was so bloody self-righteous, as though their problems were all his fault. And it was maddening, the way she would stare at him in silence whenever he lost his temper. Yet any time he was in trouble, Martha had been there for him. When he had been laid up with the flu, Martha was the one who had brought him soup, and propped him up on his pillows so she could feed him, like a baby. He had broken his ankle slipping over on the ice one winter. Martha had taken him to the hospital, looking after him until he was fit again.

'It's my duty,' she had said primly when he wanted to thank her for taking care of him. 'I'm your wife.'

She had never shown him affection, but she had always been there. Maybe that should have been enough.

It was ironic that he was in trouble as a consequence of her death, when she was the only person who would have helped him. His son was refusing to vouch for him, even though Henry had sworn he had been asleep on the sofa on Friday evening. As his son, Mark should have taken his word for it. Henry had been banking on his co-operation. Instead, Mark had as good as accused him of following Martha to the park, sticking a knife in her heart, running home again, and lying about it to save his own skin. If he couldn't rely on Mark to furnish him with an alibi, he would just have to find someone else. But only Martha would have been prepared to lie to protect him. There was no one else.

About to pour another whisky into his glass, he thought better of it and set the bottle down on the table. Drinking alone was depressing and besides, he needed to remain sober if he was going to fight his way out of his present troubles. His head cleared as he walked along the street. It was a fine evening, but chilly. Under any other circumstances he would have been happy, free at last, with money to burn.

He tried to imagine how he would be feeling if Martha had passed away naturally. Outwardly like any other grieving widower coming to terms with the death of his wife, inside he would be rejoicing at his good fortune. He wouldn't be tormented by the crippling fear that now plagued him. Without an alibi for the time of Martha's death, he was as good as convicted. Only unlike his dead wife, he was a fighter. Having wasted more than thirty years of his life tied to her, he refused to let her ruin what little time he had left. The police were on to him, but he would get the better of them yet. With a little planning he could outwit the lot of them.

He walked along the front until he came to a rundown pub. At nine o'clock it was almost empty. A middle-aged man lounged in one corner, while a couple of young lads sat laughing together at a table. An old tart was sitting up at the bar, eyeing everyone who came in. She glanced over at Henry, and turned away again. She wasn't much to look at, but she gave him an idea. He didn't have any friends to speak of, just a few workmates. But he had money. Lots of it. Instead of a short, he ordered a black coffee, strong and bitter, with two sugars. He needed to stay alert if he was going to carry out the plan that was forming in his mind. Gulping down the hot sweet drink, he turned the possibility over in his mind. The more he thought about it, the more excited he became. Nothing was a problem for a wealthy man.

* * *

Sitting at the bar, he grinned to himself. No one took any notice. They probably thought he'd had one too many. It didn't matter. It no longer mattered what anyone thought of him, because he had enough money to do whatever he wanted. Enough money to buy their good opinion if he cared to have it, which he didn't. The money was going to make it worth the thirty years of hell he'd endured with his wretched wife. Poor Martha. He couldn't help smiling as he imagined her sitting in judgement on him, up in her self-righteous heaven. She couldn't take her money away from him now. It was all his. He could do what the hell he wanted with it, and the first thing he was going to do was dish some of it out to another woman. See how Martha liked that. He swayed slightly as he stood up, drunker than he had realised. It was probably just as well. He would need some Dutch courage if he was going to carry out his plan.

As he stood up, the old tart at the bar caught his eye. He returned her gaze thoughtfully, unsure if she was suitable for his purposes. On balance, he decided she looked too shrewd. He didn't want anyone asking too many questions. Nor did he want to deal with someone living right on his doorstep. He turned and left without looking back. Before he put his plan into action, he needed to do some research. There could be no mistakes.

CHAPTER 17

Henry drove fast along the Thanet Way, enjoying the freedom of the long straight flat dual carriageway. Taking the A28, he slowed down for the speed cameras in Birchington, then put his foot down again until he reached Margate. There were signs of regeneration along the front, but not far behind the façade the High Street was virtually derelict. Almost half the shops were boarded up. Some displayed 'To Let' signs. The only place that looked as though it was thriving was a large cheap clothes store. He found a place to park and continued to explore the area on foot. Behind the amusement arcades that faced the sea he found what he was looking for: a dingy black door with a sign 'Over 21s Only'. A bored-looking bouncer stood outside, rolling a cigarette. He looked at Henry without blinking. Broad-shouldered, wearing a padded jacket over his stab vest, he had a flat square face with a big crooked nose and blubbery lips.

'I'm looking for a woman –' Henry began.

The bouncer jerked his head in the direction of the interior.

'Full price unless you're a member.'

'No, you don't understand. I need to find a woman who wasn't working here on Friday night.'

The doorman frowned. It was clearly too complicated a request for him to deal with.

'Tonight is Monday,' he said.

'Never mind.'

Henry handed over his money.

Inside, a heavily made-up woman opened a curtain and gestured for him to go in. A girl was spinning around a pole wearing nothing but a sequined G-string while music thumped out a regular beat. Normally Henry would have been mesmerised by her bouncing curves, but he was preoccupied. As soon as he entered the room, a skinny bird with unnaturally large breasts sashayed up to him. It was difficult not to be distracted by her almost naked body swaying in front of him, tantalisingly close. With an effort, he kept his gaze fixed on her painted face.

'Were you working here on Friday night?'

Immediately she stopped moving her hips and took an involuntary step back. Her eyes narrowed as she scrutinised his face.

'Are you a cop?'

'No.'

'You don't look like a cop.'

'I'm not a cop. I'm in trouble with – with my brother –' He could hardly say his wife. 'I need to find a girl who was free on Friday evening.'

The girl half turned, her eyes scanning the doorway.

'I'll pay.'

She turned back, a flicker of interest on her face.

'Twenty quid to you if you introduce me to a girl who wasn't working on Friday, and a hundred to her.'

'Fifty.'

'OK, I'll give you fifty, and—'

'Wait here.'

Although he was standing in shadow, he felt as though everyone in the room was watching him: girls gyrating on the podium, a few blokes ogling them, half-dressed waitresses prancing around with trays of drinks. He went and sat down at an empty table and watched the show, too intent on his project to be excited by the dancers on stage. Even after her death, Martha was still spoiling his fun. Once all this was over, he promised himself he would return to the club and have a good time. He seemed to be sitting there for hours, until his head was throbbing painfully at the loud music that accompanied the show. At last a blonde woman came and sat beside him. She looked very young and was wearing a short black dress that was too tight for her.

'Candy said you wanted to see me.'

'Were you here on Friday evening?'

'No. Were you?'

He scowled at her brazen smile.

'This isn't about me. Just answer the question, will you? Now, where were you on Friday evening?'

'I was at home. Washing my hair.'

Raising one hand to her head she fluffed up her blonde curls and placed her other hand firmly on his knee, speaking in staccato bursts as though she could only manage to produce a couple of words at a time.

'Aren't you going to buy me a drink?'

He waved at a half-naked waitress who brought them a couple of glasses of overpriced sparkling white wine.

'How would you like to do me a favour?' he asked.

With a practised smile she moved her hand up his thigh to his crotch. With an effort of will he moved it away. There was no denying she was achingly attractive, but he couldn't afford to be distracted.

'I'll make it worth your while,' he said and paused, uncertain how to explain what he wanted.

She waited, sipping her wine. No one appeared to be paying them any attention but he felt self-conscious.

'Can we go somewhere private?'

Without a word she stood up, took him by the elbow and steered him across the room. They went through a curtain and she led him upstairs to a small room with a bed and a cracked sink in one corner. The curtains were threadbare velvet, and the whole room had an atmosphere of shabby luxury.

Della sat down and patted the bed beside her, automatically smoothing out a few wrinkles on the cover, but the punter remained standing. He refused to look directly at her, showing no interest in her beyond a fuck. She preferred it that way. It made no difference to her, as long as he paid up without any fuss. The ones who didn't want to talk got it over with more quickly, and time was money. The men who wanted to babble on interminably about their pathetic lives were the worst. She unzipped her dress and wriggled out of it.

'Stop that. Get dressed again.'

'What's wrong?'

'That's not what I want from you.'

Eyeing him warily, she put her dress back on.

He stared at her, red-faced, struggling to control himself. She had seen more men than she could remember in his state of resentful arousal. It didn't bother her. As long as he paid, she couldn't care less that he hated himself for wanting to pay for sex. It gave them something in common: she hated him for it as well.

'I just want to talk to you,' he said eventually.

She hoped he wasn't going to sit jabbering all night.

'It'll still cost you.'

All at once he seemed anxious. He began speaking very quickly, as though he was in a hurry.

'Money's no problem. But I don't want to talk here. Follow me. Come on, we can talk in my car.'

'What's wrong with staying here?'

'I'll make it worth your while. Five hundred quid for one quick favour.' Seeing her expression, he added quickly, 'I'll make it a thousand. Don't worry, I won't touch you. That's not what I want. I only want to talk. Now, let's get out of here.'

She led him out of the back door, round the side of the building to the street, to avoid questions. If there was a thousand quid in it, she wanted to keep that to herself.

'It's worse than school in there,' she told him.

He nodded but didn't say anything. Without another word she followed him along the street to a large dark blue car. He opened the door and told her to get in. The bloke gave her the creeps but she only hesitated for a second.

'A thousand quid, you said?'

She would tell the club manager the punter insisted on having a fuck in his car and had paid the going rate, and she would pocket the difference.

'Yes, yes, now come on,' he urged. 'I told you, I'm not going to touch you. It's just that we can talk in the car. I'll give you the keys if it makes you feel better. Now stop wasting time and get in.'

*   *   *

'What were you doing on Friday evening?' he asked as he sat down beside her.

'What?'

She had met some funny blokes, but there was definitely something peculiar going on with this one. Still, it was a nice car, and he had promised her a thousand quid. She leaned back on her seat and waited.

'Don't look so scared. I'm not going to hurt you, not if you do as you're told. I just need to ask you a few questions. You weren't at the club on Friday evening, were you?'

She shook her head.

'Where were you?'

'At home.'

'Was anyone else with you?'

'No. Candy – my flatmate – was here, working.'

'So you were on your own? All evening?'

'Yes. Why? What are you after?'

She sat up, unnerved, and reached for the door handle.

'Don't you want to earn yourself an easy thousand quid?'

A thousand quid was a lot of money, but she still didn't know what he wanted from her. She gave a cautious nod.

'You're not going to mark my face—'

'How many times do I need to say it? I wouldn't want to touch you if you paid me.'

His eyes were all over her, giving the lie to his insult.

'What do you want then?'

'All you have to do is say you spent Friday evening with me. That's all there is to it.'

She hesitated, reluctant to commit herself until she knew what was going on.

'Why?'

'You don't need to know. It's a thousand quid, and no questions.'

'I don't want any trouble.'

'There's no need to worry. Look, my brother thinks I was messing about with his wife and I need to convince him he's got it all wrong, that's all. So, are you going to help me? There's a thousand quid in it for you, cash. You can have it tonight.'

Now she understood what was involved, she relaxed.

'Were you?'

'What?'

'Messing about with your brother's wife?'

'If you keep on with the questions, you can forget it. I'll ask someone else. There's fifteen hundred quid in it – a thousand now and the rest when this is over – so I won't have any problem finding someone else, someone who can keep her trap shut and just say exactly what I tell her to say.'

He turned away and opened his door. She leaned across and grabbed his sleeve, digging into his arm with her long red nails.

'No,' she said quickly. 'Don't go. I'll do it. Give

me the cash and I won't ask anything else, I promise. Just tell me what to say. I won't let you down.'

He slipped an envelope out of his pocket and held it open so she could see the contents: a wad of twenty quid notes. She seized it and, wetting her finger, flicked quickly through them, counting under her breath.

'Now, this is what I want you to say. Listen carefully. You need to be clear about the times.'

She nodded, still counting. When he finished, he made her repeat the story over and over again until he was satisfied she would remember it.

'Play your part well, and there'll be another five hundred quid in it for you,' he said quietly. 'But it you fuck up, believe me you'll be sorry. I'll make sure of that. Now get out of my car.'

'Don't you want to come back to the club and spend some time with me?' she asked.

She was thinking about the envelope he had given her. He must be loaded.

'Just get out and close the door behind you.'

Standing on the pavement she watched his car drive away before she went back indoors and slipped into the toilet. Locked in a cubicle she took the envelope out of her bag, wondering where to stash the money. Her dress was too tight to conceal anything in her underwear, and besides, someone might see it there. She ripped the inner soles out of her shoes, divided the notes and put them inside the shoes, cramming the soles back down. The hidden money made her shoes uncomfortably tight, but it was the best she could do. She didn't dare leave it in her bag. It was too much money to risk losing. She was about to throw the envelope away when she noticed it had a name and address on it. A thousand quid with another five hundred promised, and there was plenty more where that came from, if she played her cards right. Smiling to herself, she put the envelope carefully in her bag.

CHAPTER 18

At school on Tuesday nothing was the same. It wasn't only the way he was feeling inside. Other people were treating him differently too. Not teachers, who were always oblivious to everything, but other pupils seemed to regard him with more respect than usual. Even though he had only shown his knife to a couple of mates the day before, it seemed that word had spread. When a group of boys moved aside to allow him in front of them in the lunch queue, he knew for certain that things had changed. Suppressing a chuckle, he moved up the line without even acknowledging them, as though he was accustomed to such displays of deference.

After a brilliant day at school, he was so pumped up that he let down his guard. He was taking it easy in front of the television when Eddy yelled at him from the hall.

'Get your arse out here now!'

'I'm watching telly,' Ben fibbed.

There was nothing on worth watching, as usual, but he couldn't be bothered to get up. He stayed just where he was, telling himself that the days when Eddy could push him around were over. His confidence didn't last long; about as long as it took for Eddy to run in, lunge forward and grab the front of his T-shirt. Bunching the material up in a hairy fist he yanked Ben to his feet.

'I told you to get your arse out in the hall and move your stinking trainers.'

Ben twisted his head to the side but was too slow to avoid inhaling a lungful of Eddy's breath. It reeked of stale beer and cigarettes. He almost told Eddy he stank, but thought better of it. Despising himself for being weak, he was civil where he ought to have been defiant. He couldn't help it.

'Where do you want me to put them?'

'Try putting them on your feet, dickhead.'

'Mum told me to take them off when I come in.'

'Listen, you fucking moron, I don't care what she says, and I don't care where you put your fucking shoes. Chuck them out the window. Shove them up your fucking arse. Only don't leave them in the hall, stinking the place out. Other people want to be able to breathe out there.'

Ben stared straight into Eddy's eyes and swore at him. He didn't mean to, but the words slipped out of his mouth.

'You're the one who fucking stinks around here.'

He almost choked as Eddy tightened his grip.

He leaned his ugly face closer until their noses were nearly touching.

'What's that you said?'

Somehow Eddy's calm quiet manner was more terrifying than a violent outburst. Ben struggled to control his panic. No two attacks were ever the same, so Ben could never predict where Eddy was going to strike first.

'I said – I said – I said your fucking breath stinks worse than my shoes,' he gasped.

He was shaking helplessly. This was it. Eddy knew where to hit so it really hurt. This time Ben was bound to end up in intensive care. He hoped the stupid doctors would finally realise what was going on, and report Eddy to the police. Only by then it would probably be too late for the police to pin the assault on Eddy, because the only witness to his brutality would be dead. He closed his eyes, determined not to cry out however much it hurt. His mother's voice saved him.

'Eddy? Eddy? Are you here?'

Eddy swung his fist and cuffed Ben viciously on the shoulder as he let go of his shirt. Stifling a yelp, Ben fell back on his chair and stared at the screen without registering what he was looking at. He pretended Eddy hadn't hurt him. He needn't have bothered, because no one was watching. Eddy joined his mother in the hall and a moment later Ben heard them go into the kitchen. It sounded as though they were arguing. Ben waited a moment before slipping out of the living room. His legs were shaking so hard he struggled to make it up the stairs.

Sitting on the side of the bath Ben felt his arm gingerly, wincing as his fingers reached the bruised area. By kneeling on the toilet seat and craning his head sideways he could see the dark purple area of skin where Eddy had thumped him. Starting on his shoulder, the bruise was already spreading down his upper arm as the blood seeped beneath the surface of his skin. He remembered the same thing happening to his mother who had panicked, thinking she had internal bleeding and was going to die. She had gone to the hospital where a doctor had explained that it was just gravity causing the blood to spread downwards. There had been a bit of a fuss about it at the time because the doctor suspected she was being beaten up. It was a reasonable supposition as she had a black eye as well as a few nasty bruises. She had a hell of a job convincing him she had tripped over. Tripped over Eddy's fist more like.

Back in his own room he opened his wardrobe and pulled out first his school bag, and then a handful of T-shirts and an old pair of jeans. Rummaging beneath the clothes that were left in there, he took out his knife and ran his finger along the smooth surface of the blade. The cold curve of the metal made him shiver with excitement. He had made a stupid mistake, leaving the knife safely stowed away in his bedroom. From now on, he was going to take it with him wherever he went. He would keep it well hidden. Only a few people would know about it. Eddy would be one of them. He shut his eyes, picturing the fear on his repulsive face.

'I'm going to teach you a lesson you'll never forget,' Eddy would snarl, raising his huge fist.

'No!' Ben would bellow as he pulled out his knife. 'This time *I'm* going to teach *you* a lesson!'

He imagined the blade slicing through flesh, leaving a scar so that Eddy would never be able to forget what Ben had done. He would carry the mark of his shame for the rest of his life, bettered in a fight by a scrawny boy. A boy wielding a knife.

CHAPTER 19

'It must have been the husband. He's the obvious suspect, wouldn't you say?'

Rob was looking down at his desk. Under the bright ceiling light, shiny patches of scalp showed through his thinning grey hair. He raised his head. For a moment his eyes held Ian's gaze but his expression didn't alter. Ian waited.

'It's usually the husband, isn't it?' Rob said again after a few minutes. 'Has he got an alibi?'

Ian shrugged. 'You know we didn't get that far, sir. We only got as far as informing him of his wife's death. And he was desperately worried about telling his son,' he added, feeling he ought to apologise for the omission, even though it was perfectly acceptable not to have questioned the dead woman's husband straight away.

'He's our main suspect, and it makes sense that he did it,' Rob went on, as though trying to convince himself. 'It's logical, isn't it?'

Ian nodded. Henry not only automatically inherited the house on his wife's death, but he came in to a considerable fortune as well. In addition, if the neighbour's account was reliable, the Martins' marriage had been a miserable affair. Henry could have got rid of his wife and made himself rich, all in a moment.

'He certainly had an incentive to kill her—'

'Two strong motives,' Rob said.

He spoke so slowly, Ian was never sure if he had finished, or was in the middle of a sentence thinking what words to use next.

'But why would he –' Ian began.

The detective inspector raised his eyebrows at the interruption, and Ian instantly fell silent. It wouldn't do to antagonise his senior officer while he was waiting to hear if he had been successful in his bid for promotion. Before long, he hoped to be an inspector himself, holding forth to a less experienced officer who would have to listen respectfully, mindful of his or her own promotion prospects.

'The trouble is, however convinced we are that Henry Martin's guilty, there's no proof,' Rob said.

Ian nodded. He had no grounds for believing Henry was innocent. There was certainly nothing in the man's demeanour to exonerate him. Right from the start he had struck Ian as belligerent, and everything they had discovered about him since then suggested a vindictive character, prone to violent rages. On the face of it, Henry was an obvious suspect. But Ian was convinced he had been genuinely surprised to hear about the manner of his wife's death.

For the time being he decided to keep his impressions to himself. If Henry was guilty, Rob might interpret Ian's hunch as a case of poor judgement. It was a nuisance having to suck up to Rob while trying to appear intelligent and independent, but hopefully it wouldn't be for long. He had been doing well and could see no reason why he shouldn't soon be promoted.

'We're moving up the chain of command,' he had told Bev.

Determined not to let her indifference dampen his spirits when he had completed his training to become an inspector, he had taken her out for an expensive meal to celebrate.

'Some officers are content to remain sergeants for their whole careers, but I'm going all the way to the top. You're going to be so proud of me.'

'You're drunk,' she had retorted. 'And anyway, you're not an inspector yet. Let's not count our chickens before they're hatched.'

Rob leaned back in his chair and drummed his fingers on his desk.

'Proof,' he barked suddenly, sitting upright as though he had thought of something new. 'We need proof.'

'Yes, sir. We'll find it. I'll go round there straight away and ask him a few questions.'

'Yes. See if you can put a bit of pressure on him. And let me know how you get on.'

'Yes, sir.'

Ian hurried off, keen to get to work, and was soon on his way to Herne Bay.

Henry took a while to answer the bell. Ian had just about given up and was on the point of turning away when the door opened.

'Mr Martin.'

'Oh, it's you. What do you want? Have you got any news?'

The widower leaned against the door jamb and adopted a defensive stance with his arms folded across his chest.

'News?' Ian repeated.

'Yes, about who did it, who killed her.'

'Not yet. Can I come in?'

Henry made no move to let him enter but stared suspiciously at Ian.

'What for?' he demanded.

Ian took a step back. He could see the man was frightened and spoke gently.

'Mr Martin, what were your movements on Friday evening?'

'My movements? What do you mean?'

'Where were you on Friday evening?'

Henry chewed his bottom lip and scowled.

Ian repeated his question. This time he allowed a note of impatience to creep in to his voice. He was beginning to suspect the widower was deliberately stalling.

'I went out for a drive,' Henry said at last.

'Where did you go?'

Henry dropped his gaze, an embarrassed expression on his face. He rubbed his shoe against the doorstep as though trying to scrape a piece of chewing gum off the sole.

'Nowhere particular. I can't remember. I was just driving.'

'Were you alone?'

Reluctantly, Henry shook his head.

'No.'

'Who else was with you?'

Henry didn't answer.

'Who was with you?'

Henry glanced over Ian's shoulder.

'You'd better come in.'

Ian perched on the edge of a chair and took out his notebook as Henry gave him the details. The account was rather garbled but Ian gathered that he had been with a woman he called Della on Friday evening.

'What's her full name?'

Henry shook his head. He had only known her as Della.

'Where did you meet her?'

Henry mentioned a lap dancing club in Margate. Ian had never been there but he had heard the name, and knew it had been investigated for underage prostitution.

111

'Where does Della live?'

'How the hell should I know? She didn't invite me round for afternoon tea. Look, it wasn't a regular thing or anything like that. I've only seen her the once, and that was on Friday evening from around eight till about ten. I went straight home and then Mark came in just after I'd come in and put the telly on.'

Ian was busy scribbling notes.

'What time did you leave the club?'

'We weren't at the club.'

'Where did you go?'

Ian was trying to be patient, but it was hard work eliciting a straight response from Henry. He persevered, trying to keep his questions short and simple to answer.

'We were in the car. We drove out of town.'

Although Ian kept his expression fixed, it wasn't lost on him that there might be no CCTV evidence to back up Henry's story. It was unbelievably convenient for the main suspect in a murder investigation. Ian hoped the woman wouldn't back up Henry's account of the evening, if she even existed.

'Where can I find this woman?'

'Ask for her at the club.'

As Ian left, he passed a surly young man in the hall. As tall as Ian, with untidy black hair, he peered out through his fringe like a bashful girl.

'You again,' Mark said, although they hadn't met before.

When Ian expressed his condolences, Mark turned and scurried away. Ian called after him and he stopped, halfway up the stairs, and looked round.

'We'll be coming back to ask you about your movements on Friday evening.'

The young man disappeared up the stairs without a word.

CHAPTER 20

'It is nearly time,' the leader said. 'We have been working towards this day, waiting for you to carry out your sacred task. You were chosen to serve us. With Martha out of the way, the house will be in your gift. You will donate it to the cause as a token of your commitment, and your place at my right hand will be assured.'

The knowledge of his actions terrified him.

'What if someone finds out?' he stuttered. 'What if the police discover what I've done?'

'Have faith and you won't fail,' the leader interrupted, gazing earnestly into his eyes. 'There is no need to fear. You have the power to make it happen. This is your chance. Remember, every true disciple strives to prove himself worthy. For some, fulfilment takes years to achieve. Seize this opportunity while you can. It has not been offered to you by chance. It may not come again.'

He understood then that he was being tested.

'I won't fail you,' he assured the leader, but the words were more for himself than anyone else.

★　★　★

It was true he had made it happen. There had been no other choice, if he was to prove himself a worthy disciple of the one true leader. And as the leader had promised, it had been simple in the end. After all his preparations and worries, the sacrifice itself had been simple. The knife had slipped so easily into her flesh, he had almost laughed as he thrust harder, ignoring her cries, her wild staring eyes, her fingers clawing at the air. Her fear was no longer his problem. He had completed his mission and the leader was pleased.

'Your place in the afterlife is guaranteed,' the leader had assured him, with a bright smile.

'So can I come and live with you now?'

'Not yet.'

'Why not? I have done what you asked.'

'You have served the gods well. They see you are ready to leave your earthly drudgery behind and live out your days with us, free of corruption from the outside world. But your task is not yet complete.'

'What more do they want me to do?'

'Return to your house and continue as before. Be wary. We are beset all around by dangers. Our enemies are everywhere. If the police suspect you were responsible for her death, everything will come to nothing. See to it they never find out what happened. You can arrange it.' The leader's voice was gentle. 'You have my trust.'

The others were recalled and Warrior sat beside the leader, close enough to reach out and touch him. He was truly a servant of the cause. He understood that anyone who stood in their way had to be removed. It was immaterial that she had been the cause of so much trouble in his own life. She no longer existed. Her soul would perish in eternal fires. After more than fifty years of drudgery, she had left the world with nothing. It could so easily have been his own fate, but he had been enlightened. He had been granted a glorious future of everlasting peace. All that mattered was that he had discovered his calling, and he had found courage to answer the summons. The leader had invited him to follow the path of righteousness, and he had been ready. His whole previous life seemed like a distant dream, before he met the leader. Nothing happened by chance. This was his destiny. He was Warrior. He had found enlightenment.

CHAPTER 21

Martha's husband remained their only suspect so far. It seemed unlikely anyone would invent an alibi that could so easily be disproved, but Henry hadn't struck Ian as particularly shrewd, and people often behaved stupidly under pressure. He couldn't find any local record of a girl called Della which didn't surprise him, seeing as he only had a first name which was probably false. He could have initiated a search, but without a real name that was unlikely to produce a result. It would be far quicker to simply pay the club a visit and ask around. As soon as it opened in the evening, he would be there. In the meantime, all he could do was wait. With luck no one at the club would have heard of Della, and it would be obvious Henry had invented his alibi. Or if she did exist, Ian hoped she would deny having spent time with Henry on Friday evening. He imagined her shaking her head and frowning.

'Who the hell's Henry Martin? I don't know anyone called Henry. Someone's taking the piss, mate.'

The day passed slowly, livened up only by joshing

from some of Ian's colleagues who had got wind of his visit to the strip club.

'How come Ian gets all the good gigs?' a constable called out.

'Don't forget to take protection, Sarge, and I'm not talking stab vests.'

'You sure you should be going there, now you're a married man?'

Behind the laughter and ribbing, they were all curious about Henry's alibi.

At last the conventional working day came to an end. At a time when most people were heading home, Ian drove in the opposite direction towards Margate. He tried not to think about his wife arriving home to an empty house where she would spend the evening alone, while he was nearly an hour's drive away, occupied with a job he loved. He frowned. Bev had known what she was letting herself in for. It wasn't as though he had joined the police after they were married. She had no grounds for complaint. She would just have to make the best of her life as the wife of a detective.

One of the earliest English seaside resorts, Margate had attracted holiday makers in the eighteenth and nineteenth centuries when bathing in the sea was fashionable. With the advent of air travel, the town had been unable to compete with cheap holidays in sunnier climates. In spite of its sandy beach and colourful amusement arcades along the front, it had suffered a steady decline. A large sign on the front advertised the rebuilding of Dreamland, a former theme park, once a major attraction of the region. Behind the sign a huge metal skeleton of a rollercoaster towered above the high fence, visibly rusting. There was no evidence of its restoration and the whole area had an atmosphere of decay. Ian turned off the coastal road up a narrow street that led around the back of the arcades. He parked on a double yellow line next to a couple of large waste bins at the bottom of a metal fire escape.

The entrance to the club was a small dirty black door. As he approached it he felt rather than heard the vibration of music, a dull regular bass thumping. At the same time he made out the sign, 'Over 21s Only' beside the door. A massive bruiser of a man with a shaven head and crooked nose materialised from nowhere, demanding an entry fee.

'I'm a non-paying member.'

'No one goes in without paying.'

Ian squared up to him, a head taller than the bouncer, and almost as bulky. He reached into his pocket for his warrant card.

'I belong to a bigger club than this.'

With that, he barged past the other man and pushed open the door.

'Hang about,' the bouncer called after him. 'You can't just walk in unannounced—'

Ian took no notice. He didn't need to wait for permission from some jumped up thug in a stab vest before entering the premises.

A powerful, artificially sweet, fragrance hit him, making him blink in the dimly lit hallway where a voluptuous woman with long dark curly hair was standing in front of a red velvet curtain.

'Hello, handsome.'

She posed provocatively for him and fiddled with a zip on the front of her dress, pulling it down to expose an unnaturally deep cleavage. As the zip slipped down, her eyes moved suggestively up and down Ian's body. He wondered if this was what women meant when they complained about men undressing them with their eyes.

'Have you come to watch the show?' she drawled in husky tones.

It was a tawdry opening move in a game designed to fleece him, but there was something seductive about her sordid performance that was hard to resist.

'I'm looking for a girl called Della,' he said brusquely, shifting his gaze from her exposed breasts.

The woman's stance altered as abruptly as though she had been slapped. She straightened up, adjusted her dress and glared at him.

'You a cop?'

Ian hesitated only a second before pulling out his warrant card. There was no point in trying to conceal his identity. Either a woman called Della worked there or she didn't. Just then the doorman burst into the hallway.

'Pigs,' he called out.

The woman looked past Ian.

'You took your time,' she snapped.

Her voice had lost its softness, and she looked older than Ian had first thought.

'He pushed his way in—'

'Get back on the door and do what you're paid to do. Moron,' she added under her breath. 'Bloody useless moron.'

The bouncer had already disappeared outside.

She switched her attention back to Ian. Her manner was so business-like it was hard to believe this was the same woman who had been coming on to him only a moment before.

'Now, what did you say you wanted? You can't hang around here all night. Are you on your own? This isn't a raid, is it?'

'There's no raid. I'm looking for a girl called Della. Is she here?'

His hopes that she would shake her head, with a bemused expression on her face, vanished at once.

'What's she done?'

Ian was tempted to tell the woman to mind her own business, but he needed her co-operation.

'She hasn't done anything. She's a potential witness in a case we're investigating and I need to speak to her at once. It's important.'

'You're impatient,' the woman teased, twisting her body with a flicker of her practised routine. 'Quite a looker for a cop. I suppose you're going to tell me you're a happily married man?'

'Della,' Ian reminded her sharply, suppressing a smile at her shameless flirting.

She gestured to him to follow her through a side door into a small waiting room furnished with a shabby velvet sofa and a couple of large armchairs. Ian perched on a chair and the woman went out, leaving the door open. After a few moments a man in a grey coat entered the hall. Ian watched through the open door as the dark-haired woman recommenced her act, leaning back provocatively and fiddling with her dress. At one point she turned her head sideways, and smiled when she saw Ian's eyes on her. After a few minutes, his view was blocked as another woman appeared in the doorway. Wearing a very short tight black dress, she teetered into the room on absurdly high stiletto heels. Any illusion of glamour was countered by the graceless way she moved. She closed the door on Ian's view of the performance out in the hall.

'What can I do for you, big boy? I hear you been asking for me.'

She came and stood close enough to Ian for him to smell the cloying sweetness of her perfume, mingled with a stale odour of sweat and alcohol. Her heavily painted face was framed by brittle blonde curls. Her arms and legs were skinny, her thin figure oddly unbalanced by unnaturally large breasts which must have put a strain on her back. The whole package struck Ian as faintly grotesque. He thought about Bev's lovely figure, everything about her in proportion and graceful, and a wave of pity swept through him for the ungainly creature in front of him, struggling to eke out a living from her pitiful appearance. Any man who succumbed to her charms would have to be seriously drunk, or else desperate. Yet she would have been quite pretty if she had taken better care of herself. Close up, he could see she had tried to conceal a bad complexion beneath a thick layer of make-up. Dark red lipstick failed to hide several unsightly cracks in the skin on her lower lip, and she had greyish bags under her eyes from lack of sleep.

'Where were you on Friday evening?'

'Who's asking?'

Ian repeated his question.

'Are you Henry's brother?'

Ian's hopes were crushed at hearing the suspect's name on her lips. Resigned, he held up his warrant card. She waved it away without even glancing at it.

'Friday evening?' she repeated slowly.

Ian had the impression she was trotting out a story she had learned by rote, but there was nothing he could do about it. Dismayed, he held up a small photograph.

'Do you recognise this man?'

She leaned forward, squinted at the picture, and nodded without hesitation.

'Yeah, that's him. That's Henry. That's the punter I was with on Friday night.'

'I need you to go to the police station to make a statement.'

Della took a step backwards. She looked startled.

'Police station? What statement? What are you talking about? You said you were his brother.'

'No, I never said I was anyone's brother.'

'You're not his brother then?'

Ian spoke slowly, trying to get through to her.

'I'm a police sergeant.'

She hesitated.

'You don't want to get in trouble over this, do you?'

'Trouble? What kind of trouble?'

'It's not a good idea to withhold information from the police. So, are you going to go to the station to make a statement? It won't take long.'

'I don't see why I should but I suppose I can. But I can't do it now. I'm working.'

She promised to go into the police station in Margate the next day. Wary of frightening her away, Ian had to be content with that.

CHAPTER 22

Ian was going over his report once again. Sitting in Rob's office, he went into greater detail than he had felt able to record in writing, describing the club, its pole dancers and prostitutes, and Della herself, young and vulnerable.

'You're sure she was talking about Henry Martin?'

'Yes, sir. She actually mentioned his name before I did, his first name that is, and she recognised his photo. The thing is –' He hesitated. 'I'm not convinced she was telling the truth. She came up with his name so quickly, bang on cue. Why would she remember his name? She must see different punters every night of the week. She said she'd only met him the one time, on Friday, yet on Tuesday she came up with his name just like that. I think I ought to go over there and question her again, when she goes in to make a formal statement.'

'Good idea. Once she's there, we can probably be more – persuasive.'

They didn't speculate long about why a girl like Della might be telling lies about a suspect.

'How much do you think he paid her?' Rob asked.

Ian shrugged. 'Della's not put anything into her bank account. In fact, very little seems to go in and out of it. She must be paid in cash.'

'Perhaps we should get a warrant and search her rooms, see if she's got a wad of money stashed away?'

'We'd need grounds,' Rob said. 'I'm not sure if we can swing it. Ask Polly to do some digging. I dare say we'll find something on her, but it might take a while.'

'We'd better get on with it, if we're going to, sir. I doubt if she'd hang on to that kind of money for long. She didn't strike me as a saver. Clothes, drugs, booze, you know. It's already nearly a day since I saw her, and if he paid her off yesterday it could already have gone without trace.'

'See if the drug squad have any information about her being flush with cash. Of course it won't prove anything, but it all helps us build a picture.'

'Yes, sir.'

Ian went off to find Polly and pass on the instruction to carry out some research into Della's background, and her spending pattern over the past day. The constable's smile faded when Ian admitted he couldn't give her a full name.

'Della? That's not much to go on, is it?'

He told her where Della worked.

'She was jumpy as hell so I didn't press her for her real name. But the club's a start. They're cagey about giving anything away but lean on them. Find out as much as you can. Any form, and any dropped charges would be great. We need to put pressure on her, because she's giving Henry Martin an alibi for Friday when—'

'I know what happened on Friday,' Polly interrupted, grinning. 'I work here, remember? Talking of which, I've found out something that might interest you. Henry withdrew a thousand quid first thing Monday morning.'

Ian suspected that money had been given to Della in exchange for an alibi.

'We need to find out where she lives so we can scare her into telling us the truth.'

'Once I've spoken to Mark and his friend I'll see what I can find out,' she promised.

'Why don't you leave them to me, and you can get on with looking into Della?'

'Apparently he's got a young girl with him who looks petrified, so—'

'Ah, she's more likely to talk to a nice friendly woman than a big scary policeman, eh?'

'We thought she might be more comfortable talking to a woman.'

'Yes, of course, I was only joking. Come on then.'

Not convinced Henry was guilty, despite his dubious alibi, Ian was keen to hear what his son had to say.

Mark was sitting beside a girl who looked about fourteen. Her long straight hair was almost white, as were her eyelashes, while her eyes were a very pale watery blue. Everything about her was wraith-like from her extreme pallor to her emaciated figure. She was so nervous, she trembled all the time Polly was gently questioning her. The girl gave her name as Eve Thompson, said she was seventeen, and reeled off an address and telephone number. Mark fidgeted impatiently as he listened.

'The point is she was with me on Friday evening,' he blurted out suddenly. 'That's why I brought her here. You said you wanted to know what I was doing on Friday evening. Well, here she is. We split up just after ten and I went straight home. There was nothing to eat there because –' His voice broke.

The girl threw a terrified glance at him but he patted her hand reassuringly, whispering something Ian didn't catch.

'My dad was at home when I got in, about ten. I was starving, so I went out to get sausages and chips, and then I went straight home again.'

Nearly five days had passed since Martha's body had been discovered, and so far no one had come forward with any useful information.

'Someone somewhere must know something,' Rob grumbled as Ian sat in his office, bringing the inspector up to speed with the minimal progress they had made.

Neither of them held out much hope of getting the truth from Della. They discussed the chances of broadcasting a reconstruction of the victim's last hours, but they didn't have enough information about her movements in the time leading up to her death. All they knew was that she had been killed around nine at night, probably while sitting on the bench where her body had been found. It wasn't enough to warrant organising a full reconstruction, in the hope of jogging someone's memory. An image of a woman who looked like Martha, sitting on the bench in the park, would serve the same purpose.

'Were you out for a walk on Friday evening? Did you see this woman?'

Rejecting the idea of a reconstruction, Rob suggested they broadcast an appeal on television, with Henry and his son sitting on either side of the inspector. They would beg members of the public to come forward if they knew anything that might help to find whoever had committed the murder. Even if they had been in the area of the park without noticing anything suspicious, any eyewitness account could be helpful. Ian jumped to his feet.

'I'll get on to it right away, sir.'

They both knew it was best to send out such appeals as soon after the event as possible, before people had a chance to forget what they had seen. It might already be too late, but they could at least try. Anything was better than sitting around helplessly, waiting for something to turn up.

On his way out to find Henry and invite him to join in the appeal, Ian checked to see how Polly was getting on. She had managed to worm out of the manager of the club that Della's real name was Jade Higgins.

'How old is she?'

'Guess.'

He shrugged. He didn't have a clue.

'Anything from twenty-five to thirty-five.'

'Twenty.'

Ian was surprised and a little shocked.

'She looks more like forty,' he said, remembering Della's raddled face.

Ian didn't bother to call first. He wasn't expecting Henry to be at home early on Wednesday afternoon, but thought he would drive out to Herne Bay anyway and take another look at the park where Martha had been stabbed, while he was waiting for her husband to come home. He tried the house first and was surprised when Henry opened the door. He explained he had been given two weeks' compassionate leave from work.

'They don't usually,' he added. 'They're a bunch of bastards as a rule. But the case has been in the papers and they're worried I might upset some of the customers if I turn up to fit their kitchens just now. The bosses are fussy about their image.'

Briefly, Ian outlined the reason for his visit. To begin with, Henry didn't seem to grasp what he was talking about.

'An appeal' he repeated, 'what's that?'

Ian explained and finally the widower nodded to indicate he had understood.

'OK,' he said, 'go ahead. I don't mind. Why would I? Do what you have to do.'

Ian explained that he hadn't come to request permission.

'What do you want then?'

'It helps in these instances to have a family member of the victim present.'

'You want me to be there?'

'Yes.'

'What? On the telly?'

'Yes.'

Henry shook his head.

'I don't think so.'

Ian wasn't surprised. It was a common reaction. It wasn't hard to persuade Henry to change his mind, once Ian insisted that it was likely to be a real help in gathering information that would lead to an arrest.

'Well, if you're sure it will help.'

'There are no guarantees, Mr Martin, but the chances are high that it will help encourage a witness to come forward.'

He didn't get on so well when he suggested Mark join them. At first Henry was evasive, claiming he didn't know where his son was. Then he said he thought Mark might be busy, and when Ian asked for his mobile number, his father claimed not to know it. Finally, when Ian said he would trace the number himself, Henry told him bluntly not to bother.

'You won't get him on the telly to talk about his mother.'

'Not even to help find out who killed her?'

'He's too upset. They were very close. You can try if you like, but I don't suppose he'll even want to talk to you. You'd do better to leave the lad alone. He's been through enough, with all this. Now if that's all—'

'There is one other question, Mr Martin. You withdrew a thousand pounds from your bank account on Monday.'

'So? It's not a crime to spend money, is it?'

'What was it for?'

Henry didn't hesitate.

'I blew it.'

'Blew it? Do you have any receipts?'

Henry gave a bark of laughter.

'Look, I went into town on Monday night and got completely plastered and as far as I can remember I bought drinks for a load of strangers. I ended up in a cab. Someone put me in it and I got home somehow. But don't ask me where I went or how I got there, because I couldn't tell you, I was so out of it. Wouldn't you be, if your wife had just been murdered?'

CHAPTER 23

Rob was busy setting up the television appeal. Ian was relieved he didn't have to be involved in it but, at the same time, he couldn't help feeling slightly disappointed at being excluded from the bustle. He knew he was being unreasonable. It wasn't as though Rob would learn anything new from talking for a few minutes on camera. On the contrary, Ian was more likely to pick up new information if the broadcast prompted people to phone in, which was the intention. Having written up his decision log he took a quick break and was pleased to come across Polly in the canteen. Over a mug of tea, she told him she had spoken to Eve Thompson's father who had confirmed her identity. It was a disappointment, even though Mark had never really been a suspect. He had no motive for killing his mother and by all accounts had been very close to her. Meanwhile the net was closing in on Henry, whose witness seemed anything but reliable.

Jade Higgins had been working as a pole dancer for a few years. Her stint at the club in Margate was the longest she had stayed in any one place. Before she took up dancing, her history had been erratic. Her mother had given her up for adoption at birth. The couple who had taken her in had never completed the formal adoption process but had relinquished her into care when she was only eighteen months old. From there she had passed through a succession of foster homes and institutions, until she had dropped out of the system when she reached sixteen. She had turned up in Margate a year later by which time she had reinvented herself as Della. There she had embarked on a brief affair with an older man who had thrown money at her for a while, paying for an abortion, and cosmetic surgery on her breasts and nose. When he tired of her, she had found a job as a pole dancer.

'And she's still only twenty,' Polly concluded. 'It's not much of a life so far, is it?'

Ian nodded without answering.

'I remember being twenty,' Polly screwed up her face. 'With my dad being on the force, I suppose it was always there at the back of my mind, that was what I was going to do, but at twenty I hadn't grown up yet. And she's already had abortions and plastic surgery, and been a prostitute, and God knows what else besides.'

Ian tidied up his desk and set off early to meet a former colleague for a drink on his way home. He glanced at his watch and put his foot down. His previous detective inspector was waiting for him when he reached the pub. They had worked together before she left the Murder Squad in Kent for London. As a single woman Geraldine could please herself, but Ian was keen to avoid any risk of gossip and had suggested meeting in a small pub off the beaten track where they were unlikely to be spotted. It was absurd and at the same time quite exciting. He felt like a kid bunking off school.

'So what's it like, living in London?'

He shifted in his seat, trying to fit his long legs comfortably under the table without knocking into her.

'Honest truth or sanitised version?'

'What do you think?'

She gave a rueful smile.

They had worked so closely together, he could sense that she wanted to talk about her experience. An absolute trust had developed between them, a kind of intimacy that often arose between colleagues working side by side in the emergency services and armed forces knowing there might be times when their very survival depended on mutual understanding. He was beginning to doubt he would ever share such a close relationship with his wife. The thought made him almost unbearably sad. He was dismayed to hear that Geraldine was finding London a lonely place to live.

'I've got a great sergeant, though she's not like you, of course.'

He couldn't help grinning.

'We made a good team, didn't we?'

'Your turn.'

'What?'

'Tell me about married life.'

He hesitated, tempted to unburden himself. Loyalty to Bev restrained him.

'It's fine.'

She knew he was lying and smiled in unspoken sympathy.

Stopping on the way home to fill up with petrol, he bought a bunch of flowers and a bottle of wine at the garage. There was no reason not to think kindly of his wife. He told himself the flowers had nothing to do with his friendship with Geraldine. He ran up the path, hoping Bev hadn't arrived before him. The house was empty. He took some salmon pieces out of the freezer and put them in the microwave to defrost while he laid the table. Half an hour later he had made a bowl of salad, boiled potatoes and put them in the oven to brown, and had the fish defrosted and ready to grill. He poured himself a beer and sat down to wait for Bev. She was usually home by half past six. He dozed off in front of the television. When he woke up it was half past eight and she still wasn't home. Worried, he tried her mobile.

'Hi, thank you for calling. Leave a message and I'll call you back.'

Ian thought about the cases he had worked on involving missing persons; young women, teenagers, children. He tried Bev's phone once more, and again the phone went straight to voicemail. He flung himself down on the sofa, flicked through different channels on the television and opened another beer, telling himself she would be home soon. Half an hour later, he heard the front door slam and leaped to his feet.

'Where the hell have you been?'

'What?'

She took off her shoes and placed them carefully on the rack in the hall without looking up. Ian watched her, admiring the curve of her calves and her elegant hands. She straightened up and took off her coat. He noticed she was smartly dressed, in a knee-length pencil skirt that showed off her slim hips. He guessed she had gone out straight from work.

'It's gone nine.'

'So?'

She turned her back on him to hang her coat in the cupboard.

'I was worried.'

'Worried? Why? It's not late.'

Too late, he realised he had walked straight into a minefield. Hands on hips, Bev spun round and launched her attack, demanding to know how often he had been late home.

'Well? Has one week gone by when you haven't been home late?'

'That's not fair,' he protested. 'I don't work

regular hours, and you know it. You're always home by six thirty. I was worried about you.'

Any hope that she would be pleased he had missed her vanished at her verbal onslaught.

'So it's all right for you to come back at all hours, whenever it suits you, but you still expect me to be here when you get home. Well, isn't that just typical? So it's one rule for you and another for me. You can go gadding about to all hours, coming and going whenever it suits you, and that's fine, just as long as the little wife is waiting for you when you decide to come home.'

Ian sloped into the kitchen, overwhelmed by the passion of her invective. He never seemed to get it right where his wife was concerned.

CHAPTER 24

Della felt under her mattress for the envelope, pulled it out and counted the notes again. Forty-six crisp twenty quid notes. It had seemed too good to be true when the old bloke had made the offer. Fifteen hundred quid just to tell his brother she'd been shagging him on Friday night. She had never even seen the bloke before. On Friday evening she had been in the flat washing her hair, watching TV and painting her nails because the manager had sent her home on account of a swollen eye.

'You look like shit. We can't have you putting the punters off, can we?'

'But what about tips?'

'What sort of tips are you expecting to pull, looking like that? Go home and sort your face out, for fuck's sake, and don't come back before you're fixed.'

It was a blow, but she had made the best of it, like she always did. Apart from the loss of earnings, she hadn't been unhappy about spending a few days at home.

★　★　★

A thousand quid, with another five hundred to come, just when she was strapped for cash, had more than compensated for the days off. Talk about a stroke of luck. She counted the money one more time and stuffed two notes into her bag before slipping the rest back under the mattress. It wouldn't last long at the rate she was spending it, but was more than enough to tide her over. In the meantime her eye was no longer inflamed and the bruising was easy enough to conceal with make-up. She was back in the game, as though she had never been away. She took a swig from a bottle and smacked her lips. Mostly she could only afford the cheap stuff, but this was real Smirnoff from Russia, thanks to Henry messing about with his brother's wife.

There was just one problem. Henry hadn't mentioned the police might be interested, and she didn't understand their angle. She lay back on her bed and thought about it now, considering her involvement with Henry from every point of view. What it all boiled down to was that his brother suspected Henry of screwing his wife. Either the brother had complained to the police, or else Henry himself had connections with the police. He might be a cop himself. Or his brother was, more like. She sat up, leaning on her elbow, and took another gulp. The liquid slipped down her throat, burning and cooling at the same time; comforting. She couldn't help feeling sympathetic towards a man who had promised her fifteen hundred quid. So what if he was a cop? If she played her part well, he'd pay up. What the fuck did she care if she spoke to a policeman or to Henry's brother? All she had to do was stick to the same story. It was all a bit confusing, but the money was real enough.

Lying down again, she went through her lines. She had been with Henry on Friday night. He had picked her up in his car – she couldn't remember where – and they had driven out of town, along a dark road – she didn't know where. The rest was like any other punter. They had been in his car driving around for a few hours. It was past ten when he had dropped her off in the town – she couldn't remember where exactly – because she hadn't reached home until half past ten. That was important. She was to say she had been drunk, so his brother would believe her being so hazy about the details. Henry had thought of everything. Nothing could possibly go wrong. As soon as she had spoken to his brother, he said he would give her another five hundred. And it wouldn't end there. He didn't know it yet, but after that she was going to screw another payment out of him, and another. She giggled. It wasn't blackmail. She was doing him a favour. He ought to be pleased to pay up, because she was getting him out of trouble. She sat up and reached for the bottle. It was nearly empty, but she could get more. As much as she wanted.

*   *   *

The front door banged, disturbing her doze. Someone was clattering around in the kitchen. Della hauled herself up out of bed, shoved the empty vodka bottle in a drawer, and checked her money was carefully hidden before she went to join her flatmate in the kitchen.

'You look rough,' Candy said. 'Are you OK?'

'Never better.'

'Tea?'

'I'll make it if you like.'

Candy sat down and slipped her shoes off. She rubbed one of her heels and winced, grumbling about her blisters, while Della put the kettle on and wondered how much dosh she could screw out of Henry before he cut up rough.

She was absorbed in planning how to spend the thousands Henry was going to cough up when Candy's shrill voice made her jump.

'Are you making that tea then?'

'What? Oh yes, sorry. I'm on it.'

As she poured the water, she speculated how much she could squeeze out of her new benefactor: five thousand, ten thousand . . . She hoped he had plenty of cash. He was going to need it, because if he refused to pay her, she would threaten to tell his brother the truth.

'What are you grinning about? Where's that tea?'

Candy's son ran in from her bedroom and sat at the rickety kitchen table, swinging his feet. Candy warmed her hands on her mug of tea while Della switched on the television.

'Nice cuppa,' Candy said, wiggling her toes. 'Oh God, not the bloody news. Turn over for fuck's sake.'

'I want to watch a cartoon,' the little boy shouted.

Della picked up the remote control, and froze.

'Go on, what are you waiting for? Put something else on for fuck's sake.'

'Wait.'

Della leaned forward, glued to the screen, as a grey-haired policeman talked to the camera.

'Turn over, will you?' Candy repeated.

'It's boring. Mum, I don't like it. Make her turn over.'

'Shut up,' Della hissed, flapping her hand in the air, 'I need to listen.'

'But—'

'Shut *up*.'

It wasn't the police officer who had caught Della's attention, but a dour-faced grey-haired man sitting beside him.

'I know him,' she began and stopped.

The police officer was talking about a woman who had been murdered on Friday evening. Della wondered what the hell Henry was doing on the television. It was such a coincidence. She had just met him and now there he was, staring back at her from the screen. The policeman turned to Henry and introduced him, and Henry muttered something about his wife.

'Martha was a wonderful woman.'

He lapsed into silence and the detective started talking again, asking for information to help them find the killer.

'They're talking about that woman who was murdered,' Candy said. 'The whole thing creeps me out. It wasn't that far from here.'

'What woman? Where?'

'God, don't you see the papers? Some woman was stabbed in a park in Herne Bay and killed.'

Della nodded. She was trying to work out what Henry was doing there.

'Are they detectives then?'

Candy gave her a funny look. The news item changed and Della turned to her flatmate.

'Those two blokes that were on the telly, were they both detectives?'

She could hear the panic in her own voice, and looked away.

'Della, what the fuck's wrong with you? Della?'

Della shook her head.

'It's nothing,' she mumbled, and burst out crying.

She couldn't help it. She was so confused, and scared. Candy sent her son into the other room. He protested, until she yelled at him and he ran off, whining.

'Come on, Della,' Candy urged, pushing her dark hair out of her eyes and leaning forwards, her eyes bright with curiosity.

When Della didn't say anything, she sat back in her chair again.

'Look, I'll make us another cup of tea and then you can tell me all about it. You know you can trust me. And if you're in any kind of trouble, you know I'm your friend.'

Della knew Candy was only really concerned about her paying her share of the rent, but she felt grateful all the same. It was nice to have someone to talk to.

Five minutes later, she had told Candy all about her conversation with Henry.

'He told me it was because he'd been screwing around with his brother's wife,' she hiccupped, 'and I believed him. But it's not that at all, is it? It's because he killed his wife.'

She broke down again, sobbing hysterically.

'He wanted you to give him an alibi,' Candy agreed. 'Jesus, that's bad.'

'I'm so scared, I don't know what to do.'

Candy nodded solemnly.

'You've got to be careful.'

'I know. He's a killer. He could do me in—'

Candy sipped her tea for a moment, thinking.

'How much did he give you?' she asked at last.

'What?'

'Oh come on, you know what I'm talking about. He must have paid you to cover for him. You're not going to do it for nothing.' She paused expectantly. 'How much?'

Della coughed.

'Enough.'

Candy snorted.

'How much is enough?'

'He bunged me five hundred.'

'Is that all?'

Della heaved a sigh. 'I should have asked for more, shouldn't I?'

'Five hundred quid to keep the guy out of the nick. That's poor.'

'Yes, but I didn't know that then. I thought he was just trying to stop his brother finding out he'd been playing around with his brother's wife. I didn't know about – that.' Pointing at the television, she began to cry. 'But that's not important right now, is it?'

'What the hell is important, if not the dosh? He's a cheapskate! You should've told him to get lost.'

'I nearly did, but I thought, five hundred quid is five hundred quid, and I'd been off work last week. Five hundred quid for nothing, that's what I thought.'

'Five hundred quid's nothing for what he asked you to do.'

'No, but I didn't know that then. I thought he'd just been playing around. What I need to think about is, should I go to the police or not?'

'The police?' Candy sounded shocked.

'Should I tell them what I know? What would you do if you were me?'

★　★　★

Candy leaned forward and spoke in a low voice, as though she was afraid someone might be listening.

'Go and see him, tell him you need five thousand – no, say ten thousand, because there are two of us in this now. But he doesn't need to know that. Don't tell him you blabbed. He has to trust you or you might be next.'

'Next?'

'He did his wife in, didn't he?'

The two girls stared at one another and Della's eyes widened in horror.

'Look,' Candy said at last. 'There's nothing to get upset about. This is fantastic.'

Della stopped snivelling and looked up as Candy went on.

'What I mean is, five hundred isn't much, but there could be a lot more where that came from.' She grinned. 'Shit, he pulled a fast one, but it wasn't your fault. You weren't to know. But now we do know, we'll fleece the bastard for all he's got. He'll give us thousands. Because if he doesn't, he'll be banged up!'

Della began to cry again. Between sobs, she revealed that she had already spoken to the police. A detective had been to see her at the club and questioned her about Henry.

'But that's not all. I've got to go to the police station and give a statement. I was supposed to go yesterday. Only now I don't know what I should tell them.'

'What did you say?'

'I said what I'd been told to say, that I was with him on Friday evening. I never should have agreed to do it. I knew there was something not right about him. Now I've gone and lied to the police.'

'So what? He doesn't know that, does he? And in any case, it makes no difference if he finds out or not. You've given him his alibi now, and if he wants to keep things the way they are, he'll have to pay up.'

'Oh my God, what am I going to do?' Della wailed, breaking down in tears again.

'Don't worry, babes. I'm with you now. I'll come with you when you go and see him. That way you'll be safe. Now, go and get my half of the five hundred. Share and share alike now we're in this together.'

CHAPTER 25

O nce the thrill of owning such a wicked knife wore off, Ben realised he had a problem. His mother was always poking around in his room, sniffing for fags and rifling through his drawers for any spare cash. To be fair, he had done the same to her before she shacked up with Eddy. Once he had taken a bottle of gin from her room, pretending to know nothing about it when she went berserk. The poor cow was off her trolley about almost everything, but she knew he'd stolen her booze. All the same, she hadn't been able to do anything about it other than slap him around a bit. It hadn't even hurt. But with Eddy on the scene, he no longer dared risk fingering his mother's things. If she discovered the knife in his room she'd accuse him of having nicked it, which was a lie. He had found it, which wasn't the same thing at all. Eddy would give him a serious beating, after taking the knife for himself. Apart from the fact that he was a thieving selfish git, anyone in his right mind would be glad of a knife like that.

★   ★   ★

He had been puzzling over where to hide it for nearly a week. So far he had kept it out of sight, inside the trousers of his one pair of pyjamas which he never wore. His mother had given them to him last Christmas and they had been too small for him even then. He had chucked them in the wardrobe and forgotten about them. No one else knew they were there at the bottom of a pile of underwear and T-shirts. Crouched on the floor of his bedroom, alert for any sound of footsteps coming up the stairs, he stroked the flat of the blade gently. He took care not to touch the sharp edge which had already cut his thumb once. The blade sliced through his flesh like a razor. It was awesome. He might never get hold of such a knife again. The fact that he had no idea where it had come from made him shiver with excitement. It could have belonged to a serial killer who used it to carve up bodies, or it might have fallen out of an assassin's pack as he was returning from a mission. Whatever else happened, Ben had to hang on to it. Eddy must never take it from him.

Another problem with Eddy getting his hands on the knife was that it would leave Ben more vulnerable than ever at school. Until now he had managed to muddle along OK, keeping his head down. He was too small to look threatening, but not weak or weedy enough to be a magnet for the bullies. Most of the time, they ignored him. What money he had, they nicked. It never amounted to much. They had taken his phone, his second-hand iPod, and the crappy headphones he had lifted off some little kid. But by and large the bullies left him alone, only chasing him in the street when they chanced to bump into him. If they caught him they would expend more energy jeering at him than hitting him, just to humiliate him. He lay awake at night plotting horrible vengeance against every member of their gang, but he had never been seriously afraid of them. Until now.

Other pupils had begun talking. It had kicked off quietly. He became aware that pupils he barely knew were throwing him curious glances. He wasn't used to attracting attention like that. It made him nervous. Then members of the gang started coming up to him in the corridor, blocking his way, threatening him.

'Think you're hard, do you? You ain't so hard.'

'You better watch your back, faggot.'

'Someone gonna shank you, when you ain't expectin' it.'

He had only shown his knife to a couple of boys in his own year, and already his new bravado had backfired. Tougher boys thought he was issuing a challenge, and they were out to get him. He wondered what they would do to him.

'You remember Mouldy?' one of his friends said, breathless with excitement. 'Mouldy who went

151

missing from school last term? Chas done that. And he said he's gonna do for you too.'

It confirmed what Ben had already worked out: he had to hang on to his knife at all costs. Without it, he was as good as dead. The teachers said Mouldy had moved away, but the rumours told Ben all he needed to know. Teachers didn't know shit. He would have to be armed at all times. He never knew when his enemies might strike. If he wasn't ready to defend himself he would disappear, like Mouldy.

He wasn't confident about leaving the knife at home. At the same time, it was too risky to stash it at school. The lockers were like a black hole. It was one thing leaving books there, but anything worth having vanished: phones, cash, iPods, food and weapons. It was no coincidence that since he had shown his knife to a couple of mates the padlock on his locker had been busted, and his books had been scattered on the floor. Whoever had been going through his belongings wasn't looking for school books. At lunch time he slipped into the DT block and went into the textiles room. A teacher was in there. Young and blonde, she looked up with an irritated frown. Her head shook slightly from side to side as though she was nervous.

'What is it now?' she asked as though he was constantly pestering her, although he had never spoken to her before.

'Nothing, Miss. Only I was wondering if boys are allowed to do textiles in year ten.'

He sidled across the room, his eyes fixed on the teacher, and knocked into a bench. A load of sewing gear fell on the floor.

'Sorry, Miss.'

Kneeling down he grabbed a handful of cotton reels and some packets of needles and stuffed them in his pocket. Preoccupied with promoting her subject, the teacher didn't notice what he was doing. Armed with his booty he stood up, ignoring the remaining reels of cotton still rolling across the floor trailing delicate threads. The teacher went on lecturing him about textiles as an option, and how there was no reason why boys shouldn't take the subject, it wasn't only for girls.

'Thanks, Miss. Gotta go.'

'Come and see me again,' she called out after him. 'Remember, boys are welcome to do textiles.'

CHAPTER 26

Della reached down to feel around under her mattress but the envelope wasn't there. Panicking, she leaped out of bed and knelt down so she could push her arm further under the mattress until her groping fingers found the money. Clutching the envelope she climbed back into bed and counted the notes. A knock on her door made her start.

'Are you coming?'

Della swore. It was nearly time to go to work.

'Hang on,' she yelled back. 'I'm just getting dressed.'

She jumped out of bed and took another forty quid out of the envelope before shoving it back under her mattress, as far as she could reach. Then she hurried to get ready. While she was doing her face, Candy tapped at her door again.

'Are you coming?'

'Just give me a minute.'

From the living room she could hear a buzz of voices. The boy would be asleep by the time they got home. If he had been Della's son, she would have worried about leaving him in the flat by himself, but Candy insisted he was fine. When they got back she would be annoyed if she found him fast asleep on the sofa with the television blaring, but Della understood that the voices made him feel less lonely.

'Turn that off soon and get to sleep,' Candy called out as they left.

It was already dark outside. The cold was biting. They hurried along the main road and turned up a narrow side street that led behind the amusement arcades to the club. Della pulled up her collar. Her thin coat was shower proof but not very warm. There was no one else on the pavement, so they were able to talk. Glancing around, Della nudged Candy's arm.

'You won't tell anyone, will you?'

'What?'

Candy was facing away from her flatmate. Now she paused in her stride and turned to look at Della. Candy's thick mascara was already a little smudged from the cold air making her eyes water.

'You know, what I was telling you, about that man.' Della looked around nervously. 'The man on the telly. You mustn't breathe a word to anyone.'

'What about the other girls? Aren't you going to tell them?'

'No. No one must know about it, not until he's been arrested. As far as he's concerned, I don't know who he is. If he finds out I know what he's done, he might think I'll go to the police and tell them the whole truth. So you mustn't say anything. Promise me.'

Candy's grin died away at the urgency in Della's voice.

'All right, all right. Don't get in a state about it. I can't see why you're getting so worked up. He must realise you won't go to the police, not when you can make so much money out of it.' She grinned. 'No one would be that stupid. And we'd be mad to tell anyone about it. It's our secret. That money's ours. It's no one else's business.'

Della nodded uncertainly. She couldn't get her head around the fact that she was covering for a man who had killed his wife. It was all right for Candy. She wasn't involved like Della was. And then there was the detective waiting for her to go to the police station and give a statement. If they ever found out she was lying she would probably be banged up for withholding information, perverting the course of justice, or whatever they called it. But if she went to the police, and Henry found out, it would be curtains for her. Either way she was fucked. As if that wasn't enough, when she arrived at the club she was told the manager wanted to see her.

'Why?'

'He didn't say.'

The room was warm. Stinking of sweat and perfume like the rest of the place, it was furnished with a small pine desk and a set of black leather chairs. The manager sat on a black leather swivel chair which he rotated slightly from side to side as he spoke. The movement made Della feel sick as she stared at his pale bloated face. Above his dark suit and black shirt, his head seemed to hover in the air. The fat bastard made it quite clear he didn't give a toss about how Della was feeling, or that her life might be in danger. All he cared about was his own skin, which meant keeping the club out of trouble. His bald head gleamed under the central light bulb, and beads of sweat glowed on his upper lip as he spoke.

'What's this I hear about you getting in hot water?' he demanded.

'I don't know what you mean,' Della mumbled. 'Someone's been spreading lies about me. It's all bollocks.'

'So why was a police officer here on Tuesday night, asking for you?'

'I said, it's nothing. It's a mistake. He thought I was someone else.'

'Don't try to pull the wool over my eyes, you cocksucker. You think I was born yesterday? What's going on?'

'It was a mistake. He was asking me about some bloke I never met. It's nothing to do with me. I told you, I never even met the guy he was looking for.'

She scowled at him across the desk.

'Don't you fucking talk to any pig again as long as you're working here,' he said.

'I never asked to talk to him. You sent me to see him.'

Watching him fidget uncomfortably in his chair, she realised she had answered him back with a confidence she had never previously felt. For the first time, the reality of her situation struck her. Before long she would be telling Jimmy to stick his stingy wages up his fat arse.

'Don't bloody argue with me. Look,' he leaned forward on his elbows, his voice softer. 'I can't have any of my girls consorting with villains. It gives the place a bad name.'

Della gave a snort of genuine amusement.

'That's a joke. Like I said, it was a mistake. It was nothing to do with me. I don't even know the bloke they were looking for.'

'You are not to tell the police anything, you are not to even talk to them while you're here.'

'I never told them nothing. It was a mistake,' she insisted.

Jimmy rose clumsily to his feet.

'If you want to hang onto your job, you'd better start behaving yourself,' he warned her.

'You don't have to worry about me,' she assured him. 'I'm just fine and dandy.'

He scowled before dismissing her with a wave of his podgy hand.

CHAPTER 27

Ian was growing impatient. Twenty-four hours had passed since the television appeal, and so far it hadn't come up with anything more than a few crank calls. To add to his frustration, three days had passed since he had questioned Della at the club but she still hadn't shown up at the police station in Margate to give her statement. He couldn't help feeling he should have put more pressure on her to give a formal statement when he had the chance. He was sure she had been lying. If Henry was innocent he would hardly have taken so much trouble to provide himself with an alibi. Yet he wasn't convinced Henry was guilty. Something didn't add up.

'Perhaps he was scared,' Polly suggested when Ian asked her what she thought.

'Scared? How do you mean?'

'He must realise he's likely to be a suspect, seeing as he was married to the victim. So he's scared. He hasn't got an alibi. Maybe he thought he ought to sort one out, pay his way out of trouble.'

'He could certainly afford to pay for it now,' Ian

agreed. 'But a false alibi doesn't necessarily mean he's guilty.'

'It doesn't exactly suggest he's innocent.'

'No, but like you said, he's probably feeling worried, whether he's guilty or not.'

It was dark by the time Ian set off for Margate. He felt edgy. Polly had offered to accompany him, but the visit was more likely to be productive if he went alone. He had spoken to Della before, and it would be better to treat this as a routine follow-up visit. He played it through in his mind as he was speeding along the Thanet Way. Obviously Della wouldn't be pleased at his returning to the club to talk to her again. He might even have difficulty getting to see her. Staff at the club would recognise him, and certainly wouldn't welcome him back there. He was prepared to throw his weight around to gain access to her, and ready for her to be hostile towards him, and defensive about not having given her statement yet. It was likely to be a difficult visit.

The bulky doorman stepped forward and crossed his arms, peering at Ian from beneath Neanderthal brows.

'What's your game then?'

Ian brushed him aside. 'If you want to know about police procedure, you need to change your job. Now are you going to step aside, or would you rather be arrested for obstruction?'

'All right, guv, keep your hair on.'

Once again a hideously strong perfume hit him as soon as he stepped through the door. A different woman was on duty this time. Not recognising him, she opened a curtain and ushered him into the bar where a single pole dancer was gyrating on a podium. It was early but the auditorium was already quite packed. Ian had first been there on a Tuesday evening when a few men had given the place a sleazy atmosphere. On Friday the place had a different ambience, bustling and cheerful. People had gone there after work for a night out. At one table a stag party was making a racket, laughing and cheering on a lap dancer.

Ian followed the woman back out into the poorly lit foyer and explained the reason for his visit.

'Who did you say you wanted to see?'

Ian repeated his request. She denied knowing anyone called Della. When Ian pressed her, she told him to wait while she fetched the manager. Ian waited. He was prepared to be patient. Through the curtain he heard chattering voices, braying laughter and the bass thumping of music. He wondered what Bev would say if she could see him standing in the grubby hall of a sordid strip club while she was sitting at home, also waiting.

At last the woman trotted back on her high heels and gestured for him to follow her along a narrow passageway. She led him through a door into a small office where a large man sat behind a wooden desk, picking his teeth with a blue cocktail stick.

'So, Inspector,' he greeted Ian with a surly smile.

Ian didn't correct the fat man's mistake. With luck it would soon be accurate to address him as Inspector.

'I'm looking for Della.'

The other man picked his teeth thoughtfully for a second.

'She's not available right now,' he said at last. 'I can offer you another girl. Plenty more where she came from.'

'Where is she?'

'I told you, she's not available. She's working, earning her keep.'

'I'd like to speak to her, please.'

'She's working. Tell you what,' he went on, suddenly brisk. 'I'm a busy man, Inspector. I'm sure you are too. Why don't you go in and watch the show. Those girls are easy on the eye.' He winked. 'Then when they finish, you can question Della all night for all I care. But you can't speak to her before the show's over. Fair's fair. You can wait your turn like the rest of us.'

The man's suggestive manner needled Ian. Declining the offer to watch the pole dancing, he stood up and said he would return in an hour.

'Make sure Della's here when I get back.'

After the brash young detective had left the office, Jimmy sat drumming his thick fingers on the desk.

162

He had done his best to get rid of the unwelcome visitor, but the pig clearly wasn't going to give up easily. He poured himself a generous slug of Scotch, gulped it down, and called Alf who was on the door.

'Has he gone?'

Alf wasn't exactly intelligent, but he could be sharp enough when it mattered. He knew straight away who Jimmy was talking about. Hearing his bouncer grunt into the phone, Jimmy waited until he could talk. A few seconds passed before Alf came back on the line.

'He's gone, boss, but he said he'd be back.'

'Right. Buzz me when he shows up again.'

'Will do.'

Jimmy knew what to do. He opened his door and bawled out Yvonne's name. She appeared at once, as though she had been waiting for a summons. Jimmy squinted at her as she stood in the doorway, wondering what the hell had happened to her. Once she had been a real looker, with a magnificent body. Now she was just a wrinkled face on top of a spray of twig-like limbs. He glanced regretfully down at his paunch. The years hadn't improved him either. Yvonne with her drugs, himself with the drink, neither of them had weathered well.

'What did he want?' she demanded.

A pig sniffing around asking questions gave everyone the jitters. Not that they had anything to hide. The activities at the club were all perfectly legit, consenting adults having a good time. Nothing wrong with that. Still, it was bad for business if the word got out.

'He's gone,' he said tersely.

'Good riddance.'

She came into the room, closed the door and waited to hear what he wanted. Jimmy heaved a sigh that shook his large frame.

'What happened to us, Sugar?' he asked.

'Oh give it a rest. You didn't call me in here to listen to you going on about the old days. We were young. Things change. Get over it. Now, come on, for fuck's sake. I've got work to do. This joint doesn't run itself. What's up?'

Responding to her brusque tone he sat up straight and downed the rest of the whisky in his glass, wiping his fat lips on the back of his hand.

'He wanted to talk to Della.' He leaned across the desk and wagged a finger at Yvonne. 'He's not a paying customer so she can see him somewhere else. When he comes back, I'll tell him she's not here. And she can bugger off and all. He's not interested in us. It's her he wants. He can have her. But not here. Tell her to sling her hook.'

'Just for tonight, or do you want to get rid of her?'

'What do you think?'

Hands on hips, frowning, she considered the options.

'Get rid of her,' she said at last. 'Once a girl gets in trouble, there's no knowing where it'll end.'

CHAPTER 28

In the week since Martha's death, Henry had struggled to get by without dwelling on what had happened to her. Being given two weeks off work hadn't helped. It would have been easier to cope if he had been allowed to keep to his normal routine. As it was, he passed his time sitting around at home with nothing to do. His employer called it compassionate leave, but he was a tricky bastard. Henry didn't think compassion had much to do with it. Every morning he scanned the post in case there was a letter advising him that the company was reluctantly 'letting him go'. He would be entitled to a redundancy package after working there for so long, but that was beside the point. He didn't want to take early retirement. It would leave him with nothing to do. In the meantime he did his best to fill his days with chores. He wiped the kitchen worktops with a damp cloth, and scrubbed the hob which had become encrusted with dried food detritus. He found where Martha kept the dustpan and brush and swept the floor, cursing and resolving to pay a cleaner, if he could find one.

* * *

He had already been to the corner shop once for essential supplies, but decided not to return there. He didn't want any more embarrassing encounters with neighbours. Martha had always gone to the supermarket armed with a list. She would make a huge fuss about it if she ever left it at home. On Friday evening, Henry sat down to make a shopping list of his own. It gave him something to do. He called up the stairs to Mark to ask if he wanted anything, but there was no answering shout from his son's room. After waiting a moment, he trotted upstairs and knocked on the bedroom door. When there was still no response, he turned the handle and pushed the door gingerly, afraid his son might fly into a rage with him for invading his privacy.

'I knocked—'

The room was empty. Shutting the door on the temptation to go in and snoop, he ran back downstairs to continue writing his list: toilet rolls, frozen chips, pizza. There was really no end of things he could buy if he wanted. He had been to the supermarket countless times with Martha but his first solitary visit to the supermarket was proving unexpectedly stressful and he hadn't even left the house yet. By the time he got home again and put the shopping away, the evening would be half over. But he was so bored and lonely, even a trip to the supermarket held a certain appeal.

He hadn't expected the store to be so crowded. He collected a trolley and stepped out of his personal nightmare into a world of normality. Most of the shoppers were women, but there were enough men there for him to blend in with the rest of the customers. No one paid him any attention. Only once did anyone so much as glance at him, when another trolley collided with his. The woman pushing the trolley gave an apologetic scowl before moving on. Her eyes slid past his face without a flicker of recognition. Reassured by his anonymity, he felt the tension that had been growing in his neck and shoulders ease. Before long, everything would get sorted out, the police would lose interest in him, and he would settle into a new routine.

He pressed on, but his composure didn't last. Martha had always seemed to know exactly what she wanted and where to find it, but shopping wasn't as straightforward as he had expected. The store was like a maze, with no logic to the organisation of its shelves. He had to ask staff half a dozen times to direct him to the items he wanted. It was a gruelling hour. In the end he barely bought anything because, within twenty minutes of his arrival, the place was heaving. He hurried round the aisles, gathering up essential items on his list, and leaving the ones he could manage without or had difficulty finding. He would have to return during the day when the store was less busy. He had been naive to go there in the evening when everyone was on their way home from work.

* * *

At last he was done, paid up and went out of the store. The car park was busy, with cars and trolleys cruising past. Whenever he looked up, someone was watching him. He manoeuvred his trolley between the vehicles, unloaded the bags, and drove home exhausted. He was pleasantly surprised when Mark opened the front door and called to him.

'There you are, dad. I was worried about you. Where have you been?'

Henry's tired spirits lifted. Without speaking, he lifted the bags he was holding. The front door stood open. Mark looked out at the car parked outside.

'Is there any more shopping to bring in?'

'Yes. Don't worry, I'll get it.'

But Mark was already jogging lightly down the path to the street. Henry took the bags he was carrying into the kitchen and began to unpack them. Mark followed laden with more bags.

'That's the lot, dad. You wouldn't think the boot could hold so much, would you? There's enough here to keep us going for months!'

At last Henry's shattered existence was returning to some kind of sanity. In a week he would be back at work. Resolutely he told himself that from now on everything was going to be all right. No one else would ever know the dark nightmare he had endured before reaching this turning point in his life. Mark was becoming quite reasonable.

Henry had been so shocked by what had happened, and so preoccupied with fears for his own future, that he hadn't stopped to consider how the terrible tragedy had affected Mark. The boy had always been close to his mother. Now Henry would be the one to befriend and support his son. Life was definitely going to improve. He hummed quietly to himself as he stacked tins neatly in the cupboard.

Mark seemed so pleased with the shopping that Henry was taken by surprise. He wondered if his son's grief had been prompted at least in part by concern over how they were going to manage without Martha to look after them. As it turned out, they seemed to be managing very well. Over a readymade curry, they drank a bottle of red wine. Mark encouraged Henry to open a second bottle.

'It's Friday night. We've got to pull ourselves together, dad. Mum wouldn't have wanted us to mope around forever. Life goes on.'

Mark was right. Life went on, with Martha or without her.

Henry drank far too much. Despite everything that had happened, he felt happy. When Mark apologised for his recent behaviour, Henry almost cried with relief. He leaned back in his chair, more relaxed than he had been in a long time.

'I think I was in shock or something,' Mark said.

'Of course you were. So was I – so am I.' Henry paused before adding, 'You know, that business.'

'What business?'

'When I asked you to lie about being here with me *that* night, well, I should never have asked you to do that. It was very wrong of me, putting that kind of pressure on you, especially at a time like that. But you don't need to worry any more. It's sorted.'

'What do you mean?'

With a grin, Henry explained how he had created his own alibi.

'That is clever,' Mark agreed. 'But what if she wants more? If you don't keep paying, what's to stop her going to the police after she's got the money?'

'No, no, that's not how it works,' Henry assured him.

But he had a sinking feeling Mark was right. He had blundered into more trouble, and this time it could prove expensive.

CHAPTER 29

Della's outrage faded as soon as she stepped out into the invigorating cold night air. She didn't need to work at the club any more. She hadn't been planning on staying anyway. Jimmy had done her a favour, sending her packing. She had another way of making money now, and all she had to do was ask. It had felt great, telling Jimmy to stuff his poxy job.

'You think I want to work here all my life, and end up a fat disappointed slob like you? I've got other plans.'

'You can sod off then.'

'Don't worry, I'm going.'

Shoving her hands into her coat pockets, she smiled as she hurried home. All she wanted to do was get back to her room and count her money. Tomorrow she would buy herself a proper winter coat, brand new. She wouldn't even wait for the sales. Soon she planned to screw another payment out of her benefactor. She knew his name, Henry Martin, and his address in Herne Bay. It was written on the envelope he'd put her money in. It was reassuring to know he was that stupid. And with Candy to help her, it wouldn't take long to find him.

Everything was working out perfectly. She had always known her luck would change one day. This was the break she had been waiting for all her life. It couldn't go wrong now Candy had promised to go with her. She knew her flatmate was only helping out to get her hands on half the cash, but it was worth sharing the money to have company when she visited Henry. There was no knowing what he might do to her if she went to see him alone. She shivered, remembering he had killed his wife. She had barely walked ten yards from the club when a car drew into the kerb and cruised slowly behind her. At first she thought nothing of it, but when she turned the corner onto the main road, so did the car. She halted, and the car stopped right beside her. She was reaching into her bag for her phone when she recognised the car. Henry wound his window down and called out to her to get in.

'But—'

'Get in. Or don't you want the rest of your money?'

In the darkness she fumbled to put on her seat belt as they accelerated away up the road. Henry stank of alcohol. In the flickering light of the passing street lamps she sneaked a look at him but his face was hidden by his hood. From the way he was dressed, in brand new jacket and smart leather gloves, she was confident he would pay up without any trouble. In any case, he had too much to lose. She hoped he was taking her somewhere posh. Maybe their meeting would end up like in a film she had seen, where Julia Roberts played a sex worker. After her wealthy client bought her a beautiful frock, and took her out to dinner, he ended up marrying her. Della wouldn't say no to a rich man who would buy her lovely clothes and keep her in luxury so she never had to work again. But one way or another, Henry was going to be her sugar daddy, whether he liked it or not.

'Where are you taking me?' she asked.

He didn't answer at first, but spun the wheel, driving round the roundabout and back along the front.

'Somewhere private.'

His speech was slurred. Despite his posturing, he wanted sex in return for the money he was paying her. He was no better than all the other punters, only he needed to get pissed before he had the courage to fuck her. The alcohol would probably prevent him getting it up anyway. Sober or pissed, he was pathetic. She shrugged. It was all the same to her as long as she got paid.

'Where are we going?' she asked again.

'Somewhere we won't be seen.'

'Don't worry about that. I won't blab. I'm the soul of discretion.'

'Oh, I'm not worried about you,' he replied. 'You're not going to be talking. Not where you're going.'

He spoke firmly, as though forcing himself to sound confident, but he couldn't hide the fact that he was nervous. She nodded to show she understood, even though he was facing the road ahead and couldn't see her. It wasn't a problem. No one liked to advertise the fact that they spent time with women like her.

'I charge for my time,' she said as she leaned back in the seat and closed her eyes. 'It'll cost you extra,' she added.

Just because he was paying for her silence, didn't mean she was going to give him a free ride.

They slowed down and she sat up to look around. They turned off the road by a blue sign: 'Dreamland'. Driving in between high metal railings, he pulled up beside a group of overgrown shrubs in the centre of a large empty car park. Della sat perfectly still, waiting, gazing at swirling patterns the leaves made. In the artificial light they looked black. Her companion turned the headlights off, and the bushes were swallowed up in darkness. He climbed out of the car, walked around and jerked her door open.

'Get out.'

She assumed he wanted her to get in the back, but he seized her by the arm and shoved her roughly away from the car, towards the shrubbery.

'Can't we do it in the car? It's cold out here,' she grumbled.

He didn't answer but continued pushing her towards the bushes. There was a soft click beside her, and a beam from a torch lit up the ground ahead. She followed the light, while his hand gripped her arm more tightly and propelled her forward.

Reaching the paving stones around the planted area she tripped on the kerb. Only his grasp of her arm prevented her from falling over.

'Where are we going?'

When he didn't answer she asked again.

'I asked you, where are we going?'

'Shut up,' he hissed. 'Keep walking and stop your yapping.'

The shrubs were taller than both of them. After they had been stumbling along for a few seconds, she twisted her ankle on a root concealed in the darkness. She yelped in pain, and swore angrily. Enough was enough. She was limping now, and didn't want to go any further. It was dark, and cold, and she had no idea why they had left the car. There was no need to hide in the bushes. No one could see them there anyway. The whole place was deserted. They might just as well have stayed in the car. She stopped walking. He yanked her arm but she stood her ground, nearly falling over when he gave her a violent shove.

* * *

'I'm not going any further,' she said, trying to keep her voice steady. 'And you'd better be bloody careful. I haven't given the police a statement yet, so you want to look after me, or your alibi's gone. You don't want to be in trouble with your "brother" do you?'

After her careful arrangement with Candy, and her determination not to see him alone, she had walked right into this. Her voice rose in consternation.

'We've gone far enough. Where the hell are we going anyway? I can't see a bloody thing out here. You said you wanted to go somewhere we couldn't be seen, well, no one's going to see us here, are they? So come on, let's get this over with and then you can give me my money. I'm bloody freezing.'

For an instant she saw his eyes gleaming coldly in the darkness and felt a stab of fear. Then the light went out. It made no sense to get out of the car on such a freezing night. For a second she was afraid he was going to continue pushing her onwards, away from the car, into the darkness. Instead, she was relieved to feel his grip on her arm loosen.

'All right,' he conceded tersely. 'Here will do as well as anywhere. Turn around.'

'What?'

'You heard me. Turn round so you're facing the other way, away from me. I don't want you watching me. I don't want to see your face right now.'

'You can't see a bloody thing out here anyway,' she muttered as she complied.

She was used to doing whatever men asked of her. There wasn't much she hadn't seen before.

'Do you want me to struggle?'

'No. Just do as you're told, will you, and shut up while you're about it.'

'It'll cost you extra, doing it out here in the cold,' she said.

In the darkness, she thought she heard a guttural chuckle before his gloved fingers closed around her neck.

CHAPTER 30

Della and Candy rented a flat in a shabby twenty-storey block behind a greasy-looking kebab shop and a tattoo parlour, round the corner from Margate station. Ian followed Candy up a stone staircase that stank of urine and stale smoke. Inside the first-floor flat, doors off a tiny entrance hall led to two bedrooms, a bathroom and a kitchen that doubled up as a living area. There was barely enough space for two people to sit at the table. Candy nodded at an open door.

'That's hers.'

Ian turned his head to look. There was no one in the narrow room. The bed was unmade, the duvet crumpled and grubby. It looked as though someone had grabbed an armful of clothes and chucked them on the floor. A shaving mirror had been propped upright on top of a low chest of drawers beside the bed. The only other furniture he could see was a scratched dark wooden wardrobe standing so close to the end of the bed that the doors couldn't open fully. The room smelt of talcum powder and cheap perfume.

★　★　★

'Here, where do you think you're going?'

Candy stepped forward to stand in the doorway, arms folded, blocking his way.

'I suppose you think you can go poking around, seeing as she's not here to tell you to get lost. But you got no right and when Della finds out, she'll be on to your lot like a shot and then you'll be for it and serve you right.'

'It won't take long to get a search warrant,' Ian fibbed; Della wasn't even a suspect, and no one had reported her missing. 'Then we can take the place apart, room by room.'

'Well, go on then, what are you waiting for? Piss off and get your warrant. But you're not going in Della's room without her knowing about it, not while I'm here. I know your type. Always throwing your weight around. You think you're so bloody high and mighty, but you're the one who's going to be in the shit, if I know anything, if you try and force your way in there while she's out. A person's entitled to some privacy. You got no right.'

Ian was used to encountering aggressive resistance, usually when people were frightened. Women like Candy had plenty of reasons to fear the police. It didn't usually amount to much. No doubt Della had some cannabis stashed in her room, or cocaine, hardly worth the bother. He wasn't there on a drugs bust. Looking at Candy's knowing expression, he decided to proceed carefully and postpone

179

his search until he could come back accompanied. He told Candy he would return in the morning, and she stood watching him leave.

He couldn't help wondering if he had made a mistake in deciding not to search Della's room while he had the chance. If she turned up there during the night, Candy was bound to tell her about his visit. If Henry *had* paid her to lie, she would move the cash out of her room before Ian came back. But it was a flimsy sort of evidence at best, because Della might have a stash of cash that could be traced back to Henry anyway, received for services that had nothing to do with his alibi. Finding a heap of cash might help them put pressure on her to destroy Henry's alibi for the night his wife was murdered, but it was a long shot. The reality was, they had nothing to suggest Henry was responsible for his wife's death, and no other suspect under investigation.

Candy wished her flatmate would come home. She tried calling her phone, but there was no answer. Slipping into Della's room, she yanked up the mattress and felt around beneath it. For a moment she was afraid Della had thought better of revealing her secret, and had moved the money from its original hiding place. Then her fingers closed on an envelope stuffed with cash. Quickly she replaced the sheets. Clutching Della's share of the money, she sat down on the edge of the bed. Her hands trembled as she called her flatmate once more. There was still no reply. Candy couldn't wait much longer before acting. The sergeant had threatened to return with a search warrant. He might be back at any moment. Somehow she had to hide the money where the police couldn't find it. Della would understand that she had acted only to keep it safe. There was no way Candy was going to let the sergeant pocket it. And once this crisis was over, there would be a lot more cash where this came from. Even while she was thinking where to hide the money, she was making plans to increase it.

After trying Della's phone one last time, she stood up and smoothed the covers on the bed. Returning to her own room, she shoved two hundred quid of her own into the envelope with the rest. Without stopping to count it all, she hurried to the kitchen where Della kept plastic freezer bags for her drugs. Just to be sure, she sealed the envelope in three plastic bags, one inside the other. Stuffing the package down her bra, she scurried downstairs. At the bottom, she switched off the light in the hall before stealing out of the flats. With no light behind it, an observer might not notice the front door open and close. Crouching down, she crept along the narrow path and around the side of the block. Pressed against the wall, she looked back at the street. A dark car was parked on yellow lines on the other side of the road. She froze as a figure sitting inside it turned his head and looked towards the flats. He looked away. She guessed the police were waiting for Della. Or it could be the killer coming for his money.

Still crouching, she edged her way along the side of the building, thankful the nearest street light wasn't working. Dropping to her knees she used a knife she had brought from the kitchen to scrape frantically at a scrubby strip of earth, directly beneath a cracked brick. The place would be easy for her to find again. When she had dug deep enough, she buried the package under the surface and patted the soil down. Even the police searching every inch of the property wouldn't suspect it was there. Brushing her hands, she hurried back into the flat where she closed the door and felt her way up the stairs in the dark. Leaving her shoes on the mat, she ran into the kitchen where she washed the knife thoroughly and scrubbed her hands so there was no trace of mud left anywhere. The money was safe, and so was she. As soon as Della showed up, they would visit her benefactor together. Only this time they would demand a lot more, and he would have to pay up.

CHAPTER 31

As he drove away from Margate, Ian thought about Polly. She was an attractive young woman. If he had been free he would doubtless have flirted with her. Maybe he would have been tempted to consider asking her out. It was a hypothetical whimsy, like thinking about a woman he had seen on television, unreal and unattainable. Except that Polly wasn't an image on a screen. She often sat beside him in his car, chatted in the canteen with him, or at the pub, joking, laughing and interacting. On holiday he had clocked plenty of topless women without a trace of guilt. But this was different. He knew Polly. He liked her. It was uncomfortable to realise that, much as he loved his wife, he wasn't sure if he actually liked her. Polly wasn't the only woman he considered a friend, outside his marriage. He was very fond of his previous inspector, Geraldine. It seemed he had no problem liking other women, only his wife.

Back at the station, he checked in with Rob. Eager to hear what Ian had found at Della's flat, the detective inspector was dashed by the answer to his enquiry.

'Nothing at all, only a bit of dope—'

Rob looked up.

'Large enough to threaten charges?'

'Maybe enough to give her a scare. Although my guess is that it would take more than that to get her to talk. The threat of being an accessory to murder might work, if we could find her.'

Rob nodded. 'No pile of notes with Henry Martin's prints all over it, then.'

Ian shook his head. Although he hadn't expected to find anything suggesting Della had been paid a large sum of money by Henry, he was disappointed all the same. They were getting nowhere.

'And still no sign of her?'

'I reckon she's gone into hiding, to avoid being questioned again.'

Rob looked thoughtful. 'Are you saying you think she was lying about being with Henry on the night of the murder?'

Ian shrugged. It was impossible to say one way or the other. In the meantime, they were discussing the same questions over and over again, going nowhere.

On his way out, Ian glanced into the canteen. He wasn't looking for anyone in particular. In any case, if a colleague had happened to suggest going to the pub for a quick drink, he would have refused. It was gone seven thirty on a Saturday evening. All he wanted to do was get home to his wife. The question of the pub didn't arise because the canteen was empty, apart from a table of older officers engrossed in a discussion. He arrived home before eight ready for a quiet evening at home with Bev. She was in the bedroom when he trotted upstairs to change. He was momentarily surprised to see she was all dressed up.

'You look great,' he said, and hesitated.

Catching sight of his expression, she pouted. 'You haven't forgotten?'

'No,' he lied.

Desperately he tried to remember what they had planned for that evening as she pestered him to get ready.

'They'll be here soon.'

Forcing a smile, Ian went to kiss her.

'Don't worry,' he said, 'I'll be ready.'

As ready as he ever would be to spend an evening with Bev's family.

With her cold manner and supercilious remarks, Ian's mother-in-law made it obvious she didn't think he was good enough for her daughter, while Bev's sister would spend the evening bragging about her latest extravagance: a brand new car, or a luxury cruise. Ian was on a decent salary but his brother-in-law was in a different league. Ian still didn't understand exactly what he did; something in sales.

'They must be in debt up to their eyeballs,' he

once said to Bev. 'It wouldn't surprise me to learn they've remortgaged their house.'

'He just earns more than you,' she replied tartly. 'There's no need to be spiteful.'

Bev had prepared an elaborate three-course dinner, with an expensive wine. Reluctantly, Ian declined a second glass as they sat down at the table. He couldn't afford to be over the limit. Once he was on a case, it was impossible to predict when he might be summoned.

'Come on, Ian,' his brother-in-law urged him. 'Don't be a stuffed shirt. You're not on duty now. Even a policeman is entitled to a night off.'

'He's always on duty,' Bev muttered.

Ian's mother-in-law glowered at him, daring him to disagree.

With Bev's sister living in Canterbury, only eight miles from Herne Bay, it was inevitable she wanted to discuss the recent murder. As politely as he could, Ian refused to be drawn.

'It's hardly surprising, when you look at how the area has deteriorated,' Bev's sister said, grumbling about the impossibility of persuading the local council to deal with loiterers near the coast, while her husband complained about unsuitable neighbours arriving in the neighbourhood.

'Hippies and gipsies right on our doorstep,' he complained. 'You people ought to do something about it.'

'It would only come to our attention if they were committing a crime. There's no law against people moving into the area, as long as they don't cause trouble.'

'That depends on what you mean by trouble,' his brother-in-law said sourly. 'No one seems to do know anything about it.'

'Including the police,' Bev's mother remarked, glaring at Ian.

She never missed an opportunity to snipe at him.

Ian was relieved when he could escape to the kitchen to help Bev serve the main course. By the time they sat down again he was relieved to find the conversation had moved on from personal jibes to general affairs, desultory discussion about politics and a television series which Ian had never seen.

'This looks wonderful,' Bev's mother said. 'You are clever, Bev.'

'Yes, you're a lucky bloke,' the brother-in-law said to Ian. 'I wish I was fed like this at home.'

Bev's sister slapped him playfully on the arm.

'Shut up, Freddy. You do all right. And it's not like she cooks like this every night, do you, Bev?'

'There wouldn't be much point,' Bev said. 'Ian isn't often home in time for supper. We don't all work regular hours, you know,' she added quickly. 'Ian can't put off following a lead that will help him arrest a murderer, just because I've made dinner.'

She smiled complacently at Ian who lowered his eyes. He knew she was just putting on a show for her family, but was grateful for her support all the same. He wondered if, deep down, she really was proud of him.

CHAPTER 32

Henry woke up early on Sunday with a thumping hangover, wishing he hadn't drunk so much the night before. Mark wasn't up and about yet. Henry decided not to disturb him. They had been growing closer since Martha's death, but he didn't want to push his luck. He set about making himself breakfast, although he had no appetite. After a paltry stab at eating, he needed some fresh air. Slipping into his coat, he had his first inkling that something was wrong when he couldn't find his keys. They weren't on his bedside table where he expected to see them, nor were they in the kitchen on a shelf beside the phone. He checked the pocket of the jacket he had been wearing the previous evening when he had gone out shopping, and everywhere else he could think of. At last he realised he must have left them in the car. He remembered Mark opening the front door for him when he got home from the supermarket, and he hadn't been out since. Carefully propping the front door open with a shoe, he hurried outside and straight into a worse predicament. The car wasn't there.

He checked round the corner where he often left it, although he remembered parking right outside the house so it would be easier to unload the shopping.

He ran back indoors and raced upstairs, hoping no one else was in. In his present fit of good humour, Mark might have taken the car for a spin, or to the car wash. Reaching the landing, he tapped on Mark's door. When there was no response he knocked more loudly until the door opened to reveal Mark in his dressing gown, blinking. He had clearly only just woken up.

'What the hell—?'

'Have you used the car this morning?'

'What?'

'The car. Have you used it?'

'When?'

'Today.'

'Dad, I've only just got up. Haven't you got a hangover?'

'The car's gone.'

'What do you mean, it's gone?'

Henry took a deep breath and explained that the car wasn't outside, and he couldn't find his keys anywhere. House keys and car keys had all disappeared.

'Shit. Are you sure? Shall I help you look for them?'

Henry nodded miserably.

★   ★   ★

190

He could see in his face that Mark was thinking the same as him. It was too much of a fluke to suppose that someone had come along and nicked the car independently of Henry having misplaced his keys somewhere in the house. There was only one logical explanation: Henry had left the keys in the car and someone had helped themselves, a professional car thief, or some kid who had spotted the keys and taken the car for a joyride.

'Bugger,' Mark said. 'We'll have to change the lock on the front door.'

Henry groaned.

They searched for the keys without success. Finally Henry picked up the phone to call the police and report that his car had been stolen from right outside his house.

'Shall I tell them I left the keys in the car?' he wondered aloud.

They discussed whether it would be best to come clean. If car thieves had gone for a joy ride and abandoned the car just as they had found it, the police might wonder how Henry's key ring, with all his keys, came to be in the ignition.

'Someone could have stolen the keys from inside the house,' Mark said.

Henry shook his head. 'There's no sign of a break in. But if the insurance company find out I left the keys in the car, they'll say we weren't covered.'

They agreed Henry should just report the car

stolen and say nothing about the keys until he had chatted to a colleague who had a friend who worked for an insurance company. Whatever happened now, it was going to be a bloody nuisance. At least Martha wasn't there to bellyache about him leaving the keys in the car.

Ian reached carefully for his phone. He didn't want to disturb Bev who was sleeping peacefully beside him. She moaned softly as the duvet shifted, but she didn't wake up. For a while now she had been able to sleep through his night calls. It didn't happen often, and he always remembered to leave a note if he left the house before she was awake. Gradually they were reaching a reasonable accommodation, learning to tolerate one another's demands. And he was confident she would like being married to an inspector. It wouldn't be long now until his promotion came through. He padded out onto the landing in his bare feet, bemused by what he was hearing.

'A stolen car?' he repeated. 'I don't understand.'

He glanced at his watch. He had overslept. The morning was half over. It wasn't too early to be called for something that wasn't an emergency. But a report of a missing vehicle shouldn't land on his desk. He was involved in major crime, not petty theft.

'It's not the car that might interest you, exactly,' the constable explained.

'Then what the—'

'Henry Martin reported it missing.'

Ian was instantly alert. 'Henry Martin? The same Henry Martin?'

'Yes.'

'In Herne Bay?'

'Yes, it's the Henry Martin whose wife was stabbed, the same one. He phoned to report that his car's been stolen from outside his house in Beltinge Road. As soon the report came in we noticed the name and thought you'd want to know about it straight away.'

Ian hung up thoughtfully. He didn't believe for one minute that Henry's car had been stolen. It was too much of a coincidence. What was more likely was that Henry had a reason for wanting to get rid of his car himself, although a forensic team had searched the car after Martha's death, and found no evidence of a weapon, or blood spatter. Aware that he might already be too late to make use of the information he had just received, Ian had to move fast. Henry's car could be at the bottom of the sea by now, or burnt to a bare metal frame. As he drove to work he made his plans. First he needed to put a team in place to check film in the traffic cameras in Herne Bay. Once that was under way, he would go and question Henry again. He hadn't made sense of this latest development yet, but he was excited. Things were beginning to happen. He was halfway to Herne Bay when he realised he had forgotten to leave a note for Bev.

CHAPTER 33

Having checked in at the incident room in Herne Bay to discuss the report of the missing car, Ian drove on to Margate to speak to Della. Interviewing Henry about his car could wait. First he wanted to persuade Della to come clean about the alibi she had given him for the night his wife was killed. He took Polly with him. No one answered when he rang the bell. After trying several times, he hammered loudly on the front door. It shook with the impact but there was still no answer. No one from the neighbouring apartments looked out to investigate the cause of the disturbance.

'I suppose she's fast asleep,' he said crossly.

'All right for some,' Polly agreed cheerfully. 'Wish I was.'

Ian banged on the door again, as loudly as he could. Lifting the flap on the letterbox he yelled.

'Open the door, or we'll have to break it down.'

'She's really got under your skin, hasn't she?' Polly said, laughing, and Ian couldn't help smiling back.

As they were about to turn away, they heard footsteps and the front door opened. Clutching a pink silk dressing gown round her waist, Candy held on to the door, displaying dirty finger nails with chipped red nail varnish. She stood blinking up at them, her bleary eyes encircled with smudged black make-up, and traces of bright red lipstick on her cracked lips.

'Fuck it, not you again,' she muttered indistinctly. 'What now? Can't you bloody well leave us alone? It's bloody Sunday morning. Don't you people ever sleep?'

Her voice was thick, as though she was drunk or had just woken up. When she went to close the door, Ian stepped forward and put his shoulder against it.

'This is bloody harassment,' she grumbled, but she didn't sound very angry.

Ian introduced Polly. Candy glared at the constable, and then back at him again.

'Two of you now, is it? Brought her along to help you do your dirty work, have you? Well, what do you want?'

Della wasn't home yet. She had been missing for over thirty hours, in itself cause for concern, enough to justify searching her room in an attempt to discover where she might have gone.

While Polly checked through Della's possessions, Ian questioned her flatmate in the kitchen.

'Did she tell you she was going away?'

'We're not bloody married.'

Candy spoke with affected breeziness, but Ian

could tell she was worried. Her eyes flitted nervously round the room, and when she wasn't speaking, she chewed on the side of her thumb.

'Was there any reason why she might have wanted to go away?'

'What do you mean, go away?'

Ian stared at her closely as he asked whether Della had received any threats. Candy shrugged, her thumb at her lips, her eyes avoiding Ian's gaze.

'If she was in trouble, she never told me. We shared a flat, that's all. We weren't joined at the hip.'

'Was she struggling to pay off debts?'

'Who isn't? Oh – of course you're not, you on your nice fat policeman's salary. But for ordinary people like me and Della, living in debt is nothing unusual. So what of it?'

Candy crossed her arms. She watched Ian as he made a note.

'How much longer is this going to take?' she asked at last.

'Until my colleague has finished searching Della's things. And now I'd like to have a look through your room. I have a warrant, don't worry.'

'You like going through strangers' knickers, do you? Get off on it, do you? Pervert,' she added under her breath. 'What's your problem then? Not getting any?'

She squinted at Ian who didn't answer. He kept his expression bland. Jibes like that didn't bother him. He had heard too many of them.

★   ★   ★

196

To his surprise, Ian saw a small child lying fast asleep on the bed in Candy's room. He looked about eight. He had an angelic face with a tiny button nose and long thick eye lashes.

'You'd better not wake my boy,' Candy hissed.

Ian began by looking through the drawer in the bedside table. Candy stood in the doorway, arms still folded, staring at him. Ignoring her muttering, he proceeded with his search. There was a jumble of make-up in the top drawer, tweezers and mascara, lipsticks and blusher, and little bottles of nail varnish all thrown in together. Next he checked the wardrobe. He rummaged through the pockets of every item of clothing hanging there, and felt inside the shoes. Pulling a bundle of bedding down from the top of the wardrobe, he shook it all out, and checked inside the sleeping bag that was rolled up there. Next he turned his attention to the bed. He removed one of the pillow cases, but couldn't get to the other pillows or the duvet without disturbing the sleeping child.

'Are you going to move him or shall I?' he asked.

With an oath, Candy leaned over and tapped the child on his shoulder. The boy's large black eyes flew open at once, as though he had been awake all the time, waiting for her signal. He glanced up at Ian then turned to Candy and hopped off the bed without taking his eyes from her face. She leaned down and whispered in the child's ear, stroking his unruly hair as she did so, her face glowing with affection. The boy turned and scampered from the room, his curly hair bobbing up and down on top of his head.

'Do your coat up!' Candy yelled, and a moment later the front door slammed.

'Shouldn't you go after him?'

'Mind your own fucking business.'

Ian peered under the bed and lifted the mattress to look underneath it. At last, resigned to the fact that he wasn't going to find any cash or drugs hidden in Candy's bedroom, he went and found Polly. Having completed her search of Della's room, she had found nothing to suggest the girl had been bribed to give Henry a false alibi.

'I'll look in the kitchen and you take the bathroom,' Ian said.

Ignoring Candy's protests, they pursued their search.

'You won't find anything illegal here,' Candy insisted, demanding to know how long they were going to take. 'I want to get some sleep this morning, if it's all the same to you.'

'It'll take as long as it takes,' Ian told her brusquely. 'And the morning's over. It's nearly half past twelve.'

The only money they found was sixty pounds in Candy's purse.

'I'm allowed to have some cash on me, aren't I? Having money isn't against the law, is it?'

'No, but this is,' Polly replied, holding up a small plastic bag of grass she had found in the bathroom.

Candy snatched it back from her.

'Oh fuck off, it's medicinal. Leave it out, will you.'

Ian didn't even bother to caution her about it. They had more important things to do, and had just wasted the best part of a morning vainly searching for evidence that Henry had paid Della to give him an alibi. She must have done a runner with the money. He had a feeling Candy knew a lot more about the situation than she was letting on. They needed to find Della urgently, but Candy swore she had no idea where her flatmate had gone.

'If you hear from her, let us know straight away.'

'OK. I'll send you a message by flying pig. Now fuck off out of here, will you? I need to get my beauty sleep.' She glared at Polly. 'Some of us take care of our appearance.'

Neat and smart, Polly had no reason to pay any attention to such a stupid insult. Ian was surprised to see his colleague's face flush with annoyance. He would never understand women's insecurities.

CHAPTER 34

By late morning the rain had eased off. After losing what little cash they had in an amusement arcade they wandered miserably along the front, gazing at the brightly lit pink and yellow slot machines. Megan suggested going into town to look around the shops, although the place was dead on Sundays.

'What for?' Mac asked. 'We got no money.'

They walked on aimlessly, thoroughly fed up.

'This is lame,' she grumbled.

'I'm fucking starving,' Mac said. 'Let's get something to eat.'

Even the thrill of being with blonde slim Megan paled beside the thought of finding breakfast. Megan said that as far as she was concerned it made no difference what they did, as long as they did something.

'I'm so bored,' she moaned. 'For fuck's sake, let's do something.'

The problem was that they had no money which meant that all their arguments about what to do were pointless. They had nowhere to go and nothing to do.

⋆　⋆　⋆

Turning off the coast road, they went into the Dreamland car park and wandered towards the fenced off entrance to the disused roller coaster.

Megan read the sign aloud: 'Welcome to Dreamland'.

'Awesome,' Mac said, gazing up at the sweep of the metal frame.

'It must be a hundred feet high.'

'A thousand!'

On a weekday the car park would have been in use but on a Sunday it was deserted, with just a few random vehicles parked around the perimeter. Suddenly Mac let out a low whistle, his hunger forgotten. If this didn't impress Megan, nothing would.

'Get over here,' he called out. 'Some stupid fucker's only gone and left the keys in his car. Come and take a look!'

Megan frowned as though she couldn't understand his excitement.

'What the fuck are you on about? It's only an old car –' she began, and broke off as he opened the passenger door for her.

'Your carriage, my lady,' he said, grinning, and making a stupid bow.

'Bleeding hell, how did you manage that?'

'Just call me genius. Well, go on then, are you getting in or what?'

'Where are we going?' she asked as he climbed in beside her.

He was busy fiddling with the controls on the steering column and didn't answer.

First the indicators clicked and flashed, then the windscreen wipers started and stopped.

'Have you ever driven one of these before?' Megan asked.

'Course I have.'

'How come you don't know where everything is then?'

'Well, I haven't driven the exact same model, but cars are all the same. Once you know how to drive one, you can drive anything.'

Megan muttered something about him driving her mad. Mac ignored her. He was too excited about the car.

'Well go on then, drive it, if you're such an expert,' she said. 'It's boring sitting here.'

Mac turned the key in the ignition and the car jumped forward.

'Ow!' Megan called out. 'Watch out, will you? I thought you said you could drive this thing.'

'Shut up will you, and let me concentrate. It can't be that different to my brother's car and I've driven that loads of times.'

He kept his foot on the brake as the car reversed gradually. Clear of the edge of the car park he spun the wheel until they were facing the exit on the other side of the empty car park. Megan stared at him with sudden apprehension.

'Do you think we should be doing this?'

'It's not like we're doing anything wrong. We're in a car park. As long as we don't go on the road, it's not illegal.'

'Bollocks,' Megan laughed. 'You can't just nick a car and say you didn't know it was wrong.'

'Stupid twat shouldn't have left the keys in the ignition if he didn't want anyone to nick it. Serves him right. He's an idiot. I mean, come on. We'd have to be stupid not to jack it. If you think about it, the owner's had a lucky escape. We could've been car thieves, and he would never have seen this old heap of junk again. As it is, we're just taking it for a little ride, that's all. Technically, we're not even stealing it because we're not taking it out of the car park. But if you think about it, he's left the keys which means anyone can take it. The owner probably doesn't even want it any more. It's an abandoned vehicle. Whoever finds it can keep it if they want.'

'Are we going for a drive then, or are you just going to sit around gassing about it?' Megan asked.

They were soon racing around the car park. Megan screamed every time they swerved or rattled over a bump.

'Just as well the car park's empty,' she shrieked as the car spun round a corner.

'Just shut up, will you? I'm trying to concentrate.'

'Ooh, I'm trying to concentrate,' Megan mimicked him.

Mac took no notice. He was enjoying himself. Driving was easy. Not for everyone, perhaps, but he was a natural. He felt like a prince. All Megan could do was sit there, powerless, travelling wherever he wanted. He had complete control.

'How long are we going to do this?' Megan asked after they had gone round a few times. 'What if someone comes?'

Mac shrugged. He had no idea how long he was going to stay at the wheel, and what was more, he didn't care. He wished she would stop fussing. It was beginning to get on his nerves.

'We'll keep going as long as the petrol lasts,' he said. 'Chill out, will you? We're free spirits, remember?'

'Yes, I know, but don't you think we should quit before someone sees us?' she asked. 'What if the owner comes back?'

'Shut up.'

Mac wasn't sure he'd be able to stop, even if he wanted to, but once she started on at him she wouldn't give up. Typical of a girl. He was taking her out for a drive, which was more than most thirteen-year-old boys could do, and all she did was moan.

'Look, we're staying here as long as I say,' he snapped. 'Who's driving, you or me?'

The other vehicle came out of nowhere. One second they had the place to themselves, the next they were careering towards a red car. Mac saw the whites of a woman's eyes and her mouth hanging open in a silent scream. Sunlight flashed on glass and red metal. A horn was hooting loudly while at his side Megan was screaming, a long, high-pitched screech. Fear flooded through him making his legs feel numb. He could barely move his arms. If he had been on his feet he would have fallen over. The noise of the crash exploded in his ears before darkness swallowed everything.

CHAPTER 35

Sandra was late. It was impossible to keep an eye on her father who was growing increasingly confused. One night last week she had received a call from the police to say he had been found wandering along the front, lost, claiming he had gone out to buy some milk.

'You don't need to go to the shops by yourself, dad,' she had scolded him when she got him back home, past midnight. 'You just have to tell me what you want and I'll get it for you on my way over. Whatever you want, you only have to say.'

It was hard not to be angry with him. She was doing her best. She visited him at home most days, which was more than her brother managed, although he only lived in Ramsgate.

Even at the weekend, she no longer dared go a day without checking on him. But she couldn't be at his side constantly. It was the time in between her visits that worried her. As she put her foot down, a carrier bag of shopping on the seat beside her flew onto the floor. Cursing, she looked around for somewhere to stop so she could get out of the car to repack it, and saw the entrance to the Dreamland car park just across the road. Her father used to take her to the Dreamland theme park when she was a child. She smiled, remembering how terrified she had been on the Big Wheel. The whole place had closed down years ago, but the car park was still in use. She drove in, taking no notice of a warning sign that 'Cars parked here without authorisation will be clamped'. She was only going to stop for a moment. Through the gate, she glanced down at tins and jars rolling around on the floor of the car. A pot had smashed. Shards of glass winked up at her, half buried in sticky marmalade. Looking up again, she barely had time to register a dark car rushing towards her with what appeared to be a child at the wheel. His mouth was open in horror, his eyes glaring wildly at her. With a sick feeling, she realised they couldn't avoid a crash. Instead of turning his wheel, the other driver sat rigidly clinging to it while his vehicle raced straight at her.

Sandra swung her steering wheel, slamming on her brakes. The car skidded and slid to crash into the oncoming vehicle at an angle. If the other car had taken similar evasive action, they might have avoided a collision. As it was, the impact was deafening. The airbag blew up in her face as the car juddered to a halt. She was shaking so badly, she could barely manage to reach for the door handle. All she could think of was that she had to get out of the car. It might explode, or burst into flames, with her still inside it. She seemed to be sitting for hours, frantically rattling the door handle.

Suddenly the door flew open. A face peered in at her. Despite her wooziness, she saw that it was a policeman.

'Help,' she croaked. 'Help!'

She must have lost consciousness for a second, because when she looked again the policeman had vanished. Tears sprang to her eyes at the realisation that she was on her own. Gingerly she tried to move her arms and legs. Everything seemed to be working normally. She told herself she hadn't been travelling very fast when the vehicles crashed, and it had probably sounded worse than it was. She struggled to slide her legs round so she could get out and as she did so, the sound of a siren reached her. She fell back on her seat, crying with relief. Of course the policeman hadn't abandoned her. He had been calling for help.

As if in response to her thoughts, he returned and leaned down to talk to her through the open door.

'Don't worry.'

It was such an inane thing to say, she felt like laughing. It occurred to her that her father probably felt similarly helpless. She wondered what he really thought of her attempts to reassure him. He was always polite, and appreciative, but inside he must feel as tormented by the futility of her efforts as she was. The policeman was talking again.

'We'll soon have you out of there.'

He looked very young, and very grave. She thanked him quite lucidly and his worried frown relaxed.

'That's the spirit. You're going to be OK,' he said with forced cheerfulness that made her want to cry, because she understood so well how he was feeling.

The keys had gone from the ignition. The young policeman must have reached in to switch off the engine. Sensibly he hadn't attempted to move her but had left that to the experts who were already on their way. Before long two firemen were lifting her gently out of the car. They laid her on a waiting stretcher and the paramedics took over. No longer panicking, Sandra became aware that her head was pounding, and her whole body ached as though she was suffering from a serious bout of flu. A paramedic gently felt her limbs and neck and asked her if anything hurt.

'Everything,' she groaned.

Having established it was safe to move her, they carried her into an ambulance and she was taken off to hospital for a more thorough examination.

'What about the other driver?' she asked.

'They're fine,' she was assured.

She closed her eyes and felt unexpectedly peaceful. For once, other people were taking over the responsibility for what was happening.

'Is there anyone we can call?' a voice asked.

Without opening her eyes, she gave them her husband's phone number. As for her father, her brother would have to step in for once.

The first thing Police Constable Michael Rogers did on seeing the mangled vehicles was call for urgent assistance. A dark blue Honda had crashed into a red Mini. Behind the Honda, a figure lay motionless on the tarmac. He ran over to the woman who had been run over and knelt down to check for signs of life. The awkward position in which she lay made him suspect that he was too late. As he leaned forward, a putrid smell wafted towards him from the body and he gagged. Dutifully, he pressed on. He couldn't find a pulse and she didn't appear to be breathing. He became aware of a rattling sound behind him. Turning his head, he saw the driver's door to the Mini was being shaken from inside. He ran over and yanked it open.

A middle-aged woman was sitting in the driver's seat, moaning. She blinked up at him and called out for help. Michael leaned in and turned the engine off. He wasn't sure it was safe to move the woman, but she didn't appear to be in any immediate danger so he decided it was best to wait for the paramedics. They soon arrived, closely followed by a fire team ready with cutting equipment in case anyone was trapped, and a police car. Quickly,

Michael brought them up to speed: a driver in the mini, a driver and one passenger in the Honda, and a woman who had been knocked down on the tarmac. A paramedic ran over to the woman lying on the ground. After a few seconds, he stood up and shook his head.

Having passed the responsibility for dealing with the victims on to those who were equipped to help them, Michael busied himself setting up a cordon to keep the public out of the car park. It wouldn't be long before people started to gather. When more police officers showed up, he returned to the scene of the crash to find out the extent of the damage. The bodywork of both vehicles was badly damaged. The drivers and passenger were suffering from shock, but appeared to have escaped serious physical injury. The pedestrian who had been knocked down was dead. A white-faced boy of about twelve was sitting in an ambulance, wrapped in a silver blanket, shivering, while a paramedic was chatting quietly to him.

'He was driving the Honda,' the paramedic told the constable.

Seeing the policeman's uniform, the boy glared, blinking furiously. Michael had the impression he was on the point of tears so he spoke to him gently.

Macauley Hobbs was thirteen. He had found the car with the keys in the dashboard, so he had driven it round the car park 'for a laugh', no doubt intending to impress his companion, a little blonde girl who was sitting in another ambulance, crying hysterically. Even if Michael had been trained to question underage witnesses, he would have to wait for a suitable adult to be present. The two children's mothers had both been contacted and were on their way.

'Your mother will be here soon,' he reassured the boy who shook his head vehemently, and looked more frightened than ever.

'You can't tell my mum. She'll kill me if she finds out what I done.'

First to arrive was a blonde woman in a black coat who was escorted through the cordon and over to the ambulance where the young girl was still sobbing. Soon after that, there was a commotion at the cordon and a fat voluble woman marched into the car park, waving her arms in the air. Michael recognised her companion, a female constable called Susan Bailey who was trained to question children.

'Where is the little sod?' the fat woman was shouting.

Michael hurried to intercept them.

'You must be Macauley's mother?'

'Where is the little sod?' she repeated loudly.

'Mrs Hobbs—'

'It's Miss.'

'Miss Hobbs, your son has just been involved in a collision and he's in shock. You'll need to give him time—'

The woman rounded on him, her large face quivering with anger. Her cheeks were pink, and there was a faint sheen of perspiration on her forehead.

'Don't you tell me how to deal with my own son.'

As soon as Macauley's mother saw the boy inside the ambulance, her whole demeanour altered. Her shoulders drooped and she ran forward, arms outstretched, her face creased with emotion. She had to be restrained from enfolding the boy in her arms before he had been thoroughly checked for internal injuries.

Privately Michael wondered if they were all being a bit soft. The boy had stolen a car and driven it. As a result of his boyish escapade, a woman had died. They needed to establish her identity. Neither of the drivers involved in the crash seemed to know that there had even been a pedestrian knocked down in the accident.

'Who is she?' Michael asked.

'We haven't got an identity yet,' a constable told him. 'She must have been knocked down, and no one noticed, with all the noise and ruck of the crash.'

'What a sad way to die,' Michael said softly. 'No one even noticed.'

CHAPTER 36

Feeling guilty that he hadn't remembered to leave a note, Ian was home by early afternoon. He even remembered they were meeting friends for a drink that evening. But when his work phone rang soon after he reached the house, he answered without hesitation. He would never have admitted as much to Bev, but he was eager to get back to the station and find out how things were going. Checking online or by phone wasn't the same as being there, in the bustle and pressure of the physical team. Her expression darkened when he said he was on his way before he rang off.

'What did you say?'

Her eyes grew bright with anger as he gave an apologetic shrug and explained he had to go.

'Go where?'

'I've got to go and follow something up.'

'You can't. It's Sunday. It's your day off. You've only just got home.'

'Unfortunately there's no law that says people can't be killed at weekends. It would make my life a whole lot easier if there was.'

'You're not supposed to be working today. We've arranged to go out later on.'

'You'll have to go without me.'

'You know I can't.'

Losing patience, he spoke harshly.

'A woman's been run over and killed, and the car involved is registered to someone we're currently investigating. I don't have a choice, Bev.'

'You do have a choice,' she muttered crossly.

He didn't bother to answer. They had been through this many times before. She should know by now that he wasn't going to leave his job. He had been through too much, and come too far to quit now.

'You go on ahead if I'm not back in time,' he said. 'I'll join you when I can.'

He didn't stop to argue any more. Scene of crime officers would already be crawling all over the site of the car crash in Margate. A forensic tent would have been erected. A forensic medical examiner would be looking at the body where it lay, before a post mortem was carried out once the body arrived at the morgue. As far as he knew neither of the drivers was seriously injured. They had both been taken to hospital to be checked. But he wasn't going there to find out about the crash. He wasn't concerned about the underage driver, or even the fatality. The reason for his interest was that one of the vehicles involved in the collision was registered to Henry Martin who had telephoned the police to report it stolen earlier that morning. This was Ian's chance to find out exactly when the car had been moved from outside Henry's house in Herne Bay, and have it thoroughly searched again by forensic officers. There was a chance Henry had paid someone else to dump it, and the job had been bungled. He imagined finding a knife with one sharp edge and a bent blade, a knife stained with Martha's blood and Henry's prints all over the handle. With growing excitement, he put his foot down.

Apart from emergency vehicles, there were two smashed-up cars in the car park, beside a forensic tent. A pick-up truck was standing ready to tow the cars away once SOCOs had finished with them, and a row of police vehicles were waiting along one side of the car park. Looming above the scene, the massive metal structure of a disused rollercoaster swept eerily across the evening sky. After glancing at a badly damaged red Mini, Ian went over to take a closer look at the Honda that belonged to Henry. A faint stench of rotting flesh grew stronger as he approached the car and he wished he had put on a mask to diminish the smell. He called out to the scene of crime officer who was working inside the vehicle.

'Have you found anything?'

The officer clambered out of the car and

straightened up, wiping his brow with the back of his sleeve.

'You've only got to stick your mug in the boot to know she wasn't involved in a fatal accident this morning. The body was in there for a while.'

'A while?'

'I'd say a day at least, but don't quote me on that. I mean, it's pretty obvious, but we need to get the DNA results before we can say for certain that the body on the tarmac was the cause of the stench in the boot.'

Briefly, Ian told him about Martha's fatal stabbing. The forensic officer nodded and said he had heard about it. His eyes widened when he heard that the Honda belonged to the husband of the woman who had been murdered.

'So is he a suspect then?'

'He's the only suspect so far.'

Ian didn't add that he wasn't convinced Henry was guilty.

'Leave it to us, Sarge. He'll have left something incriminating here. They always do. We'll find it if it takes all night.'

With a parting grin, he climbed back in the car and resumed his scrutiny of the upholstered front seats.

Ian wasn't sure what to do next. An officer who was trained to interview juveniles had gone to the hospital to talk to the two children who had been in the Honda when it crashed. Ian was impatient to know exactly when they had taken the car from outside Henry's house, but there was nothing he could do to speed up the process. All he could do was wait for the report. He was going to speak to the driver of the Mini himself, although he wasn't sure how talking to her was going to help. Before he left, he pulled on a protective suit and went into the forensic tent to see what was happening in there. He recognised the doctor kneeling beside the body at once from his skinny frame. Dr Millard was skeletal, from the dome of his large bald head to his bony fingers. Ian stood for a few seconds, watching the doctor at work. His hands flitted deftly around the dead woman's throat, searching, probing. As though he could feel Ian's eyes on him, he twisted his head round and looked up.

'Oh, hello again, Sergeant. How are you keeping? I hear you've lost your sharp inspector.'

'She's been transferred to the Met.'

'Well, I can't say I envy her.'

Ian grunted in acknowledgement, if not agreement.

'So what have you found for us, doc?'

'If you think she was run over and killed, you can think again.'

Ian nodded. He already knew the victim had been dead for at least a day, and had probably been stored in the boot of the Honda.

'You're thinking it was the kid in the Honda who knocked her down,' Millard went on.

With a non-committal grunt, Ian waited to hear what the doctor had to say about it.

'Well, it wasn't. And before you ask, it wasn't the driver of the Mini either. Are you surprised?'

Ian didn't answer.

'Oh, I know there was a car crash,' the doctor went on briskly, 'but that wasn't what killed her.'

'Are you telling me this death had nothing to do with the crash here this morning—?'

'If she was knocked over and killed this morning, she must have been one of the walking dead,' the doctor replied, getting to his feet and facing Ian. 'She died at least thirty-six hours ago, and she wasn't run over. She was strangled and then kept in a confined space.'

Gently he lifted a tress of her hair with a plastic gloved finger. One side of her face was livid where blood had pooled while she lay on her side after she died. Her flesh was already beginning to acquire a faint greenish tinge of putrefaction but the blackened line around her neck was still clearly visible where she had been strangled with a cord of some kind.

'D's the initial on her key ring,' the doctor said. 'It might not be hers, of course, and we don't have a full name yet.'

'It's hers, all right,' Ian replied, staring at the dead girl's face. 'She called herself Della, although her real name's Jade Higgins.'

'You know her?' Millard didn't seem surprised. 'Was she connected to the owner of the Honda? I take it he's the one you're investigating.'

Deep in thought, Ian left without answering.

Polly was standing just outside the tent, chatting to a gloomy middle-aged constable in uniform. Ian joined them.

'I was just telling the detective constable here how Dreamland used to be the number one place to visit,' the uniformed officer said. 'Looking at it now, you'd hardly credit there was a time when it was one of the top ten tourist attractions in the UK, would you? Back in the day, people used to come from all over. You know we had a Big Wheel here, years before the London Eye. They're all over the place now, of course, Manchester, Liverpool, Brighton, Torquay – you name a town, they've got a big wheel. But I remember the Dreamland Big Wheel from when I was a kid, and that's going back a bit. It was something special in those days. Then they took the Big Wheel down and sold it off to some theme park in Mexico in the mid-nineties, and the whole place shut down about ten years after that.' He gazed around and heaved a sigh. 'And look at it now. It's like a graveyard.'

'Literally,' Ian muttered.

Ian led Polly back towards her car. On the way he told her about Della.

'So Henry's been unlucky and lost his alibi,' he concluded.

'Or he's stopped her from admitting she lied about being with him the night his wife was killed,' Polly said.

'Does it strike you as odd that she was strangled thirty-six hours ago and yet she turns up here, at the scene of a car crash, looking for all the world as though she'd been run over?'

Polly shrugged and he went on.

'It seems so clumsy, doesn't it? Obviously we would know straight away that she hadn't been killed in the accident, but had been brought here and left at the scene. Why would anyone do that?'

'Perhaps it wasn't like that,' Polly said. 'Perhaps she was sitting in Henry's car all the time, and she was thrown out in the crash.'

She wasn't being serious, but Ian seized on the idea.

'Of course! That's it. Millard said she had been kept in a confined space—'

They both turned to stare at the Honda. The answer was staring them in the face. The door to the boot was open. It was the work of a second to establish that it had been like that when the first officer had arrived on the scene. As the Honda had crashed, head on, the nearside doors and boot must have burst open on impact. The body had been thrown out onto the tarmac behind the car without anyone involved in the accident noticing it. Jade's body had been in the boot of Henry's car all morning, possibly longer.

'I wonder if he can come up with an alibi for that,' Ian commented grimly.

CHAPTER 37

'What can you tell us about the victim?' Rob asked when they were all assembled in the Major Incident Room that had been set up in the police station in Herne Bay. It was cramped, but saved travelling time and more importantly meant they wasted less of the precious few hours they had to question suspects before they had to release them.

It was not much more than a week since they had last gathered together as a team to investigate Martha's murder. Now a second body had been discovered ten miles away in Margate, that of a woman closely associated with the case. The mood in the room was unusually solemn.

'You met the victim, didn't you?' Rob added.

Everyone on the team knew by now that the woman who had provided Henry Martin with his alibi was dead. What had yet to be established was how she had died, and whether he was again their number one suspect.

'The victim's name was Jade Higgins. She was known as Della. That was what she called herself when I met her last week. She was barely twenty.'

All eyes turned to gaze at the image of a young woman, her flesh deathly pale and already discoloured with the early signs of decomposition.

'She was born in Clacton and brought up in care after one failed adoption,' Ian went on.

An eager young constable raised his hand to request clarification, as though he was still at school. Ian explained that a couple had applied to adopt Jade as a baby and had then changed their minds. After that she had gone to a succession of childcare institutions. None of it made any difference now. By the time she was sixteen she had moved to London and was earning her living on the streets.

'She had a sugar daddy for less than a year and when that came to an end she found a job as a dancer in a strip club, which is where I met her.'

The hushed atmosphere erupted with whistles and jeering, and a few colleagues called out suggestive comments. While Rob scowled at the light-hearted ribbing, Ian felt reassured. They couldn't afford to be overwhelmed by the scenes they witnessed in the course of their duties. Each officer had to find a way to remain emotionally detached from the case if they were to cope with the job at all; inappropriate humour wasn't a bad way of dealing with the horror.

★　★　★

Briefly Ian went over what they already knew. Jade had been involved in the investigation into Martha's murder.

'So Henry's lost his alibi in a car crash,' a constable said. 'Where does that leave him then?'

'We've still got her statement,' someone pointed out.

Rob reminded them that Jade had never gone to the police station in Margate to make a formal statement. She had given her story to Ian, but they didn't have her signature or anything in her hand writing. In a court, there was a risk Ian's account might be dismissed as unreliable, despite his detailed notes on the interview.

'It's not that detailed, sir,' Ian muttered. 'She wasn't exactly forthcoming.'

He had asked her where she had been on Friday evening. Without hesitation she had confirmed that she had been with the man in the photograph Ian had shown her. She said she never knew his surname.

'He was just Henry. I don't ask no questions. Why do you want to know anyway? What's he done?'

Although she had been adamant she had spent Friday evening with Henry, she had been vague about times, and claimed not to remember where he had taken her.

'But we was together the whole evening,' she had insisted.

★　　★　　★

225

Ian gazed at a picture of the dead woman. Her face looked horribly pale. Her eyes were closed but it was obvious she wasn't sleeping. She looked inhuman, like a dirty doll that had been thrown on the ground and left there. She hadn't looked much better when he had seen her alive, but she was only twenty when she died. If she had lived, she could have changed. There had still been some hope for her, however slight.

'Does Henry know she's been run over?' someone wanted to know.

A couple of constables were whispering together somewhere behind Ian.

'She wasn't run over,' he said loudly and the muttered conversation stopped.

Everyone was listening now.

Carefully Ian went over what had happened. As far as they could make out, kids had taken Henry's car from right outside his house on Sunday morning, with Jade's body in the boot.

'Her body was in the boot when the car was stolen?' a constable repeated.

'SOCOs are still examining the car, but that's how it appears, yes.'

'So these kids jacked a car, not knowing there was a body in the boot, and then had an accident,' Polly said with a hint of a smile.

Someone laughed.

'And we think the body somehow fell out of the boot of the car in the crash?' Rob asked.

Ian nodded, slightly irritated by the reaction in the room. What made it worse was that he had to agree the story sounded unlikely. But recalling the stench in the boot of the Honda, he affirmed there was little doubt the body had been kept there.

'The boot and back nearside door flew open on impact,' he added.

When Ian had finished, Susan, the constable who had spoken to the children in the Honda, gave her report. According to their statements, they had found the car in the car park in Margate with the keys in the ignition. Both children had insisted they had not driven the car away from outside Henry's house where he claimed to have left it.

'There was no reason for them to have gone to Herne Bay, and I don't think they even had enough money for the bus to get them there. They said they never took the car out on the road, only round the car park.'

'They might have been covering up the fact that he drove on the highway,' Rob said.

'Henry said it was taken from outside his house,' Ian reminded them. 'He was quite clear about it. He told us he left the car there on Saturday evening and on Sunday morning it had gone.'

'Yes, that's what he *said*,' Rob agreed. 'But some-one's lying. Henry, suspected of murder, with a second victim stashed in the boot of his car, or these kids out joyriding not wanting to get in trouble for driving on the road. Take your pick who to believe.'

'I think those kids were telling the truth,' Susan repeated. 'They understood how important it was not to lie. We explained it all very carefully to them and they appreciated what was at stake. There was no reason for them to lie. We made it very clear they wouldn't be in any trouble over it.' She paused. 'They weren't bad kids, sir. They've learned their lesson.'

'Let's say Henry killed Jade, in Margate or Herne Bay,' Rob said after a short pause, 'why would he drive around with her body in the boot, leave the car in Margate, make his way back home and then alert the police to look out for it?'

No one answered for a moment, then people all started talking at once. There were so many possible reasons for him acting that way: guilt, panic, confusion, or a misplaced optimism that he might somehow get away with it by claiming his car had been stolen.

'With the doors unlocked, and the keys in the ignition, the car could have ended up anywhere.'

'It might even have been taken out of the country.'

'The plates could have been changed – it's possible he might even have hoped that, by the time the body was found, the car might not be traced back to him.'

'It wouldn't have been long before the body was discovered,' Ian said, remembering the smell. He grimaced. 'Another day or two and no one could have missed it.'

CHAPTER 38

Dr Millard was in the morgue leaning over the body. He raised his head and straightened up as Ian and Polly entered. Placing gloved hands on his narrow hips, he bent backwards and winced.

'It's back-breaking work,' he greeted them. 'Good timing on your part, anyway,' he added, his face brightening. 'I've just finished. You know the victim's identity. You met this young lady, didn't you, Ian?'

He squinted across the table at the sergeant and grinned, one eyebrow raised quizzically.

'I questioned her as a witness,' Ian replied curtly.

He tried to put Della's voice out of his mind, but couldn't help remembering the jerky way she had spoken, her heavy cheap scent mingled with the smell of her sweat when she was alive. Tacky and stupefied by alcohol or drugs, she had been a living human being. Given different opportunities in life, she could have been standing in Polly's place.

The doctor shrugged and looked down at the body. The greenish blue tinge was more evident, spreading upwards from her belly, while her limbs had taken on a marbled pattern.

'Right then, let's get on with it. As you know, the victim was about twenty. She was generally in a pretty bad way before she was killed, due to her unhealthy life style: poorly nourished, a heavy smoker, and her liver's suffered severe damage as a result of frequent binge drinking and other substance abuse. She had an abortion, not recently, and suffered from arthritis in her left arm, probably due to a fractured ulna and dislocated radius some years ago, and there's scarring from an infected navel piercing. She had breast implants and cosmetic surgery on her face. She was killed by strangulation with a rough narrow green cord, probably garden twine. You can see the marks on her neck quite clearly.'

'How do you know it was green?' Polly failed to hide the excitement in her voice.

'We found a few threads, too tiny to be seen with the naked eye, caught in the hair at the back of her neck. They've gone off to be identified in case there's anything they can tell us – like a trace of Henry Martin's DNA.'

The three of them stood around the body for a moment, thinking, before the doctor continued.

'It looks like she might have known her killer. Either that, or he crept up on her unawares from behind, which is possible, because it would have been dark and there's every chance she might not have been completely compos mentis, given her life style. Whatever the reason, there are no signs of defence wounds.'

'That's exactly what you said about Martha,' Ian said quietly.

'Indeed, but the methods of killing are very different,' Millard replied. 'One stabbed, the other strangled. From the post mortem results alone there's nothing to suggest the two murders are linked.'

'Are you saying you don't think the same person killed them both?'

Millard shook his head.

'That's not for me to say. If I could tell you who killed them, that'd be you out of a job, wouldn't it?'

'Is there anything else you can tell us?'

'She was dragged along the ground, probably while she was unconscious, since there's no indication of a struggle.'

He pointed to bruising underneath the tops of her arms, and then to some scratches on her heels and lower calves.

'These bruises on her arms were caused by someone grabbing hold of her here. She was wearing shoes when she was found, but they must have fallen off during the attack because the backs of her feet were grazed as she was pulled along the ground. The shoes must have been replaced afterwards, when she was packed into the boot of the car. She was shut inside a protected environment until Sunday morning, where it was dry and cold, good conditions to preserve the body. There's no insect activity yet.'

He touched the dead woman's hair lightly, in a gesture that was almost a caress.

Having gathered as much information as they could from the pathologist, Ian was pleased to leave the morgue. The antiseptic smell that failed to mask the stench of dead flesh made him feel sick. It didn't help that Polly kept glancing at him with a concerned expression all the time Millard was talking to them.

'Are you all right?' she asked before they had even left the building.

'Of course,' he answered shortly. 'Why wouldn't I be?'

Ian knew perfectly well she must have noticed him turning pale in the morgue.

'I'm fine,' he repeated and was rewarded with a grin.

'Thank God for that,' she said happily. 'I thought for a minute back there—'

'What?'

'Nothing, sir.'

'It was just really strange, seeing her like that. I'd been speaking to her less than a week ago.'

He turned away. Polly was right. At one point he had nearly succumbed to the nausea he always experienced in the morgue. He could just imagine Polly and Millard's reactions if he had run to the toilets to throw up. The doctor was bound to make some quip: 'Was it something I said?' Polly would look concerned and embarrassed. He wondered if she would tell all their colleagues. Word might even reach Rob, who was writing a report to support Ian's application for promotion.

'Are you sure you're all right?'

'I said I'm fine,' he replied sternly, his tone warning her to back off from this familiarity with a senior officer.

Leaving the morgue, they went to the hospital to speak to the driver of the Mini, Sandra Brice. She had been kept on the ward for observation for twenty-four hours, and was due to be discharged later that day, once the doctor had done his rounds. From the doorway she appeared to be reading a woman's magazine, but as they approached they saw that her eyes were closed. One of her wrists was in a cast, but there was no visible sign of any other injury above the bed covers. A nurse bustled past without challenging them as they crossed the ward. Reaching the bed, Ian hesitated.

'Do you think she's asleep?' he whispered.

Polly leaned forward.

'Sandra?' she said softly. 'Sandra Brice?'

The woman's eyelids flickered and she opened her eyes. Briefly Ian introduced himself and his colleague.

★   ★   ★

233

'There was no way I could have avoided a collision,' Sandra said quickly. 'The other car drove straight at me. He didn't even try to avoid hitting me. If he'd swerved, the accident might never have happened. I turned my wheel, and skidded, but he just kept on coming straight at me. It was crazy. He must have been drunk or on drugs or something. There was nothing I could do to avoid it. He drove into me. If anyone wants to pin the blame on me, or say it was fifty-fifty –' She broke off, frowning. 'I did nothing wrong. I'm the victim. Now I'd like you to go please. I've got nothing more to say to you.'

'No one's saying you were at fault, Mrs Brice,' Ian reassured her. 'We're not here to throw any accusation at you.'

She glared suspiciously at him.

'The driver of the other vehicle was underage.'

'Underage?' She sat up, an alert expression on her face. 'You mean he didn't have a licence? He was driving illegally?' She leaned back against the pillow again and closed her eyes. 'Yes, I seem to remember he looked young, but it's all such a blur.'

'He was thirteen.'

Sandra's eyes flew open in alarm. 'Oh my God. Was he hurt?'

'No. He and his young passenger were badly shocked, and shaken up, but they weren't seriously injured. Just a few bumps and scratches.'

She closed her eyes again.

'Thank God for that.'

★   ★   ★

234

Sandra confirmed the circumstances of the accident. Everything she said agreed with the account the two youngsters had given of the crash, apart from the boy indignantly blaming the collision on the other driver. None of them had noticed anyone other than the drivers of the two cars and the passenger in the Honda.

'You're sure you didn't notice anything fall from the boot of the Honda when the cars hit?'

'When he drove into me, all I saw was the airbag.'

'And you didn't hear anything?' Ian asked, aware he was clutching at straws.

'Apart from a deafening crash?'

They thanked Sandra and left. Neither of them had expected to hear anything that would move the investigation forward. They were just ticking boxes while they waited for the forensic report on Henry's car.

As they drove away from the hospital, Rob called. Henry was in custody in Herne Bay and a warrant to search his house had been granted. Proof that Jade's body had been kept in the boot of his car was all the evidence they needed.

'We'll go and take a look at his house,' Ian said, 'and then we'll have a word with Henry himself.'

'Can't we leave the house to a search team, and go straight to the interview?'

'No. The more pressure we can put on him, the better,' Ian said, aware that he was dodging the question.

The truth was that if incriminating evidence was discovered at Henry's house – a hidden bloody knife, or length of green garden twine – Ian wanted to be there when it was found. He would be happy to discover he had made a mistake in doubting Henry's guilt. Much as he hated to be proved wrong, seeing justice for Martha and Jade was more important than anything else.

CHAPTER 39

By the time Ian and Polly arrived the search team was already hard at work, scouring Henry's house for evidence to link him to the killing of two women.

'What if we find evidence there were more murders, sir?' Polly asked as they walked up to the front door.

'What?'

'Well, if he's killed two women, there could have been more. We might find—'

'If,' Ian interrupted. 'We don't even know he's guilty, so let's not start jumping to conclusions. It's vitally important to keep an open mind.'

'Yes, I know all that. But what if he *is* guilty, and these two aren't the only victims, and we find evidence of more murders?'

'Let's hope we don't.'

Henry had been taken away to the police station for questioning. He hadn't yet been charged but it was beginning to look as though that was only a matter of time. Meanwhile, it wouldn't harm to let him sweat in a cell for a while. His son was at home when they arrived. He looked stressed.

'Are you in charge here?' he demanded in a thin high voice, 'because whoever I speak to just says they're following orders and there's nothing they can do. But someone must be in charge. Is it you?'

Ian nodded and the young man stepped forward, shaking with pent-up fury.

'Well, perhaps you can tell me what's going on. As soon as I got home they were here. They must have been waiting for me. I opened the door and all these policemen rushed in. They're running around all over the place. This can't be legal. I'd like you all to leave right now or I'll – I'll call a lawyer and have you thrown out. This isn't a police state, you know. You can't just march in here and behave like you own the place. Just take all your policemen and get out of our house. And let my father come home. He's done nothing wrong,' he concluded petulantly.

Calmly Ian explained that they had a warrant to search the house. Without disclosing any details he said that another body had been found. The young man flicked his fringe back off his face and stared at Ian, wide-eyed and listening intently, as he explained that a second woman had been murdered and they had reason to suspect she too might be connected to Henry. Mark's eyes shone with unshed tears and he shook his head in disbelief. For a few seconds he appeared too upset to

238

speak. Ian felt sorry for him. The young man had just lost his mother and now his father was being accused of murder.

'I'm sorry,' he said, 'we're just doing our job. Best let us get on with it.'

Mark nodded and asked what they were expecting to find.

'I'm afraid I can't tell you that, sir.'

Leaving the distraught young man in the living room with a constable, Ian put on protective clothing before going upstairs. The search team had been instructed to hunt for a knife with a blade bent out of shape, bloodstained clothing, and a ball of green garden twine. Ian wasn't so clear about what he was looking for. He just wanted to take a look around and get the feel of the house, and its residents. First he went into a large square main bedroom furnished with two single beds, fitted wardrobes, an iron fireplace that was probably decorative rather than functional, and a wide bay window that looked out over the back garden. The curtains and carpet were grey, the cupboards and bed covers white. He noted the absence of a mirror, or any pictures. It was a cold room. He could have been standing in a hospital ward, it was so impersonal. He thought of his own bedroom, decorated in lilac and white, with patterned duvet cover on the double bed, and his discarded clothes strewn around the room despite all Bev's protests.

'It's not a bloody show house,' he would complain when she nagged him about being untidy.

The fitted wardrobe was half empty and contained only men's clothes, apart from one section where a woman's winter coat hung from the rail.

A uniformed officer was looking in the cabinet in the en suite bathroom. He looked round when Ian entered, and shook his head.

'Nothing here,' he said.

He nodded at two shelves, the top one containing shaving accoutrements, toothpaste and athletes foot powder, the bottom one hand cream and various pots of moisturising lotions, female deodorant and a bottle of Vitamin C tablets. There were two toothbrush mugs on the sink, two tubes of toothpaste, and two sets of towels were neatly folded on a wide window ledge, one white, the other blue.

'We'll send this away, anyway,' the SOCO said, picking up the container of powder. 'Just in case it's not what it says on the label.'

Ian grunted in agreement but they both knew it wasn't likely to be of much interest since they were investigating a stabbing and a strangling.

The second bedroom on the first floor clearly belonged to Martha's son. An officer was sifting through the wardrobe, checking in jacket and trouser pockets, and beneath piles of vests and pants. He too glanced up at Ian and shook his head. Beside the bed there was a photograph of Martha, smiling complacently into the camera. Mark had probably taken the photograph himself. Ian wondered if he always slept with her picture at his bedside, or if he had put it there after she was killed. He had clearly been close to his mother. There were no pictures of her in her own room, the one she shared with Henry. The second bathroom was large and clean. There was no one in there when Ian peered inside, but it would doubtless be scrutinised during the course of the search.

There were three more large bedrooms on that floor, two of which were empty, and another four rooms in the converted loft. The last room Ian looked at on the first floor was decorated in pale pink and white. A single bed stood against one wall. On a small chest beside it were a lamp and a bible. A grey night gown was folded on the pillow. Ian gazed around the room where the dead woman had evidently slept. There was an air of tranquillity in that room that was lacking in the rest of the house. He wondered if she had been at peace in there, alone with her Bible. The room had not yet been searched. He was about to leave for the station to question Henry, but decided to spend a few minutes in Martha's room first. He wanted to try and picture what her life must have been like, sleeping apart from her husband. He opened the drawers of the bedside chest and searched through them. At the back of the bottom drawer was a small black leather jewellery box. He took it out and opened it. A small silver cross lay inside. Carefully he lifted out the lining of the box and found a key carefully concealed in the folds of silky fabric. If Henry had considered this a good hiding place, he had miscalculated. Ian slipped the key in his pocket.

Before he left, he felt around under the bed covers. Stooping to peer beneath the bed, he lifted a rug and was surprised to see the carpet at the side of the bed worn almost threadbare in two small patches just a few inches apart. He hurried back into the main bedroom to call a forensic officer to examine it, and remove a sample for examination. It looked as though a stain had been rubbed away, taking most of the carpet fibre with it.

'If there's a trace of her blood there,' Ian said to Polly, 'that could be all we need.'

'It won't prove he killed her,' she pointed out. 'There could be all sorts of reasons why she bled in there.'

Ian shook his head.

'She was fifty-three. Her medical records will confirm it, but she must have been past her menopause, and there were no signs of any cuts or abrasions on the body—'

'Apart from the one that killed her,' Polly added.

There was little that Ian and Polly could do but watch the uniformed team going about their systematic search. It was frustrating, but they couldn't afford to hang around for long. Searching the whole property could take days, and they needed to get back to the station to question Henry. He couldn't be held for more than twenty-four hours without charge, and for that they needed evidence of his guilt. Ian hoped it would be enough to tell Henry what was happening at his home. Of course it was possible the murder weapons had been concealed somewhere else. Perhaps the key Ian had found would lead them to the hiding place.

'Let's hope they find the evidence soon,' he said.

'You think he did it then?' Polly asked. 'What made you change your mind?'

'I'm still not convinced he's responsible,' Ian replied. 'I'm only saying that it would be great to get this case sewn up.'

'Before any more bodies are discovered,' Polly added.

CHAPTER 40

Polly couldn't hide her excitement when Ian told her about the key he had found.

'Don't you see,' she said, 'we can't find a murder weapon, or any traces of blood on Henry Martin's clothes, or in his wardrobe, and there's nothing in his bins. If he's guilty, he must have disposed of the weapon and the clothes he was wearing. They must be somewhere.' She held up the small bag containing the key he had found. 'This could be the key to the place where he's stashed the evidence. It could be that simple. All we have to do is find out what the key opens.'

'How are we going to do that?' Ian asked.

Ian set up a team to go through all of Henry's bank statements looking for a transaction that could be connected to the purchase of a key. It had a generic number on it so shouldn't be difficult to trace. At the same time, he instructed a couple of constables to contact every locksmith and hardware store in Kent for a cash sale of a padlock or other key, anything that could be connected to Henry. Finally, he intended to put pressure on the suspect to confess.

'So he's a suspect now, is he?' Polly asked, smiling. 'You just can't make up your mind, can you? Typical man!'

'He's not a suspect yet, not officially, but we have to keep an open mind.'

'So keeping an open mind basically means you can change your opinion whenever the mood takes you?'

'Something like that,' he grinned.

Once the necessary and lengthy preamble had been completed, the interview commenced. Henry gazed levelly across the table, apparently relaxed, as though Ian was a neighbour who had just invited him in for a chat. Ian stared back, registering the calm expression on the suspect's face, his hair as neatly combed down as when they had first met. If anything he looked less tired than when Ian had last seen him. Being widowed didn't seem to trouble him much. After a moment he leaned back in his chair so he could stretch out his legs. He folded his arms and waited, his eyes fixed on Ian's face. No one spoke. The solicitor cleared his throat. Resigning himself to the fact that Henry wasn't going to be unnerved by waiting, Ian reached into his jacket pocket. They had already wasted part of the twenty-four hours they could keep him in custody. The clock was ticking.

Doing his best to remain deadpan, Ian lay a small evidence bag on the table. Still pokerfaced, he watched Henry closely as he spoke.

'We found this.'

Henry looked down at the bag.

'Is this your key?' Ian leaned forward, speaking in what he hoped was a menacing voice. With a glance at the solicitor he sat back and lightened his tone. 'We found it hidden in your house. Was it yours? Or perhaps it belonged to your wife? Come on, Henry, let's drop the pretence. Did you think we wouldn't be interested in it because we found it in her room? If it's yours, it wasn't a very clever hiding place, was it?'

Henry frowned, perplexed rather than worried. 'What's it for?'

'Oh, we'll find out soon enough, you can be sure of that,' Ian told him, 'so you might as well save us time and help yourself by co-operating. What does the key belong to?'

'I don't know what it's for,' Henry replied simply. 'You're making a mistake. It's not mine.'

'What does it open?' Ian insisted fiercely.

It was frustrating. This wasn't how Ian had hoped the interview might progress. Henry seemed so calm, and was so convincing. The solicitor stirred.

'My client has already answered that question. He's told you the key doesn't belong to him.' He turned to Henry. 'You don't need to answer that question again.' He looked back at Ian as he added, 'The police have no right to hector you.'

Ian looked at the solicitor. Grey-haired, slim and elegant, he looked effete beside his rough-looking

246

client. The solicitor smiled, an easy, debonair smile, no more intimidated by Ian's aggressive stance than his client, who appeared oblivious to the significance of the key. The solicitor looked pointedly at his watch.

'Are you intending to charge my client, Sergeant? Or are you going to let him go?'

Ian terminated the interview and sent Henry back to the cells, but he knew he couldn't hold him for much longer.

'So do you still think it was him now,' Polly asked, 'or have you changed your mind again?'

Ian didn't answer.

The next morning there was finally a positive development when a constable traced the key through the number engraved on it. If it had belonged to a padlock there would have been virtually no hope of tracking down whatever it had been used to secure. But they were in luck. The key belonged to a locker at a self-storage site in Canterbury. Ian broke into a grin on receiving the information. He almost ran along the corridor to Rob's office to share the news. Catching Ian's excitement, Rob seemed to bounce up and down on his chair as he spoke. Ian had never seen him so animated. They both knew this could be the break they needed.

'Well, what are we waiting for?'

Rob sprang to his feet, grabbed his jacket, and they hurried out of the office. As he followed, Ian checked he still had the key in his pocket, safely in its bag. He passed Polly in the corridor. She had heard the news.

'Do you want me to come with you?' she asked.

'Thanks, Polly, but the DI's coming.'

'But—'

Without giving her a chance to protest, he walked away.

Superior Self-Storage was located on an industrial estate a mile outside Canterbury. The warehouse was easy to spot, the name printed in huge red and yellow letters above the entrance. They followed the sign to reception where a skinny dark-haired girl sat slumped behind a large desk with a blank expression on her face. She straightened up as they entered and asked if they were existing customers. When Rob told her they weren't she launched into an account of the different storage spaces on offer, starting with fifteen square feet.

'All of our units are eight-foot high.'

The inspector interrupted her to explain the reason for their visit. Her bored recitation halted abruptly and her eyes lit up with excitement.

'The police?' she said, clapping her hands to her cheeks. 'Oh my God, don't tell me someone's stored a dead body in one of the units?'

She looked disappointed when Rob asked to see a manager. Tapping at her switchboard, she motioned them to take a seat. A few moments later, a shambling bear of a man appeared. He was wearing blue overalls and walked with an ungainly motion, as though his huge frame was too bulky for his legs to carry.

'What seems to be the problem, officer? I hope there isn't going to be any trouble. We had a case of stolen goods a couple of years back, but that was straightened out and we were cleared of any involvement. All we do is hire out the units. If customers don't adhere to the terms and conditions, well, there's not a great deal we can do to stop people lying to us, is there? I mean, we're not mind readers.'

Ian interrupted his moaning to show him the key, explaining there was reason to suspect the contents of this unit might contain items that would help them with an investigation. The girl behind the desk was listening. As soon as Ian finished, she jumped up and offered to take them to the relevant unit.

'We need to rely on your absolute discretion,' Ian said quietly to the manager who nodded.

Instructing the girl to remain at her post, he led Ian through a maze of white slatted walls punctuated at intervals by bright blue doors. A couple of times Ian's guide checked the number on the key and once he turned back with a muttered apology.

At last they came to a halt beside a blue door.

'Here it is,' the manager announced, 'fifteen

square feet and eight-feet high. What are you expecting to find in there, then? Drugs? Guns?'

'Nothing as dramatic as that!'

'What then?'

'I'm not sure,' Ian lied.

He hoped his companions wouldn't notice he was sweating as he put on his gloves and turned the key. Rob sent the manager away while Ian opened the door and switched on the bare light bulb. As he looked inside the large cupboard, his jaw dropped in astonishment. Behind him, he heard his colleague exclaim out loud.

CHAPTER 41

A frown creased his white forehead. The corners of his thin lips curled down. A faint sigh whispered through the assembled disciples, and their shoulders drooped. The leader was displeased. Ten pairs of eyes gazed accusingly at Warrior who didn't dare speak, not even to defend himself. Usually uplifting in the presence of the leader, the silence grew painful.

Somewhere in the room a clock was ticking.

He stared into the leader's huge dark eyes and waited. After what felt like a long time, the leader shifted in his seat. He rose from his chair and crossed the room in long strides until he was standing right in front of his cowed follower. Both were tall, about the same height. For a moment the leader stared calmly into Warrior's eyes, then he spun round on his heels and faced the disciples.

'Leave us,' he said.

The others lowered their heads submissively before they turned and filed out of the room in silence. The last in line closed the door to the meeting room behind them.

Although the leader's voice was soft, every word could be easily heard in the still room.

'What is it that troubles you?'

'I've killed another woman.'

He dropped his face in his hands, resisting an impulse to throw himself on the floor at the leader's feet.

'What made you do that?'

'I was afraid,' Warrior admitted.

'Tell me about your fear.' The low voice invited confidence.

'I killed the prostitute, Della.'

'Did you distrust her?'

'I didn't know what she was going to do. I still don't know.'

The leader asked him what happened and then closed his eyes for a moment, as he listened to Warrior's account of the second death.

'Did you want to kill her?' he asked in a voice that sounded unexpectedly tender.

'Did I *want* to do it?' Warrior repeated. He wasn't sure what to say.

'Did you enjoy killing those two women?' the leader repeated his question patiently.

'What do you mean?'

'You understand my words perfectly, just as I understand you. Through your actions you have shown your dedication. You have done no more than was required. Many would have done less.'

Warrior felt as though a weight had lifted from his shoulders. The leader was smiling at him.

'Would you like to kill more women? Is that what you want?'

Warrior trembled. He felt as though the leader had penetrated deep into his mind, and observed him more accurately than he could ever dare to see himself.

In spite of his relief he was afraid, as much of himself as of the leader.

'I did it for you,' he said desperately. 'I did it to protect you. I didn't mean any harm—'

'It is of no consequence,' the leader reassured him, dismissing his words with an elegant wave of his hand. 'The gods see your motives. They gave you strength, and will protect you. You have nothing to fear. Now tell me, what troubles you? Regrets are foolish.'

The leader always understood.

'I need to know,' Warrior said. 'Was it wrong to kill her?'

The leader's face relaxed into a solemn smile.

'She would have died anyway. Everyone dies. It is what happens after death that concerns us. Nothing that happens here on this earth is of any lasting significance.'

'But killing – doesn't that matter?'

'You had no choice. You had to remove her. She

was a threat to us all. A man has the right to protect his own.'

'What about the police?' Warrior asked. He couldn't believe it was really going to be all right. 'What if they suspect me?'

'You were careful. Only have faith, and the gods will protect you. We are the enlightened ones.'

'We are the enlightened ones,' he repeated the familiar chant. 'We follow the path to eternal salvation. We will be saved.'

The leader himself stepped out to recall the disciples into the meeting room. Seated once more in his high-backed chair, he announced that Warrior had earned the right to sit as one of them.

'Our number is growing,' he intoned. 'Warrior has performed another sacrifice, and proved himself worthy to serve us. He is no longer a follower, he is a disciple of the sacred cause.'

'He is a disciple of our sacred leader,' the others chanted.

'I am a disciple of our sacred leader,' Warrior cried out.

He tried to remain subdued, as fitted the occasion, but he couldn't contain his joy.

'His name is no longer Warrior,' the leader announced when they had finished chanting. 'He has a special calling. He will be called Assassin.'

CHAPTER 42

Rob stepped inside the unit behind Ian, closed the door and pulled on his gloves. The two men stood side by side, their arms nearly touching in the confined space. Attached to the wall in front of them was a twelve-inch crucifix. Carved in wood, painted flesh colour, the figure had glass eyes and was wearing a white loin cloth. Beneath it on a white table stood a twelve-inch statue of the virgin Mary, her hands pressed together in prayer, her robes painted blue and white, her skin a similar pale flesh colour. Both Mary and Jesus had bare feet and were crowned with bright yellow haloes. The floor in front of the icons was dust-free in two places. There was nothing else in the storage space. Ian was in no doubt about the identity of the customer. At the same time he understood that the carpet in Martha's bedroom hadn't been scrubbed to clean away blood stains; it had been worn away by someone kneeling in prayer.

Rob swore. It was far from the conclusive evidence of murder they had been hoping to find.

'We'll get finger prints and send a SOCO team down to see if there's anything,' he said.

On their way out they confirmed that the lock-up had been rented by Martha Martin.

'Is there a problem with it?' the manager asked again.

'Oh my God,' the receptionist cried out suddenly. 'I recognise that name. It's the woman, isn't it? The one who was stabbed to death in Herne Bay!'

Her eyes grew round with excitement. Ian swore under his breath. So much for discretion. There was no way they could keep this silly girl quiet. If they asked her to keep this information a secret, she would probably blab to the press as well as to her friends.

'It's a common name,' was all he said.

They didn't speak in the car on the way back to Herne Bay. Ian was thinking about Henry, who had been released. They didn't have enough to hold him. They knew Martha had been brought up as a Catholic. Henry wasn't a practising Christian and, as far as they knew, his wife no longer adhered to her religion. If their neighbour's report was reliable, the marriage had been unhappy but they had stayed together. Perhaps Ian's first instinct had been correct. Henry had wanted a divorce, but his wife had refused, because she still clung to her Catholicism. She had kept her faith secret, storing her iconography in a secure unit in Canterbury, and hiding the key from her husband. It gave Henry another motive for wanting to be rid of his wife. Desperate to escape from a miserable marriage, killing his wife offered him the added bonus that he would become a wealthy man. But they still lacked proof, and there remained the problem of the alibi which Della had given, an alibi which could no longer be corroborated.

'If we could prove that Henry paid Della to give him an alibi,' he said, 'that would be something.'

Rob shrugged. There was no need to point out the futility of the idea. Even if they were able to establish that Henry had handed a substantial amount of money to Della, there was no way of proving he had bribed her to lie for him. Men paid women like that all the time. 'Maybe she told her flatmate about it,' he suggested.

'Hearsay,' Rob replied. 'But you can go and talk to her again if you want.'

Ian dropped the inspector off in Herne Bay and drove on to Margate. Questioning the dead girl's flatmate gave him something to do and he couldn't bear to sit at his desk fiddling about. He had to be out doing something. At least that way there was a chance he might uncover a new lead. At the moment, they were completely in the dark. After his excitement at finding the key, his disappointment was acute.

Gaining access to the block was easy, but no one came to the door when he rang the bell to the flat where Della had lived with Candy. Cursing, he rang the bell again. There was still no answer. On the off chance that the bell wasn't working, he knocked violently. The door shuddered as though it wasn't securely in place. He turned the handle and the door opened. The whole time he had been ringing the bell, the flat had been unlocked. He went in and pulled the door shut behind him, intending to take a quick look around. He opened the door to Candy's room and stole inside. Turning, he almost yelled in surprise. Candy was lying on the bed, propped up against the headboard in an awkward position. She seemed to be staring straight at him, without moving or crying out. Gazing into her vacant eyes, he reached out to feel her neck for a pulse.

As he leaned over the bed, she raised one hand and pointed her finger at him. Startled by her movement, he drew back.

'You,' she mumbled.

The lifeless expression in her eyes didn't alter. Her pupils were dilated, her voice slurred. Clearly she was out of her head on alcohol or drugs, or a cocktail of both. She spoke slowly and deliberately as though it was an immense effort to articulate the words.

'You,' she repeated, her eyes fixed on his face. 'Why're you here? What you doing here? 'S my room. My room. Get the fuck out my room, pig.'

Her eyes closed, as though she had exhausted

her energy. Ian wondered whether she might be more likely to tell the truth when she was high, if he was able to get any sense out of her at all. She was in no state to challenge his entering her flat without permission, yet lucid enough to know who he was. The next day she wouldn't remember that he had let himself in, if she remembered speaking to him at all.

'Why're you here?' she asked again, raising herself up with a grunt and resting on one elbow.

Ian determined to make the best of the situation. Time was pressing. He might not have another chance to speak to her when she was out of control. It was unethical, but she would have no recollection of his visit. In the meantime, he had a double murder to investigate. If he could advance the investigation by ignoring the niceties of protocol just this once, so be it. No one would know. The ends would justify the means. Aware that he was taking advantage of her vulnerable state, he spoke quietly.

'I came here to ask you a question.'

Candy sniggered.

'The question,' she repeated in a singsong voice, 'the question.'

Ian cleared his throat. But before he could continue, she flopped back against her pillows again, giggling hysterically. On hearing her former flatmate's name, she stopped laughing abruptly.

'He done for her,' she muttered. 'He done it.'

'Done it? What did he do to her? Candy, talk to me.'

'He did for her.'

'He? Who is he?'

Ian took a step forward.

'Candy, it's very important you tell me who he is. Who did for Della? Who was it?'

She didn't answer.

'Did a man give her money to lie for him?'

Candy stared at her feet, stretched out on the bed in front of her.

'Who killed Della?'

Candy closed her eyes. Her mouth dropped open and she began to snore gently. Ian waited a moment, then began to search once more through piles of soiled clothing, cheap jewellery, bottles and jars of perfume, hand cream, make-up, and hair accessories, but he found nothing to help his enquiry, and only thirty pounds in cash in her purse. If she knew about money Henry had given to Della, she had probably spent it herself. He glanced at her prostrate form on the bed. It didn't need a detective to work out how she would have disposed of a windfall.

CHAPTER 43

Ben had no option but to carry his knife with him at all times. It was only just over a week since he had found it but the knife had already changed his life so much that he couldn't imagine living without it. The question was how to carry it around without anyone seeing. It didn't matter that other kids knew. On the contrary, the more of them who heard about it, the better. But he had to make sure no adult spotted it. If his mother, or Eddy, or any of his teachers got their thieving hands on it, he would be in trouble with everyone. The adults would punish him for carrying a knife, and his classmates wouldn't hesitate to beat him up once they were no longer in awe of him. It would be unbearable. He could just imagine the taunts.

'Not so tough now, are you?'

Ben had never learned how to sew. As if! But he needed to create a pocket inside his school jacket where he could keep his knife out of sight. It was surprisingly easy to get hold of the essential materials. He thought he would have to go to Canterbury or Faversham, but it turned out there was a sewing shop in the High Street right there in Herne Bay. The needles he had nicked from school were useless so he bought one that worked better, telling the woman in the shop that his mother had sent him to buy the biggest needle there was, and some really strong thread. He was afraid she would laugh at him, but she just asked him what colour he wanted. The most difficult part of the task would be lining the pocket with something that would protect him from the sharp blade. After casting around for something to use, he finally nicked his mother's leather jacket. Locked in the bathroom, he chopped off a sleeve, grinning as his new knife sliced through the leather with ease. He bundled the remainder of the jacket into a carrier bag which he dumped in a skip outside a house round the corner. He covered it with a pile of rubble. His mother would never find it there. No one would notice it hidden beneath a load of rubbish. Then he raced home, eager to start.

Armed with needle and thread he painstakingly sewed a secret pocket inside his jacket. It took days. Not only was it difficult, but he could only work on it when his mother and Eddy were out. Even then he locked himself safely in the bathroom before getting down to it. When the pocket was finished, he turned his attention to the leather. That was more difficult to sew. He soon regretted having chucked the rest of the jacket away. If he ruined the one piece he had kept, he would have to find something else to use. By the time he finished sewing, his fingers were sore from pushing the end of the needle through the fabric. But he had done it. He slid the knife into its leather sheath and slipped it into the pocket inside his jacket. Staring at himself in the mirror in his mum's room, he thought he looked OK. He couldn't bend over, but at least the knife didn't show. The only danger was if some dick of a teacher told him to take his jacket off. But for now that wasn't going to be a problem. By the time the weather grew warm again, he would have assembled his own gang to protect him.

Ben didn't take much notice of a group of older boys hanging around just inside the school gate. It was no big deal. He was armed. One of his mates came running out of the school grounds to join him.

'You seen them?' Col's eyes were bright with anger.

Ben grinned at him. Small and wiry, Col was always over-excited about something.

'Stay cool, bro. What's going on?' Ben asked nonchalantly.

'It's them, innit. Chas's lot. All of them in the playground.'

'They better not mess with me.'

Col giggled nervously at Ben's bravado and stood aside to let him go in first. Ben flung his shoulders back and strode into the playground. He felt ten-feet tall.

★   ★   ★

Just inside the gate, his way was blocked by a thickset boy who towered over him, a vicious grin on his ugly face.

'Where do you think you're going, faggot?'

The other boys joined in, jeering and calling Ben names. By the time he realised how many of them were there, he was surrounded. He couldn't see Col, not that he would have been much help. There was nothing for it but to tough it out. It was time someone taught Chas a lesson. Everyone said so. But fear made his legs feel weak, and he was too frightened to speak.

Chas stepped forward and shoved him roughly on the shoulder. Ben staggered and nearly lost his balance. He could hear laughter. When he glanced around, looking for an escape route, he saw that he and Chas were hemmed in by a crowd of jostling kids all chanting, 'Fight! Fight! Fight!'.

With a burst of adrenaline he reached inside his jacket, pulled out his knife, and brandished it in the air. The blade shook in his grasp as he struggled to hold his arm steady. His hands were sweaty with panic. He wasn't sure how he managed to keep hold of the knife and stay upright. All he wanted to do was barge his way through the throng and run as fast as he could.

'Get away from me!' he screamed, swinging his arm wildly.

Chas faltered and took a step back. Thrilled,

Ben advanced on him, waving the knife with a slashing movement. The gang closed in on them.

'Get back or I'll kill him!' he yelled at the assembled crowd.

He was beside himself with terror and excitement, hungry to draw blood. They would all see who was in charge. The new general had arrived and his triumph would be sealed with the blood of his enemy.

The chanting was suddenly hushed. For an instant, Ben didn't notice what was happening and continued ferociously brandishing his weapon. He saw the deputy head at the same time as he heard him shouting, 'What's going on here?'

Ben's relief lasted less than a second. This wasn't a reprieve. Instead of standing his ground, maybe having time to think of a way out of his predicament, he was going to be expelled for bringing a weapon in to school. Worse, they would take his knife away. He was in so much trouble. Wretchedly he lowered his arm and obeyed the deputy's summons to follow him. With every step his legs felt heavier until he could barely put one foot in front of the other. He hardly noticed the howls of derision behind him.

'I don't feel well,' he whined, stopping to lean against the wall as they reached the corridor. He thought he was going to collapse.

The maddening part of it was that he could so easily have avoided trouble. He should never have brought his knife to school. It would have been better to have taken a beating. The knife was never going to protect him in the long run.

'I'm going to be sick.'

The teacher's expression remained deadpan.

'When will I get my knife back?'

'We'll be handing that to the police.'

There was really no point trying to argue his way out of it, but he had a go anyway, whining that they had no right to confiscate his knife.

'It was self-defence,' he insisted, staring at his feet. 'He started it.'

'Enough!' the deputy barked. 'Keep quiet.'

Ben stopped babbling and looked up. The teacher's pale complexion was suffused with a pink glow. He looked as though he was enjoying himself.

CHAPTER 44

Rob was away at a meeting and Ian was working with Polly, trying to find out more about Della. Early on Wednesday afternoon they arrived at the club where she worked to find the shutters closed and everything seemingly locked up. Ian tried the bell anyway and was pleased to hear footsteps approaching inside. A woman in a blue overall opened the door and peered up at him.

'We're closed,' she announced in a thin sharp voice, 'so you'll have to come back later. None of the girls is here at this time of the day.'

Catching sight of Polly, she broke off abruptly and gazed at the visitors in surprise.

'What was it you wanted, anyway?'

Ian told her who he was and introduced Polly. After a bungled attempt to close the door, the woman began to bleat that she was only the cleaner, and had no idea what went on in the club.

'I keep myself to myself, always have,' she said. 'You can't expect me to answer your questions.'

Ian explained they weren't there to quiz her.

They just wanted to know what time the manager would arrive.

'Could be any time.'

Polly stepped forward.

'Perhaps we could come in and wait for him,' she said, 'and then we can let you get on. We don't want to hold you up. It must be a full-time job, cleaning this place. But you must have a team of people working for you.'

The cleaner snorted.

'Chance would be a fine thing. No, it's just me.'

'What?' Polly sounded really shocked. 'You are kidding, aren't you?'

'I wish I was.'

'You mean you keep this place clean all by yourself? With no help?'

'Well there's Bill, the caretaker, but he does bugger all. He's never here when you need him. And the bouncers are supposed to keep it tidy out the front, only they don't. And if it isn't swept, who gets it in the neck?'

'None of the men,' Polly commiserated with her.

'You're right there. Anyway, you come on in, dear, and you can wait at a table. You go and sit down and I'll bring you a cup of tea, you and the young chap.'

Ian followed Polly and the cleaner, who was telling the constable she must be the same age as her own daughter. When the two detectives were seated in the small auditorium, facing the empty stage, the cleaner bustled off to fetch them some tea. Polly grinned at Ian who returned her smile with developing respect. Ingratiating herself with the cleaner had been smart. It might help them pick up on some useful gossip.

'You did well to get us in here like that,' he said.

Polly went red.

'It's only because I remind her of her daughter,' she said, flustered.

Before long the cleaner returned clutching two mugs of steaming tea.

'Where's yours?' Polly asked as she took her tea.

'Oh, I need to get on, dear.'

'Not until we've asked you a few questions, so you might as well fetch yourself a cup of tea and come and sit down.'

The woman hesitated before going to fetch a third mug of tea.

'Well, seeing as you have to speak to me, I suppose I might as well take the weight off, if you really think I can help you.'

She let out a loud sigh as she sat down. Ian leaned back and left it to Polly to find out as much as she could about the club, the manager, and the girls who worked there.

'They call them dancers, but there's more goes on here than you might think.' She leaned forward and lowered her voice, although there was no one else there but Ian. 'It's not just what you see on the stage. The girls are expected to take customers upstairs.'

Although the cleaner was eager to tell them every-thing she knew, she was unable to reveal anything they hadn't figured out already. She thought she had heard of Della and said she knew a girl called Candy worked there, but wasn't sure who she was. Every few minutes she glanced at her watch and became increasingly uneasy, until finally she said it was time for her to return to her work. She must have had a shrewd idea when the manager would arrive, because a few minutes after she had left them the door flew open and he stomped in, looking down at his iPhone. He was halfway across the room when he caught sight of them watching him. The complexion of his large face darkened, and his heavy brows drew together.

'What the hell are you doing here?' he roared. He strode over to their table and stood over them, his face red and bloated. 'Who let you in?'

Ian rose to his feet, towering over the other man. The manager took a step back.

'What do you want?' he asked in a lower voice. 'We're not open. How did you get in?'

'We'd like to ask you a few questions.'

'Go on, then, now's as good a time as any. But make it quick. We open in two hours. Is it about Della?'

'What do you know about what happened?'

The fat man pulled a chair over to their table and sat astride it with an air of resignation.

'The trouble with these girls is they're none too bright. We warn them not to go off with men. They don't need that kind of shit. I mean, they got a good job here, as long as they keep the customers happy. But after a while they start thinking they can do better for themselves. They all think they're going to find themselves a man who'll take care of them, keep them in clover. But what man's going to want them? We're in the twenty-first century, for fuck's sake. If they knew what was good for them, they'd be satisfied with what they get here and not keep looking for something better. That was what Della did, and look what happened to her.' He shook his head. 'She didn't know when she was well off. We do our best to look after our girls here, Inspector, but they don't help themselves.'

It was clear that the manager believed Della had been killed by a frustrated customer. He had no idea that her death had anything to do with the recent stabbing in Herne Bay. Just as Ian concluded that they were wasting their time at the club, his phone rang. A knife matching the description of the one used to stab Martha had been discovered. It had the hand guard and, more significantly, the blade was bent out of shape in a manner that exactly matched the blade they were looking for. It was being examined for traces of blood, which would give conclusive proof that it had been used in the fatal stabbing. In the meantime, the young boy who had been carrying it had been taken to the police station where he was being held pending questioning.

In the car, Ian told Polly everything he knew about this new development.

'When you say young boy—'

'He's thirteen.'

'Jesus.'

'We don't know he was the one who stabbed her,' Ian pointed out.

He hoped the boy wouldn't turn out to be implicated in the murder.

CHAPTER 45

Susan Bailey was waiting at the police station in Herne Bay when Ian arrived. With an officer trained to question children present, Ian could sit back and observe the boy.

'Ben, do you know why you're here?' Susan began.

The boy looked sullen. Susan repeated the question.

'Yeah, yeah. It's because of my knife – the knife.'

'Well done. Now, would you like someone to be here with you? Do you want us to call your mother?'

'No way. She'll tell Eddy.'

'Who's Eddy?'

'He's her boyfriend. He's not my father. What I do is none of his fucking business.'

He dropped his gaze, incapable of hiding his disquiet.

'That's fine, Ben,' Susan said gently. 'We won't tell Eddy. But we'll have to let your mother know you're here. Would you like to wait for her before answering a few questions?'

'Fuck off. You don't know my mother or you'd never ask.'

'Now, Ben, you do understand that we have to

273

ask you some questions about the knife that was found on you. You know this is really important, don't you?'

'I'm thirteen. You don't have to talk to me like I'm a child. And I'm not dumb. I know what you're doing.'

'What are we doing?'

'You're trying to scare me. Bloody hell, it's only a knife. Everyone has one. It's for protection. No one messes with me.'

He glared first at Susan, then at Ian, with pathetic bravado. Small and skinny, he could have been eleven although he was nearly fourteen. With his shoulders thrust back and head held high, he stared defiantly across the table. His straggly light brown hair looked as though it could do with a wash, and his face and hands were grubby. He was wearing a dark green anorak, faded jeans and muddy trainers. In any other circumstances he wouldn't have attracted a second look, just another kid loitering on the streets.

'We've sent your knife away for forensic examination,' Ian said bluntly.

There was something about the boy's insolent stare that needled him. It worried him that youngsters had so little respect for authority.

The boy didn't answer. He licked his lips and looked from Ian to the constable and back again.

'We've been looking for your knife,' Ian added.

'Why?'

'We've been looking for a knife with a bent blade.'

At a nod from Susan, he put a photograph of the weapon on the table.

'Your knife,' Ian repeated. 'A knife that was used to stab someone.'

'Yeah, well, that's what knives do, innit.'

He glanced at the photograph.

'How do you know it's my knife? There's thousands of knives like that. Millions.'

'It was found in your pocket. A pocket sewn into your jacket.'

'Yeah, well, someone put it there, didn't they?'

'It's got your prints all over it.'

'Yeah, well, it's mine. I recognise it now. I never said it wasn't mine.'

Susan flinched as the boy raised his filthy thumb to his mouth and began chewing his nail.

Ian sat forward and spoke very slowly, glancing at Susan.

'This knife was used to kill a woman.'

'It wasn't me,' the boy blurted out.

His cocky bearing slipped and he blinked nervously. His face went pale.

'A woman was stabbed to death in a park near your house.'

'What's that got to do with me?' The boy wriggled in his chair. 'That's got nothing to do with me.'

'Listen, son. Your prints are on the handle. We're

275

going to find a dead woman's blood on the blade. It's not looking good for you. So why don't you tell us exactly what happened, because lying isn't going to help you. We'll know.'

'You're the one who's lying,' the boy said.

'A dead woman's blood on your knife is going to take some explaining,' Ian said.

'Yeah, well, I found it, didn't I?'

'You found it?'

'Yeah, I found it.'

Even though he was clearly rattled, there was something calculating in the boy's expression.

'I took it,' he amended his statement. 'I thought it would be cool.'

'Cool?'

'A knife like that, I thought it would get me some respect!'

He scowled at Ian then, for no apparent reason, his whole demeanour changed. His eyes lit up with excitement and he began fidgeting. All at once he had come alive, bursting to leap up out of his seat. He should have been out kicking a football around with his mates, not sitting in a police station answering questions. No longer craven, he stared boldly across the table. Even his voice changed, aping a Jamaican drawl.

'Yeah, well, it was me, man. You got me bang to rights.'

'Are you telling us you killed a woman with this knife?'

'Yeah, like I told you, it was me, man. I'm the killer you're looking for. It was me all along.' He grinned at Susan, avoiding Ian's eye, and dropped his affectation of an accent. 'Will it be in the papers that I done it? Because you can't put me in the nick, can you? Not at my age.'

'You don't know what we can do,' Ian said softly. 'Now, why don't you tell us the truth? Because one way or another whoever did this is going to be locked up for a very long time. And you can imagine what would happen to a boy like you, in a young offenders' institution.'

Ignoring Susan's warning frown, Ian pressed on.

'Locked up, day after day, with all those older boys, testosterone levels out of control. Is that what you want?'

Ian didn't believe the boy's mindless boasting for a second. He wondered if he was covering up for someone else, or if he wanted to be labelled a murderer, someone to be feared. He clearly had no idea what it would actually mean if he was found guilty. Ian tried another tack.

'We know it wasn't you stabbed that woman, Ben. Who are you lying to protect? Is it your stepfather?'

At his side he heard Susan give a disapproving sniff but Ben responded to the provocation.

'I told you he ain't my fucking stepfather and I'm not lying.'

He no longer sounded sure of himself.

★　　★　　★

277

'Ben, you can see now why it's so important we know whose knife you had on you,' Susan said. 'We really need to know and you're the only person who can help us. We won't tell anyone if you don't want us to.' Ian kept quiet. He could see the boy was ready to talk.

'Whose knife was it, Ben? Did someone give it to you?'

Ben appeared to be considering.

'What about my money?' he demanded after a pause.

'Money?'

'Yes, what you pay me for being an informer. You pay for information, don't you? You can't expect me to do this for nothing.'

Susan looked at Ian who nodded.

'Yes,' she agreed slowly. 'As long as you tell us the truth.'

'Do you want to know who gave me that knife, and told me to keep it hidden?' the boy asked eagerly. Too eagerly.

Ian wasn't sure the boy was telling the truth but he went along with it. He had an inkling where this was leading.

'Yeah well, it was Eddy,' Ben said, making no attempt to conceal his satisfaction.

'Eddy? You mean your mother's boyfriend, Eddy?' Susan asked.

'Yeah. He give it me and says look after this for me, lad. So I done it. Until Mr Kelsey took it off me at school. There wasn't nothing I could do.'

'Why did Eddy give it to you?' Ian asked.

Ben shrugged.

'How should I know? He told me to hide it and not to show it to anyone, not to let anyone know anything about it. He said he'd be for it if anyone found out. And he said I should keep it on me all the time because it would stop the other kids bullying me.'

'Even though he told you not to show it to anyone.'

'Yeah, well. He's thick, innit.'

Ian had no doubt the boy was making up his story as he went along, but Susan was looking triumphant.

'Well done, Ben,' she crowed. 'You've been a very brave boy.'

Ian cringed at her patronising tone, but Ben seemed too pleased with himself to care. Ian couldn't tell if he was smiling with relief at having unburdened himself, or because he thought it was payback time for his mother's bullying boyfriend.

'How much do I get?' he demanded. 'And can I have my knife back now? And don't let on I said anything. Eddy'll kill me if he finds out.' All at once he looked terrified. 'Tell him I never said nothing.'

CHAPTER 46

'He could have been lying,' Ian pointed out to Polly as they drove to Ben's flat to question Eddy. Polly was so cheerful that Ian felt like a heel undermining her conviction the case was solved. But Ian was sufficiently experienced not to take anything he heard at face value.

'Why would he lie?' she countered. 'He's only thirteen.'

Ian couldn't help laughing.

'Thirteen-year-olds lie. I know I did when I was thirteen, every time I forgot to do my homework.'

'That's completely different,' Polly protested. 'He must realise he could get his stepfather into a lot of trouble.'

Ian grunted.

'Either he has no idea how serious this is, or else he's taking the opportunity to drop Eddy in it, big time. I can't say I blame him, not really. He's only a kid, and Eddy sounds like a vicious bastard. He's been done for GBH before now. As a kid living in the same house as him, I'd probably be inventing lies to get rid of him as well.'

'OK, he might be making it all up, but it could

be true, that's all I'm saying. You're always telling me to keep an open mind.'

Ian smiled bleakly.

A skinny woman of indeterminate age came to the door. Ian thought she was probably younger than she looked. Her skin was lined and she had an unhealthy complexion, pale and pimply, with grey pouches under her dull eyes.

'We're looking for Eddy.'

'He ain't here.'

Ian stepped forward and blocked her attempt to shut the door. He held up his warrant card.

'What you want with him anyway?'

She squinted suspiciously from Ian to Polly and back again.

'We just need to ask him a few questions.'

'Well he ain't here.'

'Where does he work?'

'Work? Him? You're having a laugh.'

Ian tried a different approach.

'You must be Ben's mother.'

'What's the little shit gone and done now?'

Ian was slightly shocked that she had no idea her thirteen-year-old son had been caught carrying a knife at school. He wondered why the school hadn't been in touch with her and whether social services would be alerted. In the meantime, he turned his attention back to the woman's boyfriend.

'What time do you expect Eddy back?'

Ben's mother just shrugged.

'Whenever.'

It was obvious that as soon as she shut the door she was going to warn Eddy the police had been asking for him. He could decide to disappear for a while. By the time they had conclusive proof of his fingerprints on the knife, and perhaps his bloodstained clothing hidden in the flat, he might be impossible to track down.

Ian nodded at Polly who understood at once what he wanted. She took a few steps away down the path and spoke rapidly into her phone. As soon as Polly finished, Ian called to her.

'Why don't you accompany her round the corner to the station for a while?' he suggested quietly.

'What the fuck are you talking about?' Ben's mother shrieked in sudden alarm, jumping away from the door.

'Just to help us with our enquiries,' Ian went on smoothly. 'Don't worry, you're not in any trouble. But you could be if you don't go quietly. We just want to show you a few photos, and see if you recognise anyone.'

He was making up the story as he went along. Ben wasn't the only one who could be inventive. Suddenly she was transformed into a solicitous mother, flapping about Ben and who was going to look after him.

'I can't go nowhere. I need to give my boy his tea.'

'Don't worry about Ben,' he reassured her. 'We're taking care of him.'

The woman was genuinely frightened now and began squawking about her son. Polly stepped forward and took her firmly by the arm.

'Come along, this won't take long. My colleague is going to be busy for a while, and you're coming with me to look at a few pictures. There's a car on its way from the local station which will be here any minute.'

'What are you on about? What pictures? What car?'

'Come along, and we'll have a nice cup of tea.'

'I don't want no tea, not from you.'

But she accompanied Polly out of the house, moaning and complaining. Half way down the path, she darted away from the constable with surprising agility, and ran into the arms of a stout uniformed officer who had just arrived at the gate. Swearing foully, she was hustled into the waiting vehicle. Before Polly closed the door on her, Ian was reassured to see that the constable had taken a mobile phone out of the angry woman's grasp. There was an unmarked police car outside the back entrance to the block of flats and a second one was in position near the front gate. Now all they had to do was wait for Eddy to return home.

To pass the time, Ian conducted a quick survey of the flat. He started by looking in the kitchen.

Mould was growing on the wall above a grimy sink which had once been white. Rotting food lay in the bottom of the sink, impossible to identify, and there was a putrid stench which Ian suspected came from a blocked drain. But on the draining board clean plates and cutlery had been neatly stacked, apparently washed in that filthy sink. The oven and hob were encrusted with burned food detritus, and the greasy floor was speckled with crumbs of food. A patch of dried custard or egg yolk made a bright splash of yellow on the one chipped white worktop. Ian hesitated to search the room and went instead into the main bedroom where clothes littered the dirty carpet, soiled underwear and muddy shoes lying together in disarray. He wanted to call the station and ask if Ben's mother had been persuaded to give them any information about when Eddy would come back but he couldn't risk making a sound. Eddy might return at any moment, and he didn't want to alert him to a police presence inside or outside the flat. They couldn't afford to lose a potential suspect.

Ian decided against rummaging through the bedroom looking for tell-tale evidence. The nature of the wound meant the killer would have been heavily sprayed with Martha's blood in the course of the attack. Nevertheless, finding bloodstained clothing in itself would be of no help until the blood had been identified as belonging to the victim.

By himself, Ian could prove nothing, and the flat would be thoroughly searched once they had Eddy securely in custody. In the meantime, he didn't want to do anything to arouse Eddy's suspicion when he entered the flat. He was known to be a violent man. Ian wanted to apprehend him as quickly and simply as possible. He went into the sitting room and perched on the wooden arm of a grubby upholstered armchair to wait, listening for the sound of a key in the lock.

CHAPTER 47

As long as he had kept busy, Ian had been fine. Now he was nervous of moving in case Eddy came in and heard him. If the flat hadn't been on the ground floor he wouldn't have been so bothered. As it was, Eddy could escape through the window in any one of the rooms, if his suspicions were aroused. There was nothing Ian could do but wait in absolute silence and gathering darkness for Eddy to return. He was exhausted. Only the arm of the chair digging into his backside stopped him drifting off. He kept checking his watch, forcing his eyes to stay open. Time crawled by until he must have dozed off. He woke with a start to discover that he needn't have worried about Eddy entering the flat unnoticed. There was an unnecessary racket from a key rattling in the lock. Eddy yelled out his girlfriend's name before slamming the front door so forcefully that the walls trembled. Ian held his breath, waiting to hear what he would do next.

'Natalie!' Eddy shouted once more. 'Where the fuck are you? I'm here.'

He sounded impatient, as though he expected to be greeted as soon as he arrived. Still hollering, he went into the kitchen.

Ian tensed when he heard Eddy open and close a cupboard door. There would be sharp knives in the kitchen, and glassware. Eddy was likely to react aggressively towards an intruder. Ian hardly dared breathe in case he was overheard. Too late he regretted his rash decision to wait alone in the flat instead of outside in a patrol car. Silently he rose to his feet and stole across the room to stand behind the open door. Peering round it, he saw Eddy emerge from the kitchen. Ian pulled back without being seen, just before Eddy entered the room. He was clutching a bottle of beer in one hand. Without making a sound, Ian drew in a deep gulp of air and pounced. Seizing Eddy's arm, he twisted it up behind his back. The bottle fell to the floor as Eddy bellowed in pain and surprise.

'Fuck off. I'll bloody kill you,' he groaned. 'I'll have the law on you.'

'Whose law is that, Eddy?'

'Fuck off. What do you want? I ain't got it, if that's what you're thinking. I know what you're after.'

Ian didn't answer.

'Well, you can piss off because I ain't got it any more. Duffy took it, so you can just get lost. Go ask Duffy.'

★　★　★

Ian didn't know what Eddy was talking about, but was reassured to learn he hadn't been mistaken for a random intruder.

'Duffy hasn't got it,' he replied in an even tone, giving Eddy's arm a vicious jerk as he spoke. 'The police took it.'

'What?'

Eddy stiffened. He stopped wriggling and stood completely still. Stupid with exhaustion, Ian relaxed his hold for an instant. That was all Eddy needed. With a sudden surge of energy he shoved Ian backwards, knocking his head against the edge of the door. Momentarily stunned, Ian let go of his arm. With a sideways lunge at Ian's guts, Eddy spun round and darted out of the room while Ian doubled over, gasping. He staggered after Eddy who raced into the bedroom and flung open a window. Ian threw himself forward too late to stop the other man leaping out. Ian scrambled after him, landing awkwardly in a bank of brambles beneath the window. There was no time to stop and examine his injuries. Although the bushes had scratched his face and hands, they had broken his fall. Apart from jarring his elbow, he didn't think he was hurt.

Frantically he looked around but couldn't see anything in the moonless night. As he fumbled for his torch there was a low rustling in the bushes nearby. Shining his light in the direction of the sound, he caught a glimpse of Eddy's squat frame hurrying away. They were at the back of the property, in a strip of garden bordered on three sides by high fences. Eddy was running towards a path that led round to the front of the building. In pursuit, Ian punched the keys on his phone to alert the officers who were waiting in the street.

'He's on his way,' he panted as he ran.

He was too winded to say more. He could only hope his colleagues would spot Eddy in time. In the beam from his torch, Ian followed a narrow grassy path along the side of the flats to the road, cursing himself for being unable to run any faster. But although Eddy was strong his bulk slowed him down, so that despite being winded Ian almost caught up with his target by the time they reached the pavement.

Ian's guts were aching. Just when he thought he couldn't run any further, a patrol car screeched to a halt and two officers jumped out. Eddy tried to barge past them but he stood no chance. Only when he stopped running did Ian realise that he was in agony where Eddy had punched him in the stomach. He sank to the ground, groaning, overcome with nausea.

'Are you all right, sir?'

'Just cuff him,' Ian gasped, 'before he can do any more damage.'

'Yes, sir.'

Leaning back against the car, Ian heard Eddy shouting abuse at the officer who was restraining him.

'Gotcha,' he muttered as he threw up in the gutter.

★   ★   ★

He looked up and saw Eddy grinning at his discomfort.

'I wouldn't feel too cheerful if I were you,' Ian growled. 'You're in real trouble, Eddy. Assaulting a police officer—'

'It was self-defence,' Eddy protested. 'I thought you were an intruder. No, fuck it, you *were* an intruder. What the fuck were you doing, breaking into my house like that? Fucking pigs.'

'It's a flat,' Ian retorted, 'it's not yours, and I didn't break in. I was invited.'

He nodded to the uniformed officers.

'Take him away.'

Complaining loudly about wrongful arrest and police brutality, Eddy was dragged into the car.

CHAPTER 48

Although he was tired and his elbow ached where he had fallen on it, Ian was keen to question Eddy. Rob was at his desk in the Incident Room in Herne Bay. He took one look at Ian and offered to take over. Ian shook his head, insisting he was absolutely fine. His stomach no longer hurt, which was a relief.

'You don't look fine,' Rob said, staring pointedly at Ian's muddy clothes and the scratches on his face. 'What the hell happened to you?'

'I fell through a hedge backwards,' Ian replied solemnly. 'Let me question him, sir.'

Eddy had given them the run around, but now Ian had regained control of the situation he wasn't going to forego the pleasure of watching him squirm. He had a feeling of excitement that he hadn't experienced on first meeting Henry, even though Martha's husband was the more likely suspect. Other than the knife they knew of no connection between Eddy and the victim who had been stabbed, yet Ian had a feeling Eddy was somehow implicated in her death.

★   ★   ★

Eddy was slumped in a chair. Beads of sweat glistened on his wide forehead. His face looked almost sickly, while his dark eyes shone with furtive desperation. He had spent two years in the nick for aggravated burglary when he was a youngster. Such an experience could scar a man permanently. It would certainly explain why he was looking so stressed at the prospect of being apprehended again. Ian barely managed to hide his satisfaction as he opened the interview.

'We just want to ask you a few questions.'

Eddy glowered at him.

Ian didn't reveal straight away that he had discovered the identity of the man Eddy had mentioned. A few questions around the station had quickly disclosed that Duffy was the name of a local drug dealer.

'He isn't one of your quiet "go away, I'm stoned" dealers,' the drug squad officer had explained. 'Some of them just want to pursue their illegal activities discreetly. Not Duffy. He's as vicious a piece of work as you'll find anywhere, and tricky with it. We've never managed to nail him though God knows we've tried. Don't be shy about muscling in on our patch, mate. If you can get anything on Duffy, you go for it. Do us all a favour. Go for the jugular.'

Ian recalled how Eddy's voice had trembled when he had spoken about Duffy. He clearly wasn't someone Eddy wanted to cross.

★　★　★

Ian stared closely at Eddy as he started questioning him.

'Why did you run?'

'Huh?'

'Why did you run away from me this afternoon? Come on, Eddy, you know perfectly well what I'm talking about.'

Eddy said he had mistaken Ian for an intruder. It wasn't an unreasonable claim, considering he had been attacked in his own home by a stranger. It was hardly an indication of a guilty conscience. Ian listened with growing impatience as Eddy refused to admit he had given Ben a weapon to hide.

'Now why would I do that to the poor kid?' he protested. 'The boy's like a son to me. He's only twelve,' he added, reminding Ian, man to man, that they were discussing a child. 'Kids make stuff up all the time. You don't want to go taking it seriously, for fuck's sake.'

Eddy's implication was clear. Ben's word couldn't be trusted.

'He says you asked him to look after a knife for him,' Ian said quietly. 'Do you deny it?'

'Course I bloody deny it. I never carried a knife in me life. Don't hold with them. I'm a pacifist.'

Ian slapped a photograph of the knife on the table between them.

'You gave it to him because you needed to hide

it. You thought it would be safe with him. You couldn't afford to let the police get hold of this knife.'

Ian's suggestion that he had trusted something important to Ben seemed to surprise Eddy more than the accusation itself.

'You think I'd trust him?' he spluttered indignantly, dropping any pretence of affection for Ben. 'I wouldn't trust that little sod if my life depended on it. The lies he tells his mother about me would make your jaw drop. She never believes a word he says, and you're a fool if you listen to him. What's the big deal anyway? It's not illegal to own a knife.'

'But it *is* illegal to use a knife as an offensive weapon. A woman was killed on Friday, with a knife just like this one—'

'Now you look here,' Eddy interrupted.

All at once he seemed so jumpy, he could hardly sit still. He began to slag Ben off, going all out to discredit the boy who had accused him of owning a murder weapon. It was hard to determine which of the two was the worse liar. Eddy was a fool if he believed Ian hadn't seen his record. Nevertheless, he winced when Ian opened a folder and read out the list of his previous convictions. Three of the charges involved carrying knives, and he had twice been convicted of GBH.

'That last one was never proved,' Eddy exclaimed, with pointless bluster.

Ian had made his point, not only catching Eddy

out in a lie, but establishing a history of threatening behaviour involving knives.

'It was just bluff,' Eddy muttered, still determined to defend himself against the odds.

'Until now.'

'No, I'm telling you, that's a lie. Jesus, just
because I was carrying a blade when I was a kid,
doesn't mean I'm going to be running around with
one now. But I get your game. Someone's been
stabbed here in Herne Bay and I've got form. So
you decide I must be guilty. As if I'm the only
person in Herne Bay to have walked around with
a blade when I was a kid. I'm telling you, I never
knifed no one. And that ain't mine.'

He pointed at the photograph.

Eddy folded his arms and pressed his lips together,
as if to signal he had said everything he was going
to say on the subject.

'Where were you the Friday before last, at about
nine in the evening?'

'Why?'

Ian tapped the picture of the knife.

'A woman was stabbed in Herne Bay on that
Friday evening with this knife. Now answer the
question. Where were you on the Friday before
last between eight and ten in the evening?'

'In the pub,' Eddy replied promptly.

'Which pub?'

'Do you know, I can't remember the name.'

★   ★   ★

All at once Eddy seemed to be enjoying himself. He leaned back in his chair with a nonchalant smile.

'You'll need a witness who can vouch for you for the whole evening, from around eight until midnight.'

Eddy laughed.

'Someone stabbed your woman for four hours? Well, that rules me out. I wouldn't have the stamina.'

'This is a murder enquiry,' Ian snapped, irritated by Eddy's frivolous tone.

'Well why don't you get on with it, then, and stop wasting time.'

'Was anyone with you at the pub?'

'Well, as it happens, I went out for a quiet drink, all by myself.'

Ian had an uneasy feeling Eddy was toying with him.

'I can't remember the exact time I got there, but the landlord will tell you. Ask him. He'll tell you. I was there all evening.'

'And let me guess, you've forgotten his name too,'

'If I ever knew it. But I have just remembered the name of the pub. It's the King's Head.'

'The King's Head,' Ian repeated. 'There are a lot of pubs with that name.'

'I can't help that, can I? I don't name the bleeding pubs.'

'So where is this particular King's Head you're talking about?'

'Newcastle'

'Newcastle?' Ian repeated with sudden misgiving.

'Yes, I was up there visiting my old mother. I'm a good son.' He grinned. 'Now can I go?'

'Wait here.'

It didn't take long to check out Eddy's story. For a start, his car was picked up on CCTV en route to Newcastle. Then the pub was traced. A local constable was despatched to question the landlord. Ian was bitterly disappointed to learn that the publican recalled seeing Eddy the previous weekend. He wasn't sure about the time, but confirmed Eddy had been drinking alone in the bar on both Friday and Saturday evenings. He recalled Eddy trying unsuccessfully to pick up a local tart who had lost interest when she discovered he was broke. The encounter had turned out luckily for Eddy in the end because the landlord remembered his face. Nursing his sore elbow, Ian watched him go.

CHAPTER 49

Rob was as disappointed as Ian. Even when they weren't sure they had the right suspect, the hope that he might be guilty kept them motivated. Now they had to accept that the weapon they had sent off for examination might not have been used to kill Martha after all. The lab had confirmed there were traces of human blood on the blade. The blood group matched Martha's, but that was by no means conclusive. Getting on for half the population shared that blood group. It would take more than that to prove the knife had been used in the fatal stabbing.

'Bugger,' Rob said. 'Now look, why don't you get home to your wife? Nothing's going to change overnight. Go home and start again tomorrow.'

Ian shook his head. The prospect of starting out all over again was depressing, just when they had thought they were getting somewhere. He knew he wouldn't be able to go home and forget about the investigation. Instead, he decided to go back to the club in Margate and see if he could find out more about Henry's connection with the young prostitute.

★   ★   ★

The stocky doorman responded to Ian's greeting with dour monosyllables. 'Have you seen this man?'

The other man barely glanced at the mug shot of Henry before turning away with an incoherent grunt. Ian leaned forward to hear more clearly.

'What did you say?'

The bouncer shrugged. Realising the other man wasn't going to give anything away, Ian dropped his amiable facade.

'If it turns out you've been withholding information, you'll be in serious trouble.'

The bouncer ignored him.

'Is this worth risking a prison sentence over?'

For the first time the bouncer turned to face Ian full on as he responded with a question of his own, while his colour rose until his cheeks were flushed.

'Is that a threat?' he asked softly.

The bouncer was clearly used to fending off awkward customers. Ian abandoned any effort to worm information out of him. Instead he went inside, breathing in the sweet stale smells of perfume, tobacco, alcohol and sweat. He didn't recognise the woman in the entrance hall but she seemed to know exactly who he was.

'You again, Inspector.'

He didn't correct her. The decision could already have been made. He might be an inspector, without yet knowing it.

299

'Don't you people ever give up?' she went on.

'Don't you people ever stop giving up?' he retorted.

The place irritated him, from the defiant bouncer, to the stale odours of the place, and the insolence of the girls who worked there. He was too tired to cope with their contempt.

'You're not the first one who can't keep away,' the woman added with a sly grin. 'Some of our girls don't mind what you do for a living.'

Ian had heard enough.

'I'm not here to see your slappers displaying themselves. I'm a married man.'

He was afraid the young woman would despise his pompous words, but she lowered her eyes and was silent.

'I want to see Jimmy Randall.'

Without meeting his eye again, she led him to the office. Muffled music and cheering were audible as she tapped on the door.

The manager looked up and grimaced.

'What do you want now?' he asked, shifting awkwardly in his chair.

His bloated face grew red. Ian went straight to the point, asking how far back the CCTV film in the entrance hall went.

'What CCTV? What are you talking about?'

'Your security cameras in the entrance hall. I need to see the footage, as far back as it goes.'

'You are joking.'

Jimmy did his best to convince Ian that it simply wasn't possible to view the film but Ian insisted. He had to resort to threats before the manager finally caved in.

'Go on then, take the whole bloody lot. Take the cameras. Take the bloody furniture. Take everything. You want the shirt off my back?'

'I'm afraid it's not my size. I'll just take the film. For now.'

Having sorted out access to the security cameras, Ian set about asking the staff and the performers whether they recognised Henry, and how often they had seen him visit the club. It was quickly apparent he was wasting his time. If anyone had seen Henry at the club they weren't admitting to it.

'We know he was in contact with Della. It's important we discover how they met.'

The manager shrugged.

'That's nothing to do with me. Now if you don't mind, I've got a club to run.'

Ian made arrangements to download the CCTV footage to enable a team back at the station to start checking customers who had entered and left the club over the past week, looking for visits from Henry. If they could establish that he had frequented the club, they might discover a pressing reason for his wanting to kill his wife.

Henry might have been having an affair, perhaps with Della. It was possible he had killed his wife in order to be with his mistress. Then, if Della had rejected him after he killed his wife, he might have had a motive for murdering her too. In order to turn this hazy speculation in to a genuine lead, they had to find evidence that Henry had been seeing Della. The club was as good a place as any to look for indications that they had known one another for a while. But although Ian quizzed all the girls who had known Della, apparently none of them had seen Henry in the club or anywhere else.

He tried asking them about Della herself, hoping to discover she had been seeing a man they didn't know by name.

'Della was OK,' they all said vaguely, one after another. 'She was all right.'

None of them was able or willing to reveal anything specific or personal about their dead co-worker. Even the girl who had lived with Della didn't seem to know much about her.

'I'll have to find another flatmate now,' she grumbled, as though Della was somehow responsible for her own murder.

'Do you have any idea who might have done this?'

'For fuck's sake, how many times are you going to ask me that?'

'I thought you might have remembered something new since we last spoke.'

'Well, you thought wrong.'

'Did she have any enemies? Any disgruntled customers? A boyfriend?'

'No. None that I knew of.'

'Would she have told you?'

'I don't know what was going on with her that she didn't tell me about.'

By the time Ian left the club, he was worn out and thoroughly dejected. He might as well have gone home and spent the evening with his wife instead of driving all the way to Margate to waste his time among strangers. Miserably he drove back to Tunbridge Wells. He wondered if Bev was right after all. Maybe he was crazy not to pack it in and find himself a steady job with regular hours that would pay his mortgage and support his wife and a couple of kids, if that was what she wanted. Murder Investigation was a single man's career. He was in his mid-thirties, married, mature enough to settle down to a regular lifestyle. But he couldn't forget a simply dressed grey-haired woman who had been stabbed to death, or Della with her painted face, breast implants, dyed hair, false nails and fake identity, both relying on him to champion their cause. Bev would have to wait, at least until he had seen this killer behind bars.

'I don't care how long it takes,' he said aloud, 'I will hunt you down.'

CHAPTER 50

It was nearly two by the time he reached home. The house was silent. He made himself toast and peanut butter, and a mug of tea. Creeping upstairs, he undressed in the dark so as not to wake Bev who was lying on her back in bed, snoring softly. When he climbed in beside her, she let out a low moan and turned away from him without waking up. Some homecoming, he thought wretchedly. He might as well have been sleeping alone. He wondered what it would be like to be married to someone who understood his life, someone like Polly. He felt disloyal even thinking about another woman, but his visit to the club had unsettled him. Having started he couldn't stop thinking about Polly, wondering what she was doing. At two in the morning, she must be fast asleep. He realised he didn't even know if she had a boyfriend. Finally he drifted into disturbed dreams. Although he was tired, he was relieved when the alarm went off.

Bev rolled over and sat up.

'What time did you get in last night?'

'I can't remember,' he lied as he pulled her towards him and embraced her. 'Not too late.'

Bev had the day off so Ian offered to bring her breakfast in bed. He grinned as she lay back on her pillow and smiled up at him. He threw on shorts and a T-shirt and pottered about in the kitchen, humming to himself. Carefully he laid out the tray with a pot of coffee, a jug of milk, toast and marmalade, just as Bev liked it. He laid the tray across her legs and climbed carefully back into bed beside her, warm and comfortable.

'Stay here today,' she urged, munching toast. 'We can spend the day together, do something—'

'You know I can't. I have to go to work.'

'Why? One day won't make any difference. I never see you any more.'

He wasn't sure what she meant by that. Nothing had changed. It was always the same when he was involved in an investigation. He resented having to apologise for going to work.

'Phone in and say you don't feel well, just this once. We don't have to go out. No one will be any the wiser.'

'You know I can't. It's not like other jobs—'

It was the wrong thing to say. She jumped on him at once, accusing him of being self-important.

Although she felt nervous about intruders, she didn't support him in his work to make society safer for everyone. All she cared about was her own personal security. It seemed impossible for

305

him to fulfil his duty to his wife and to society. Loving his wife as he did made it hard to bear, because it was impossible to ignore her complaints. Her wretchedness cut right through him. He tried to imagine how he would feel if he had stayed in a desperately unhappy marriage for thirty years to a wife who refused to divorce him. Thirty years was a long time. But having endured the relationship for so long, it made no sense for Henry to have snapped now, when his son was eighteen and old enough to cope with his parents splitting up. It wouldn't have required a divorce for Henry to pack his bags and move out. There had been no need to kill his wife, except for the fact that her death made Henry a wealthy man. If Henry was responsible, Martha wouldn't be the first person to have been murdered for money.

As soon as he arrived at work, he forgot about Bev. She would be there when he got home. Right now he had more pressing matters to deal with. Confirmation had arrived from the lab that traces of Martha's blood had been found on Ben's knife. Yet after their initial excitement at finding the murder weapon, they were no further advanced. Eddy's alibi was unassailable. Ian wondered how Ben was managing, now his mother's boyfriend had been released. There was nothing Ian could do to protect the boy in his own home. Social services had been alerted and Ian could only hope they would keep a close eye on the family. At the very least, Eddy knew the authorities were aware of him. It was horrible to think that Ben's dealings with the police might provoke Eddy to assault the boy. Ian could imagine the conversation.

'What the fuck were you playing at, telling the police I gave you a knife that was used to stab some old woman?'

It sickened him to think that one repercussion of the investigation might be a severe beating for the boy. The act of murder signified so much more than one terrible death; it triggered worlds of unseen suffering.

There were no developments that morning, so he decided to investigate Henry further. The evidence – inconclusive though it was – all pointed to him. Although Ian wasn't convinced Henry was guilty, they had no other suspects. It was clear the two deaths were linked. It would be too much of a coincidence for two women connected to Henry to have both been murdered by chance within the space of a week. Since they were dealing with a stabbing and a strangling, Rob was convinced they were looking for two culprits, the second possibly covering up for the first. Ian was inclined to think one killer was making use of whatever came to hand in attacks that were either poorly planned or else completely unpremeditated. There was nothing to indicate the two victims' paths had ever crossed: Martha, a picture of bourgeois respectability, and Della, a sex worker with a history of drug abuse. There was nothing to link the two women, or their deaths, other than their connection to one man. Suspecting Henry made sense. All they needed now was proof.

Ian knew how dangerous it was to be seduced by a theory rather than focusing on gathering evidence. But it was impossible not to speculate. If Henry was the kind of man to lose his temper easily, he might have killed his wife in a fit of rage. Having persuaded Della to provide him with an alibi, possibly by means of a generous bribe, he might have strangled her if she had threatened to go back on her word. She had possibly attempted to black-mail him. Ian wanted to build a picture of the suspect. The more he thought about it, the more certain he was they must have known their killer all along. But they had to prove his guilt.

Henry installed washing machines for a local branch of a nationwide chain that supplied and fitted kitchens and bathrooms. The receptionist in the showroom didn't realise Ian was a police officer. When he enquired about washing machines, she began reeling off a list of pros and cons of various appliances, with a clear bias towards the more expensive models.

'We can get a fitter out to you within a week,' she assured him earnestly. 'We've got a bit of a backlog right now. One of our fitters is off sick.'

She didn't seem surprised when Ian introduced

himself, but she couldn't tell him anything about Henry.

'I don't know the fitters. You need to ask the other men. I just work in the office.'

Henry didn't have a partner who regularly accompanied him on jobs. The fitters generally worked by themselves. Those of them who knew him considered him a 'decent bloke'. If Henry's bonhomie concealed a dark secret, Ian would have to discover it for himself.

CHAPTER 51

Now she had Della's money safely stashed, Candy was keen to screw as much out of Henry as she could, and get the hell out of Margate before her rent was due. Lots of girls went to London, but when they arrived they were all desperate enough to take any work they could find. Most of them ended up on the streets. With thousands of pounds in her pocket, she could afford to rent a place and take her time finding employment. There must be plenty of well-paid jobs in London for girls like her. She would be able to look around and suit herself, while Joey settled in to a new school. Della had been given the money in an envelope addressed to Henry Martin. Candy had memorised the address before burying it. It wasn't exactly blackmail, because he deserved whatever was coming to him. And as soon as Henry had paid up, Candy planned to go to the police and drop him right in it before she and Joey disappeared to London. That way he would never be able to come after her.

Although it was February, and cold, she put on dark glasses and tucked her hair underneath a blonde wig so Henry wouldn't be able to recognise her again. It would be to her advantage to catch him off guard. Besides, she knew better than to give the police a record of her movements on the CCTV cameras they had everywhere, spying on innocent and guilty alike. Joey was fast asleep on the settee. His duvet had slipped down, exposing a small arm in a yellow T-shirt as he lay on his side, snoring softly. She tapped him lightly on the shoulder before covering him up.

'I'm going out,' she said softly. 'I won't be long.'

He opened one eye and grunted, half awake. He was used to her irregular hours.

'Things are going to be very different soon,' she whispered. 'You won't be left on your own at nights once we get away from here, I promise.'

Joey didn't stir again. This time when she left the flat there was no car parked outside in the street. She wondered if she ought to have told someone where she was going, but it would have been tricky without explaining what was happening, and she had made up her mind she was going to keep all the money for herself. She wasn't soft in the head like Della.

It was exciting setting off. She felt like a spy, skulking in the shadows on the platform dodging cameras. She kept her head down on the train to Herne Bay, and scuttled out of the station as quickly as she could. She might miss the last train back, but with what she had coming to her she could afford a taxi home. It took her almost half an hour to walk to Beltinge Road. As she drew near to Henry's house her legs began to shake until she could barely walk. One of the street lights was flickering. Mesmerised by the trembling shadows on the pavement in front of her, she forced her feet to keep going. The scheme had been for her and Della to call on Henry together. Without her friend, Candy either had to abandon the idea, and give up the chance of a lifetime, or go and see him by herself. Driven by the prospect of getting her hands on thousands of pounds all at once, she hadn't paused to consider the potential danger. Henry had murdered his wife, and then Della. Candy could be his next victim. Now she had arrived, she was terrified.

She almost turned back, but the opportunity was irresistible. She would be able to go to London and start all over again with a proper life, where she wouldn't be forced to go out leaving Joey alone at night. Trembling, she rang the bell. Her legs almost gave way when the door swung open. It wasn't him. The man sitting next to the detective on the television had been middle-aged, with grey hair and a long, sad face. The man in the doorway was in his twenties, with black hair and piercing dark eyes. Her relief turned to disappointment.

'I think I've got the wrong house,' she stammered.

She felt foolish in her blonde wig, chattering to

a stranger. As she spluttered her apology, another figure appeared in the hallway behind the young man. She recognised the long, gloomy face at once.

Her fear must have shown in her face.

'Are you all right?' the older man asked.

The younger man stepped back and slipped away along the hallway, leaving Candy face to face with the man who had killed two women, maybe more for all she knew. Ignoring the temptation to turn and run, she stood her ground, reminding herself this was what she had come for. This was her ticket to a better life, not only for herself but for Joey too.

'I want to speak to you, Henry.'

'How do you know my name?'

He stepped forward as he spoke, curious rather than suspicious. She stared at him, unable to drag her eyes from his face, while he frowned, puzzled.

'Do I know you?'

Candy drew in a deep shuddering breath.

'You knew my flatmate.'

'Your flatmate? Who are you?'

He made a move to close the door.

'Wait! I need to speak to you. It's really important. Please. Don't shut the door until you've heard what I have to say. You'll be sorry if you do.'

'Are you threatening me?'

'Della was my friend.'

'Della? I don't know anyone called Della. You're

making a mistake – you've got me mixed up with someone else.'

'No, I'm not,' she interrupted him urgently. 'You're the one who's making a mistake, if you think you can get away with lt.'

Henry scowled.

'I've no idea what you're talking about. What is it I'm supposed to be getting away with?'

Taking heart from the fact that he hadn't shut the door in her face, Candy ploughed on.

'With killing your wife, and then killing my friend Della.'

Henry didn't look worried. If anything, he looked faintly amused. Candy was puzzled. This wasn't the reaction she had been expecting. He shook his head.

'Look, I've no idea what you're talking about. I didn't kill my wife, and I don't know anyone called Della.'

Candy took a step towards him.

'Della was my flatmate. She's the girl who gave you your alibi after you killed your wife. She was your second victim. But don't think you can do the same to me, because—'

Without warning Henry lunged forward, seized her roughly by the throat and dragged her into the hall. He was unbelievably strong. Slamming her up against the wall, he kicked the front door closed behind them.

'Shut up,' he hissed. 'You can't go around

throwing accusations at respectable people like that. Don't be a fool. As if anyone would take a whore's lies seriously.'

She felt his hot breath on her skin and felt sick with fear.

There was a faint noise from upstairs. She remembered the young man who was in the house with them. At the same time, she thought of Joey, at home by himself. Whatever happened, she had to get back to him.

'If you don't let me go, I'll scream.'

Henry loosened his grip on her throat. As soon as she recovered her wind she took a deep breath and kneed him in the balls, hard. He cried out and doubled over. Resisting the temptation to make a run for it, she stood her ground. She hadn't come all this way to leave with nothing.

'Now you listen to me,' she shrieked, buoyed up by terror. 'I know what you did. I know you killed your wife and paid Della to give you an alibi. If you do what I want, I won't go to the police. But you have to give me what I want.'

She named her price. Straightening up with a groan, he swore at her.

'Twenty thousand pounds? You're insane.'

'It's that or I go to the police.'

'Oh, fuck off.'

Reckless with greed and dread, she knew she couldn't keep this up for much longer. Already her legs were shaking so hard she was afraid she would collapse.

'Don't think I won't do it.'

'And where do you suppose I'm going to get hold of that kind of money?'

He hadn't refused. He was willing to pay her all that money to buy her silence, and she would still go to the police. The man was an idiot.

'That's your problem. Sell your car. Sell your house if you have to. But if you don't find me my money, you'll be sorry. And don't try to stop me, because I'm not dumb like Della. If anything happens to me, I've left a letter for the police with a friend, and it'll drop you right in it,' she lied. 'Three murders. You'll go down for a long time. I'll be back here at the same time tomorrow and you'd better have my money, twenty thousand pounds in twenties, or you'll be sorry.'

Without waiting for a reply, she turned and fled, slamming the front door behind her. She ran along the street not daring to look back.

CHAPTER 52

There was no longer any doubt that the knife found on the young boy was the murder weapon they had been looking for. Rob was convinced they knew the identity of the killer as well.

'It must have been Henry who killed her,' he insisted. 'Look what he stood to gain. His freedom from an unhappy marriage, and a fortune into the bargain. It must have been him. Now all we have to do is prove it.'

He gazed morosely at a photograph of the knife that was contaminated with Martha's blood.

'We know it can't have been Eddy Baldock who killed her, more's the pity. He's a nasty little swine, and vicious with it. This is just his kind of job, but the bastard's gone and got an alibi.'

He thumped his left palm with his right fist in annoyance. It was certainly infuriating. When they had discovered the murder weapon belonged to a violent man with form for GBH, they had all allowed themselves to hope the case was as good as wrapped up.

★　　★　　★

Ian shared Rob's disappointment, but there was no point wasting energy on regrets. Eddy might be a vicious thug, but he had a cast-iron alibi for that Friday evening. He had been sitting in a pub over three hundred miles away, attempting to chat up another woman. It was impossible for him to have been in Kent when Martha was killed.

'So,' Rob said firmly. 'We're back to our original suspect, only now we have a murder weapon. What we have to do next is to find something that links the two.'

He looked at Ian who responded with a helpless shrug. If only life was that simple. It was all well and good for the detective inspector to demand evidence. Finding it was another matter.

'Let's get him in again and see what we can find out,' Rob suggested.

They had already questioned Henry twice. In a way it seemed pointless to bring him back to the station for yet more questioning. But the suspect might crack if they could keep up the pressure on him – assuming he was actually guilty of stabbing his wife to death. Ian took Polly with him. She chattered as they drove along, going over and over what they knew about Henry until they drew up outside his large house.

'Here we are again,' she said, 'I'm beginning to feel like I live here.' She looked along the street appreciatively. 'Chance would be a fine thing. These houses are massive.'

Ian thought about his own semi-detached house, located in an affluent area of Tunbridge Wells. He wondered where Polly lived, and nodded.

As they were walking up the path to the front door, Polly nudged Ian's arm and pointed to a Mercedes parked on the drive. They stopped to take a closer look.

'That's a brand new S-Class Saloon Mercedes,' he murmured. 'What a beauty. That set someone back a few bob.'

'It's a nice set of wheels all right,' Polly agreed. 'Very nice.'

They exchanged a quick glance of understanding. Someone had been on a spending spree since their last visit, an impression that was confirmed when the front door opened. Henry looked different from when they had seen him three days earlier, younger and better turned out, in a new shirt and smart jacket, with expensive leather shoes gleaming on his feet.

He didn't seem surprised to see them.

'You again. What is it this time?'

He sounded resigned rather than angry. He must have thought he was off the hook as they had already questioned him and let him go. 'We found the murder weapon,' Ian said simply.

'That's good, isn't it?'

'We found the knife that was used to stab your wife.'

319

Henry's eyes almost disappeared between narrowed lids, but the pupils remained fixed on Ian's face.

'So I take it you've found whoever did it then?'

'Did it?'

'You've found whoever killed my wife.'

'We're hoping you can help us with that.'

'You are kidding, aren't you? We've been through this. I've got nothing more to say to you. Believe me, I'd help you if I could.'

'Good, because we just want to ask you a few more questions.'

'I've got nothing more to say to you. I already told you everything I know about that night.'

'Don't you want to help us try to discover who did this?'

Once they had driven Henry to the police station in Herne Bay, he insisted on having a lawyer present before he would agree to answer any further questions. While they were waiting for the solicitor to arrive, Ian sent Polly to investigate Henry's financial affairs. She came up with some interesting information. Henry had started behaving like a man who had just won the lottery. As well as the brand new Mercedes, he had run up a substantial debt on his credit card, buying expensive clothes and shoes, a large television, and new bedroom furniture. The death of his wife had made him a seriously wealthy man and he was clearly enjoying making inroads into his inheritance.

* * *

Once they were settled in an interview room, Ian went over Henry's movements on the night his wife died.

'I've already answered that question,' was all he said, whatever Ian asked.

After a while, Ian changed his approach. He leaned back in his chair, gathered his papers together in a pile and adopted a conversational tone, as though the interview was over. Henry seemed to relax. The lawyer sat rigid, his expression impassive.

'That's a nice car you just bought,' Ian remarked.

'The Mercedes?' Henry nodded complacently. 'Do you like it?'

'Who wouldn't? To be fair,' he added, 'it *should* be a nice car, after what you spent on it.'

Henry shrugged, wary again.

'I could hardly keep the Honda after what happened. And you don't know the Mercedes is brand new—'

'We know. Sixty thousand quid, wasn't it?'

'So what if it was? It's my money, isn't it?'

Ian smiled. 'So it would appear, Mr Martin. It's all yours now you're wife's dead, isn't it? The house, the money, everything.'

Henry glanced at his solicitor.

'It's not illegal to buy a car, is it?' he muttered. 'Now I'd like to go home, if it's all the same to you, sergeant. I've already told you, I've got nothing more to say to you.'

The lawyer gave a brisk nod.

'Charge my client or let him go.'

CHAPTER 53

Joey was often up before his mother. Whenever she had been working late the previous night, Candy struggled to wake up in the morning. In the days before Joey started school, she never used to get up before midday. Even now she sometimes overslept, and he would be late for his first lesson. She hated herself when that happened. Getting a proper education was important for his future. She couldn't bear the thought of him ending up like her, struggling to survive from one day to the next. Her son was going to have a decent job when he grew up, and have his own house. She was dimly aware of him clattering around in the kitchen. By the time she dragged herself out of bed, he was tucking into a bowl of cornflakes, and wisps of smoke were rising from the toaster. Candy bent down and kissed the top of his tousled curly head.

'I'm gonna be late for school if you don't get a move on,' he lisped.

'Don't worry. I'll be ready.'

They raced out of the house hand in hand, heads down against the wind. Joey trotted cheerfully at her side. If she had been up any later, she would have sent him off by himself. Joey was a good kid. He didn't mind the half-mile walk to school on his own, but she liked to see him safely into school and watch him run into the midst of a group of boys who milled around the playground shouting and cuffing one another. It cheered her up to see how they welcomed Joey into the group. As she turned away, she noticed a tall man in a hooded jacket standing on the opposite side of the road, watching the children. She might not have noticed him at all if he hadn't caught her attention by turning his head away abruptly when she looked across the road in his direction. He didn't move off, but stood perfectly still, waiting. There was something creepy about him. She hoped he wasn't a pervy paedophile. But Joey was safely at school and that afternoon he was going home with his best friend, Tom. Although Joey had caused her nothing but trouble ever since he was born, she couldn't imagine her life without him. She worried about him constantly.

As she hurried along the street it began to rain, a thin driving rain that seemed to have set in for a while. She cursed, because she had left her umbrella at home. It wasn't long before the bottoms of her jeans were wet. She stepped in a puddle and water soaked through her trainer. Zipping her flimsy jacket right up to her chin she thrust her hands deep into the pockets of her jeans, feeling the warm solidity of her hips through the fabric. She didn't think anything more about the tall man she had seen outside the school until she went into her local newsagents on her way home to buy a bag of mini chocolates for Joey and a packet of cigarettes for herself. She almost bought a packet for Della, out of habit, but stopped herself just in time. It was weird to think that Della wouldn't be there when she got back. They had only been living together for a few months but they had grown used to one another. Della used to play with Joey and he was going to miss her.

After paying, she turned to leave the shop. Behind a couple of women standing in the queue she saw a tall hooded figure. He was looking down so she couldn't see his face. She had a feeling he was the same man who had been hanging around outside the school. Dismissing her disquiet, she marched out of the shop. Only after she was back on the chilly street did it strike her like a slap in the face that Henry might be following her. She walked faster, reminding herself that she had warned him about the trouble he would be in if anything happened to her. There was no way he would be careless enough of his own safety to risk harming her, unless he realised she had been lying about the letter she had written for the police. Glancing round fearfully, she caught sight of the man, his face hidden in shadows beneath his hood.

★   ★   ★

Losing all self-control, she dashed round the corner and through the entrance to her block. Not waiting for the lift, which was often out of order, she raced up the stairs to the first floor, slammed the door to her flat, dropped her shopping bags and pulled out her mobile, ready to phone the police. She was shaking, expecting to hear someone banging at the door at any moment, but all she could hear was the faint buzz of voices raised in an argument somewhere overhead. Going over to the window, she peered out. The street below was deserted. With a sigh of relief she kicked off her shoes. Della's death had unnerved her, making her imagine dangers wherever she went. Emotionally drained, she lay down on her bed. She had only intended to rest for a few minutes but she must have fallen asleep because she was dimly aware of a dream about breaking glass. A faint noise disturbed her. She opened her eyes. A hooded face was leaning over her. The light was behind him so she couldn't see his face, but she knew who it was. This wasn't a nightmare. She was wide awake.

'What are you doing here?' she gasped, pulling herself back on her elbows, away from him. 'How did you get in? What do you want?'

'What did she say?'

'What? Who? What are you talking about?'

She stared wildly round the room. There was nothing within reach that could help her. If her phone had been on the bed she could have slipped it under the covers to make an emergency call, but it was on the kitchen table. Her voice trembled uncontrollably as she asked what he wanted. But she already knew the answer. Knew what was going to happen. His black leather gloves curled around the edges of a pillow like gigantic spider legs.

CHAPTER 54

The two boys were mesmerised by the flickering screen. Shelley smiled as she watched them, tucked up together under a blanket, giggling at the antics of cartoon characters. She shivered and pulled her jumper over her knees as she sat hunched in an arm chair. Throwing her big old bed cover over the two kids when they complained of the cold was the best she could do. They seemed happy enough with the arrangement. Their two heads stuck up, side by side, motionless, Tom's curly brown hair light compared to Joey's darker crop. Shelley's smile faded as her gaze lingered on Joey.

Shelley didn't mind collecting Candy's kid from school. It made no difference to her as she was there in any case, picking up her own son, and they lived in the same block of flats. If anything it helped her, because it entertained her Tommy when one of his classmates came home with them. In principle, the favour worked both ways. There had been a time when Shelley was regularly asked to stay late at the cafe, especially after two of the

327

other waitresses were laid off. She had been only too pleased to do the additional hours whenever the boss asked her. But as the High Street grew quieter her overtime disappeared. Eventually even her basic hours were reduced. These days the place was barely busy enough to pay wages for two of them, let alone any extras. There was nothing Shelley could do about the loss of the additional income. She was lucky to have a job at all, so she was as pleasant as could be when the boss was around. She and the other remaining waitress grumbled incessantly whenever the boss went out, but they knew better than to rock the boat.

Shelley and Candy were both single mothers, both working. It made sense to help one another out. Only recently Shelley had been the only one collecting the two boys from school. It wasn't Candy's problem that Shelley didn't need her help any longer, but nor was it Shelley's fault her circumstances had changed. She had tried mentioning it to Candy.

'So if you want to find someone else to pick Joey up, that's fine with me,' she had finished lamely.

Predictably, Candy had preferred to continue with their current arrangement. There was no reason for her to be dissatisfied.

'Joey really likes Tom,' she added, 'and I know I can trust you. I can't see any point in changing anything.'

★   ★   ★

It was bad enough being used as an unpaid child minder, only now Candy was late picking her son up. She was supposed to collect him before six, in time to take him down to her own flat on the first floor and give him supper before she went out. Shelley didn't know who kept an eye on Joey while his mother was at work, but that wasn't her business. Right now it was nearly seven and there was no sign of Candy. Shelley tried calling her mobile, but there was no answer. She would have to give the boys supper – she could hardly feed her own son and not Joey. Fuming, she decided to demand Candy paid for his food, at least. It was unreasonable to expect her to shell out for him, and as long as she put up with it, Candy would continue to impose on her.

'Did your mum say anything about what time she was going to pick you up, Joey?'

He just squealed with laughter at the cartoon on the telly. He didn't seem bothered that his mother was late.

The cartoon finished and the two boys began to fidget. Shelley glanced at her watch again. It was gone seven o'clock.

'I'm hungry,' Tom announced, sitting up.

'Where's my mummy?'

Tom flung himself on top of the other boy.

'Joey can stay here. He can stay here with me. He can stay, can't he, mum?'

Shelley tried Candy's phone one last time,

although she had given up any hope of her answering. It was nearly half past seven. Candy would be on her way to work by now. It was infuriating, the way she assumed Shelley would take care of Joey. This was the last time she was going to allow Candy to take advantage of her like this.

'Come on, boys, it's time for supper,' she said in a falsely cheerful voice, 'and then you're both off to bed.'

'Where's mummy? I want to go home,' Joey wailed.

Joey cheered up once he was tucking into beans on toast. He seemed perfectly content to spend the night at his friend's flat. Shelley had the impression he was used to being moved around. The two children lay in Tom's bed together, wriggling and squeaking. Shelley considered taking Tom into her own room with her. It seemed the two children would never get to sleep if they stayed in the same bed, but at last they settled down. Tom lay flat on his back, snoring softly, while Joey curled up beside him. Shelley couldn't imagine abandoning her own son as Candy had done. Still, at least she knew Joey was safe and well cared for. It didn't really matter that he would have to wear the same clothes two days in a row. Worse things could happen to an eight-year-old boy.

CHAPTER 55

They had kept Henry in overnight but would have to let him go again at the end of the day. Rob had managed to retain him in custody for a second time on the grounds that new evidence had turned up. The trouble was, they couldn't prove the murder weapon had ever been in his possession. In the meantime, Henry had shown no signs of weakening. In a deadpan tone of voice he had acknowledged that although deeply shocked at the manner of his wife's death, he wasn't distraught at losing her.

'We'd been together a long time,' he had said, as though that explained his lack of passion.

Ian wondered whether it was inevitable a husband and wife would take each other for granted after a while.

Whatever questions were thrown at him, Henry had persisted in denying that he had anything to do with his wife's death. If Henry remained firm, Rob was equally obdurate.

'There must be something we can do to make him confess,' he insisted. 'Keep on it, Ian, break him, break him down. Find a way to crank up the pressure. You know we can't hold him much longer. Just get him to confess, one way or another. Whatever it takes, just do it.'

They both knew perfectly well there was nothing either of them could say or do to try and force an admission of guilt out of Henry. Any evidence they put forward would be immediately thrown out if there was any suggestion of coercion by the police. Despite the constraints of constantly having to watch what he said, Ian supported the Police and Criminal Evidence Act. Prior to that, there had been no rules and regulations governing the treatment of suspects. But there was no question the restraints on police powers could be frustrating.

After a few hours in a cell and more hours of questioning, Henry was no longer composed. His hair was a mess, his shirt was creased, there were sweat stains under his arms, and he looked thoroughly disgruntled.

'How am I supposed to get home? It's chucking it down out there. And just look at my shoes,' he added, raising one foot in the air.

'Very nice,' Ian remarked airily.

'You're not looking properly or you'd see how scuffed they are. It's a bloody disgrace the way you treat innocent people in here. Who is it pays *your* wages, I'd like to know. Poor bloody mugs like me. And then some careless bugger goes and throws my shoes in a cupboard and scrapes the leather. Look! These are brand new shoes. What am I supposed to do now?'

He ran a hand through his thinning hair, his face contorted with exasperation.

Ian shrugged. 'It's a pair of shoes, not the crown jewels. They weren't going to look new forever. Come on, I'll drop you home. I'm going that way anyway,' he lied.

It was possible Henry might let something slip if he thought he was speaking off the record; in reality nothing was off the record in a murder investigation.

The ploy failed. Henry was taciturn on the way back to Beltinge Road, answering only 'Yes,' or 'No,' or merely grunting in response to every question. Ian persevered, but learned nothing new on the short journey. Although he was reluctant to admit defeat, he was actually quite relieved when Henry got out of the car and he could finally stop trying to worm information out of him. He felt as though he had been questioning the man for days. Images of the hookers at the club slipped into his mind, not that he felt any real interest in them. Apart from the fact that he was a married man, he was too knackered. If he was honest, his decision to drive to Margate was partly influenced by his reluctance to go home. It was gone seven and Bev would be annoyed with him for being late again. He hated upsetting her, but lately he didn't seem able to avoid it. He guessed she must have been expecting his work pattern to change once they were married. He was too tired to deal with another row and, besides, he was already in Herne Bay, halfway to Margate. It would be an inefficient use of his time not to go and call on Candy, in the hope that she might have something new to tell him.

The bruiser on the door dipped his head between his huge shoulders and stepped aside without comment. Ian didn't recognise the girl on duty but she knew who he was and asked straight away if he wanted to see the manager.

'I'm here to speak to Candy,' he said, when he had been ushered into the small office where the manager was sitting behind his wooden desk, puffing on a cigar.

'You just can't keep away, can you?' the fat man drawled.

He leaned back in his chair, blowing smoke rings at the ceiling. Ian felt as though he was trapped in a treadmill, going round and round visiting the same places without making any progress.

'Tell Candy I want to see her. Now. I'll wait here.'

'You could be waiting all night then, mate. She's not here. Didn't show up this evening.'

Ian had a sinking feeling. If Henry *had* paid Della to give him an alibi, Candy might have scarpered with the money. It was equally possible she had done a runner because she was heavily in debt.

Or she might have done a bunk because she knew what had happened to her flatmate and the killer was putting the frighteners on her. Whatever the reason for her disappearance, there was no way of getting at the truth unless they found her.

'I can offer you another girl. Your choice.' Jimmy winked at him. 'First one's on the house. I can't say fairer than that.'

Ian turned on his heel and strode to the door.

'Come back any time you need some relaxation,' the manager called after him. 'You look like you could do with loosening up.'

With the manager's mocking words echoing in his ears, Ian hurried away.

There was no answer when he rang Candy's bell. He knocked, tried her phone, rang and knocked again. Still no response. Glancing round, he pushed the door. Pissed or high, she had forgotten to lock it again. It was an invitation to enter. Without hesitation, he slipped inside and pulled the door shut behind him.

'Candy?' he called out softly into the darkness. 'Hello? Is anyone home?'

No one answered. Shadows in the hallway quivered in the light from his torch. With an effort, he tensed his arm so the beam shone steadily as he moved it around.

The hall was empty. It was silent in the flat. His senses strained for any sound as he gazed around at the walls, grey in the half-light. A soft scuffling startled him as his foot kicked against a shoe, shifting it across the threadbare carpet. Glancing down, he nudged it away to the side of the passageway before making his way forwards. He was careful not to make a sound as he stole towards the nearest door. A distant cacophony of noise started up in one of the flats upstairs. Someone was playing music that beat out a muffled rhythm through the ceiling. It was reassuring to hear sounds of life carrying on as normal, somewhere in the building. He had been irrationally spooked by the darkness and the unnatural silence. Realising that he was crouching, his shoulders hunched, he straightened up and relaxed his grip on the torch.

Taking a deep breath, he decided against turning on the hall light. He wasn't supposed to be there. The sensible thing would be to turn round and leave. There was nothing to see in the flat. Girls like Candy and Della were paid in cash for their services all the time. No amount of money hidden in the flat could link them with Henry. It would mean nothing, even if the suspect's prints were all over it. But there was a chance Candy might give him vital information, if he could persuade her to talk.

He paused for a second, aware that he was lurking in a prostitute's flat while his wife waited for him at home. Then he continued to make his way furtively along the corridor. Mentally and physically alert to the thrill of danger, he couldn't resist the rush of adrenaline flooding through him. Even in the darkness objects looked sharper than usual. Sounds reached him with astonishing clarity as the allure of a possible lead drew him into the flat, heedless of protocol. Without any clear plan he went into the kitchen and paused. Glistening in the beam of light from his torch, shards of glass shimmered at his feet. He raised the torch and saw that a window above the sink had been smashed, and hung open. Someone had broken the glass so they could reach in to undo the catch and climb through. A forced entry on the first floor. The front door unlocked for an easy exit. The intruder might still be in the flat. Ian held his breath as he silenced his phone. He hoped he hadn't already put himself in danger by calling out from the hall.

CHAPTER 56

Ian had been home late every night for the past two weeks. He made the excuse that his time wasn't his own when he was on a case, but when he was going to be late he used to make a point of phoning to let her know. Now she was his wife his attitude had changed. It was barely two months since they had promised to love one another 'for better or worse', since when he had been leaving her on her own almost every evening. He claimed that promotion was in the offing, and he didn't want to blot his record. She had no way of knowing whether that was true. He never discussed his work with her, brushing off her questions by telling her she wouldn't want to know.

'Of course I want to know,' she had protested, more than once. 'Why else would I ask you about it?'

'We're not allowed to talk about the case until the details have been made public,' he had told her firmly.

It was humiliating. She was his wife, but he made her feel as though he didn't trust her not to blab about his investigations.

'Why did you marry me if you don't trust me?'

'Trust you? What are you talking about? Of course I trust you.'

It was hopeless.

Ian had never spoken much about his work but throughout the early years of their relationship he used to ask about her job at the recruitment agency, making her feel as though she was the centre of his world. Now he never asked to hear the gossip about her colleagues, or what her shameless boss was up to. It seemed that he wasn't interested in her life outside of their marriage after all. When he was home, he claimed he was exhausted. Meanwhile, she was well into her thirties. Another ten years and her looks would start to fade. Already her boss overlooked her in favour of younger women, as though her experience counted for nothing. She was beginning to think she had wasted the best years of her life on a horrible mistake.

They had agreed to spend Saturday evening with friends, meeting at a restaurant at eight. Ian had promised to be home in time. Bev glanced at the kitchen clock. It was nearly eight now, and there was still no sign of him. She tried his phone again and left a message.

'Where the hell are you? You're late.'

She would have been better off single. Her husband constantly made her look like a fool in front of other people; first her family, now her friends. It was almost eight. Thinking about it, she wasn't sure which would be more embarrassing, to cancel at such short notice, or to go alone. She had already cancelled several arrangements with these friends because of Ian's work. If she cancelled again, they might think she was giving them the brush off. After a moment's hesitation, she decided to go by herself. There was no reason why she should sacrifice her social life to Ian's work commitments. It was typical of him to behave with utter disregard for her wishes. All he cared about was his work – if that really *was* what was keeping him busy in the evenings.

Usually Ian drove when they went out. Bev felt a surge of independence as she accelerated along the main road. Ian and she had been together since she was eighteen, on and off. She had never really experienced life as a single woman. They had been through periods of estrangement, but she had always known she could get him back if she wanted. Speeding along the road, she was no longer sure she had been right to pursue him. Increasingly absorbed in his work, he had blatantly lost interest in her. Even their once dynamic sex life had fizzled out. She was often asleep by the time he arrived home. He claimed he didn't want to disturb her, although she had told him she wouldn't mind being woken up. It wasn't the sex she missed – although that was a visceral part of his betrayal – so much as his attention. She had tried to tackle the subject, but Ian always pleaded exhaustion at the end of a day's work. When she had protested they had only been married for two months, he had retorted irritably that they had been together for years. Predictably enough, the conversation had deteriorated into a row. Thinking about her husband as she drove into town, Bev put her foot down. She would show him she was fine by herself.

The verges at the roadside were looking vibrant, the grass speckled with a few tiny dots of white and yellow early flowering weeds. Most of the trees were covered in tight buds, their leaves waiting to uncurl in warmer weather. A few remained bare. An occasional conifer stood out from the other trees, its rich green foliage almost black in her headlights. She hoped Ian wasn't thinking of pulling the same stunt at Easter. They had agreed to go away for the weekend with her parents, but he had as good as admitted to her that he hadn't booked the time off. He maintained he didn't want to do anything that might jeopardise his promotion prospects.

'I want you to be there,' she had told him firmly, but he had merely shrugged.

It was a painful betrayal from a man who had vowed to devote his life to her.

'It's nice to be married to someone who worships you,' her mother had said once, smiling complacently.

341

Bev and her sister had agreed. All three of them shared the same striking features and elegant figures, lean yet voluptuous. Her mother and sister had both used their looks to attract husbands dedicated to pleasing them. Bev had expected the same commitment from Ian, but her marriage wasn't turning out like that.

As soon as she arrived at the restaurant she regretted the decision she had reached in anger. What made it worse was that Ian was probably on his way home. She should have waited for him. All she could do was smile, and pretend to ignore the raised eyebrows.

'Is Ian all right?'

'Yes, he's fine. He had to work late today. They don't give him much notice or I'd have called to let you know.'

'He's working late on a Saturday? You poor thing. Come and sit down and have a glass of wine. Red or white? Or are you driving?'

'Actually,' Bev announced rather too loudly, 'Ian's working on a very important project right now, keeping the streets safe for everyone.'

'Is he a traffic cop?' someone asked.

Bev felt herself blush.

'He works for the Murder Squad.'

No one spoke for a few seconds, and then the conversation moved on.

In the ladies, one of Bev's girlfriends met her eyes in the mirror while she was washing her hands.

'Are you sure you're OK?'

'What do you mean?'

'I mean, are things OK between you and Ian? Only this is the second time he's cancelled, and we were all wondering—'

Bev gave a short laugh to indicate her friends' concern was not only misplaced, but ridiculous.

'Everything's fine. I told you, he's doing a very important job. I'm really proud of him.'

'Yes, I know, but – what I mean is, he's not thinking about you, is he? Going out like this by yourself on a Saturday night. You are married. You deserve better.'

Bev could hear defiance in her voice as she repeated her assurance that everything was fine. But everything was far from fine. Her friends were right to talk about her behind her back. Her marriage was a failure. It was Saturday night, she was out without her husband and, wherever he was, Ian was certainly not thinking about her.

CHAPTER 57

There was no sound in the flat. Ian hoped the tremor in his voice wasn't noticeable as he muttered softly into his phone, summoning back-up. His message delivered, he switched the phone off completely. Even on silent it had buzzed a few times. He couldn't risk discovery. There were several voicemails from Bev, but they would have to wait. For a moment he stood perfectly still, muscles tensed, listening. At any second he might be attacked, his assailant possibly armed. It was slight relief to recognise that the only sounds came from above his head. Meanwhile, with reinforcements on their way, he couldn't justify hanging around in the kitchen any longer. It was possible someone was in need of urgent medical attention. Faced with the likelihood of a violent intruder skulking in the flat he would have waited for back up to arrive before investigating, had Candy lived alone. But she had a young son who might be hiding in the flat, terrified. It shouldn't make any difference whether it was a child or an adult whose life might be threatened. But remembering the small boy, Ian trembled with a primal fear. The child might be in danger, or dying for want of medical attention, while Ian stood in the kitchen, dithering. He couldn't afford to waste any more time before checking the rest of the flat.

Drawing in a deep breath, he muttered a quick prayer to a God he didn't believe in, before creeping out of the kitchen. His back to the wall, he edged sideways along the passageway. Above him, music played for neighbours oblivious to the drama taking place beneath them. Reaching the door to Candy's room, he pushed it open and slipped inside. It was very quiet. Even the rhythm of distant music was muffled. The light from his torch illuminated a woman lying motionless on her back on the bed, her face concealed beneath a pillow.

'Candy, Candy!' he whispered urgently.

Gently, he lifted the pillow off her face. Placing it on the bed beside her, he put down his torch and examined her for any signs of life. She was staring up at the ceiling, her bloodshot eyes further evidence of suffocation if any more was needed.

Sure she was dead, he turned and looked around the room. There was a kind of temporary nest in one corner: a tattered sleeping bag spread on top of a long cushion that must have belonged to an old piece of furniture that had seen better days. The little boy must have slept there. The sleeping arrangement hadn't been in place on Ian's previous visit. On that occasion the sleeping bag and cushion had been rolled up and stowed on top of the wardrobe. He wondered where Candy's son was now, and if he had been in the flat when his mother had died. Her death could have been the result of an accidental overdose, but the likelihood was that she had been murdered. Whatever the truth, the homicide team had to be summoned straight away. As he took out his phone, he heard voices in the hall. Back-up had arrived.

'Stay right where you are!' he shouted, 'this is a crime scene!'

He hurried out of the room to intercept them.

The sight of two sturdy officers in uniform was reassuring, but they had arrived too late to save Candy. Flicking on the light in the hall, Ian sent the pair of them straight out again to make sure no one else entered the flat, while he summoned the Homicide Assessment Team. The last thing forensics would want was multiple sets of foot-prints traipsing through the flat, contaminating any evidence the killer might have left behind. It was damaging enough that Ian had shuffled along the hall to the kitchen, and then into Candy's room. He had been wearing gloves when he entered the flat. No doubt the killer had done the same. Apart from DNA, possible footprints in the kitchen could provide crucial evidence.

'You might as well bring a forensic team with

you,' he told the Homicide Assessment Team. 'A woman's been murdered. Don't worry, you won't have to take on the case, she was a witness in an existing murder investigation. That is, she would have been if someone hadn't got to her first,' he added bitterly.

While he waited for the HAT car to arrive, Ian quickly glanced in the other rooms. There was no sign of Candy's little boy anywhere in the flat. Ian was relieved, but apprehensive at the same time. The constables were outside watching the front door, the assessment team were on their way to make an initial report on the scene. There was nothing else that Ian could do now. He would have liked to take another look around for any evidence to link Candy with Henry, but was reluctant to move around the flat any more in case he disturbed anything the killer had left behind.

'One stabbed, one strangled, and now this victim's been suffocated,' he muttered to himself. 'What the hell next?'

The methods of killing had been different and the victims had met their deaths in different locations, yet there was no doubt the three victims were linked. Caught up in a macabre game the killer was playing, Ian had no idea what the rules were.

CHAPTER 58

This time Polly didn't chatter cheerfully as she drove. When he glanced over at her she was staring straight ahead, her face rigid. He knew her well enough to understand she was troubled by their third visit to the morgue in little more than two weeks. It wasn't the post mortem itself that bothered her, but the fact that they were investigating yet another death and were still no closer to making an arrest. At last Polly broke the oppressive silence.

'What if we never stop it?'

'We'll get him,' he assured her.

'How do you know?'

'He's bound to slip up sooner or later.'

'Later?' she burst out. 'How many more women is he going to kill before we finally catch him? It could take years. He's already killed three women in two weeks, that much we know. And that's all we know. Three victims in two weeks is seventy-five victims in a year, if he carries on at this rate.'

'He won't.'

'How can you be so sure?'

'Because we're going to catch him.'

★ ★ ★

In an investigation that was spiralling out of control, Ian struggled to suppress his memories of two women who had been brutally murdered shortly after he had met them. He had established no particular rapport with either Jade or Candy, but he had heard their voices, and gazed into their living eyes. He had witnessed Jade's vulnerability, and Candy's affection for her child. The last thing he wanted right now was to allow Polly's fears to undermine his confidence. They had to find this killer. He told her so, in as forceful a voice as he could muster.

'How can you be sure?' she asked again.

'We have to be sure. We have to proceed on that basis. We can't contemplate it not being the case.'

'OK, I get it. You're scared as well, aren't you? But we have to be brave. Failure is not an option.'

He wondered if she was mocking him.

It was so difficult to understand what women meant. He was failing in so many aspects of his life right now, he couldn't afford to fail in his career as well. As if all that wasn't worrying enough, he had to prepare himself to view Candy's sliced up corpse. As far as he had been able to tell, the murderer had left her physically intact. The pathologist would hack her open and expose her innards to a group of gawping strangers. Ian felt sick and they hadn't even reached the morgue yet. He drew in a deep, shuddering breath and tried to focus on something else.

* * *

'Have you got any plans for the weekend?'

To his relief, Polly didn't appear to find his question incongruous. He wished he could switch off from work as easily as she did; but perhaps she was just making a better job of hiding her feelings than he was. It was hard to believe she was completely unmoved at the prospect of seeing another body.

'A friend of mine's having a hen night,' she announced cheerily, dispelling his doubts about her composure. 'I've booked tomorrow off. We're going to get so wasted tonight, I can't wait.'

She laughed. Glimpsing his expression, she added quickly, 'I would have said I can't go but she's my best mate and there's a group of us who were at school together. The trouble is, we're meeting in Central London and I don't know how I'm going to get home again at that time of night so I'm thinking I'll probably go home with one of the other girls. They all live near each other. It's only me that's moved away, and if I got a cab home by myself it would cost a fortune.'

She prattled on about her friend's hen night until they arrived at their destination.

The post mortem revealed nothing they didn't already know. Candy, born Caroline Clare, was thirty-one when she was killed. Brought up in care, she was on the street at fifteen, working in South London. When her pimp died, she moved to Central London where she found work as a pole dancer. She had three abortions before giving birth to a son when she was in a relationship with a man who subsequently died from an overdose. That much they knew before they heard the medical details confirmed by Dr Millard.

'Perforations here,' he pointed up her nostrils, 'and the nasal septum is about to collapse. Cocaine's probably also the cause of a developing stomach ulcer. Her liver is in a bad state from alcohol, probably binge drinking, and she certainly didn't eat a healthy diet. Far from it. Fatty fast foods and not much else, I'd say.'

He sounded fleetingly outraged, as though the victim's poor diet was the most repulsive finding of his entire examination.

Having described the victim's generally poor state of health while she was alive, he moved on to the cause of her death. It was clear from the outset that she had been suffocated. All he could do was confirm what they already knew.

'The killer must have taken her by surprise,' he concluded. 'There are no defence wounds.'

Ian swore. All they needed was one speck of DNA that would link the victim to Henry, one cell of his skin under her fingernails, or on her face, and they would have him. They didn't stay long at the morgue as Millard was clearly in a hurry to leave. There was nothing more he could tell them until the toxicology results came back.

* * *

Polly dropped Ian back at the police station and went straight off without stopping.

'I would come in, but I've got this hen party,' she explained. 'You ought to go home and get some sleep too. You look terrible.'

Ian nodded. She didn't have to apologise for having a life. He remembered when he had been a constable, keen on his job, enjoying his social life, in love with his girl. Life had been good back then. But he was only in his thirties now, too young to have lost the joy of living. At any time he might end up like Martha, Jade and Candy, denied any further opportunity to enjoy life.

'I'm going to take my wife out this weekend,' he called out after Polly's car, as it disappeared through the gate. She couldn't hear him, but he wasn't saying it for her benefit anyway.

Pushing the thought of Candy's son to the back of his mind, he went to his car without going back to his desk. He was already halfway home when he remembered Bev's arrangement to go out with friends that evening. Cursing, he slowed down, hoping she would go without him. He was too tired to put on a decent pretence of having a good time. If Bev had seen what he had seen that day, she might agree that her social engagements weren't really all that important.

CHAPTER 59

On Sunday evening Ian offered to take Bev out, but in the end they decided to stay in and watch a film instead. Bev had been so bad-tempered lately, he had forgotten how lovely she was. Her smile still took his breath away. Although they weren't going out, she had changed and put on make-up. Wearing skintight jeans and a sparkly jumper, she looked stunning. Pleased that she had gone to so much trouble just for him, he felt a stab of guilt at seeing how happy his appreciation made her. After dinner, they took their wine glasses into the living room and settled down together on the sofa. They had saved an old film on the planner, and sat comfortably watching together. Bev's hand felt warm in his. Ian hadn't felt so relaxed for months. When his work phone rang, he groaned but didn't stir.

'Aren't you going to answer that?' Bev asked.

'Not tonight.'

To demonstrate his point, he pulled the phone out of his pocket and tossed it onto a chair the other side of Bev. Laughing, she leaned forward

353

and picked it up. As she held it on the palm of her hand, it beeped.

'You've got a text,' she said.

Ian reached for the phone.

'Don't look at it,' he said sternly.

She laughed again, with a determined look in her eyes and in the set of her chin.

'I'll look if I want to. Child found.' She looked up. 'What child?'

Ian couldn't control his excitement. 'Did you say the child has turned up? Are you sure? Let me see.' He held out his hand. 'Come on, give me the phone.'

'What child?' she wanted to know.

'It's a little boy who was missing.'

'I thought you were investigating a murder.'

'We are. This is the son of one of the victims. He's been missing since his mother was killed. He's only about seven.'

'Oh my God.'

He was taken aback to see that she was almost crying.

'Seven? And his mother's been murdered? How awful. What about the father?'

'We don't know who the father is. I don't suppose anyone will ever know now. His mother's dead, and she's the only person who could have told us, if she even knew.'

Bev turned to face him, her eyes glistening with unshed tears.

'What's wrong?' he asked.

She shook her head. 'I was just thinking about that poor child. It's terrible, Ian. I had no idea.'

'There's nothing for you to get upset about. We've got it all under control,' he lied.

More than anything, he wanted her to have confidence in him as a detective. If his own wife didn't believe he would sort out this mess, how could he feel positive about himself?

'A little boy of seven, and he's got no father, and his mother's been murdered. That's one of the saddest things I've ever heard.' She reached out and clutched at his arm, staring earnestly at him. 'How do you cope with stuff like that?'

'All in a day's work,' he said quietly and saw her mouth tighten.

It was so hard to share his work with Bev. While he had to remain doggedly detached from the brutality he encountered, she was bound to react differently to it. She probably found him monstrous, shocked that he could be so unfeeling. But he couldn't allow his emotions to muddy his thinking.

'I didn't realise – that is, I had no idea how terrible it was for you. How awful for you.'

Relieved that she wasn't appalled by his objectivity, Ian felt a rush of gratitude for her compassion.

'I'm fine,' he assured her gruffly. 'It's what I'm trained to do.'

He nearly added that he wouldn't manage

without the support of his colleagues. Just in time he thought better of it.

'And I've got you, and that makes it all bearable,' he said instead, and was rewarded with a lingering kiss.

After a minute, Bev pulled away from his embrace.

'Don't you want to go into work?'

'I'm not going in now. It's Sunday evening and I'm spending time with my wife.'

'But—'

'Do you really want me to go into work on a Sunday evening?'

'Ian, there's a child involved.'

'Does that make a difference?'

'Yes, of course it does.'

Bev was right. He remembered huge black eyes peering up at him, Candy's tenderness as she stroked the mop of tight curls, and tiny feet padding across the carpet. Until now, he had tried not to think too much about the front door closing on the small figure, or to worry about where he had gone. Now the memory flooded back.

'I'd better go then,' he muttered, and bent to kiss her again.

As he drove to the police station, he felt elated. He was happy the child was safe, but it was more than that. Bev wanted him to pursue his all-important investigation. For the first time, she seemed to grasp why his work had to take priority over their time together. He was whistling by the time he arrived in Margate. Finding the child was just the start. He had reached a turning point in his life. They would soon find the killer and wrap up the case, and Bev would never resent him working long hours again now she understood. Once his promotion was confirmed, they would relocate, moving away from Bev's parents who had never thought Ian was good enough for her. He had already applied for a vacancy up north, although he hadn't told Bev yet. Together they would make a fresh start. He never should have agreed to go and live in Tunbridge Wells, so close to his in-laws. His imminent promotion offered their marriage a chance to start again somewhere new. Everything was going to be all right. He had always known it would be.

A large woman was sitting in the waiting room accompanied by Joey and another little boy who was grizzling, rubbing his eyes with his fists.

'I want him to stay with us. Why can't he stay with us?' he was nagging the woman.

'Because I said so.'

Leaving the two children with a constable, Ian took the woman into an interview room. She introduced herself as Shelley, and explained she had collected Joey from school on Friday for her neighbour.

'We do that for each other, collect each other's kids from school. They're in the same class, and we're neighbours. Candy's supposed to pick him up from me at six on Friday. Only she never came for him, did she? And she still hasn't turned up. So I've brought him here. I'm not sure what I'm supposed to do with him. When I see her, I'm going to give her a piece of my mind. I'm guessing she had one too many and she's sleeping it off somewhere, or she's off with some geezer. But her kid isn't my responsibility. I've had him since I picked him up after school on Friday. It's time someone else took a turn.'

'I'm sorry to tell you Joey's mother is dead.'

Shelley stared blankly at Ian for a few seconds. Then she dropped her head in her hands. Ian waited. After a moment she raised her head again. She looked pale and was clearly shocked.

'I wondered if there was something up,' she said. 'To be honest with you, I was afraid she'd just buggered off.'

Ian leaned forward. 'You said you thought she'd probably had one too many. What exactly did you mean by that?'

'Just what I said,' she replied cagily. 'I meant just what I said. She used to drink, nothing wrong with that. That's all I meant. It's not a crime to have a drink now and again, is it? Was it the drink that did for her, then?' She shrugged. 'She's better off out of it, if you ask me. Only her boy's not for me to look after. She wasn't family, nothing like that.'

Ian sat back in his chair and said he hoped she might be able to help the police in their investigation into

358

Candy's murder. Shelley looked startled, then frightened.

'Murder?' she repeated. 'Who said anything about murder? You never said she was murdered.'

Ian took advantage of her momentary confusion to prompt her with another question.

'Why did you leave it so long before coming here to report her missing? Didn't you think something was wrong when she didn't collect Joey from you?'

She shook her head.

'She was –' she hesitated, 'she was forgetful.'

'You mean because she took drugs?'

'No. I mean because she forgot things.'

'Had she ever forgotten to collect her son before?'

When he was assured Shelley knew no more than she had already told him, Ian let her go. Given the circumstances, she agreed to take Joey home with her again while social services were contacted.

'I had no idea,' she kept repeating. 'I feel awful now. I was annoyed with her for not picking him up. I had no idea she was dead.'

CHAPTER 60

While they continued casting around for leads, Rob brought in a profiler on Monday morning. Gerard Greer was a short small-boned man with delicate features and a pale clean-shaven face. Apart from his square chin he looked quite effeminate, with dainty hands, and light brown hair that reached down just below his ears. He peered around the team through rimless glasses, blinking nervously, although his voice was calm.

'I wonder,' he said, 'and I'm only raising it as a question, if you haven't been barking up the wrong tree? We don't know it's the same man who killed all three women, do we?'

'It's a bit of a coincidence otherwise,' Rob murmured.

Ian grunted in agreement.

'Jade and Candy, granted,' Gerard went on in his measured tones. 'They were both likely to be victims of violent attacks.'

A muttered protest passed around the assembled officers.

'They're prostitutes, so they're fair game,' a female officer called out angrily. The profiler looked at her, his eyebrows raised.

'You know perfectly well that's not what I meant at all,' he responded evenly, 'but given the line of work they followed, they were putting themselves at risk from violent men acting out fantasies and frustrations, often the worse for drink, things getting out of hand, that sort of scenario. A man looking for someone to punish is likely to seek out sex workers. That's what I meant.' His bland tone had an edge of cold anger as he added, 'only a fool would think otherwise.'

No one answered.

Rob prompted the profiler to share his conclusions.

'No conclusions, only questions. Let's deal with Martha first because that case appears to be straightforward. It seems highly likely the husband killed her. Assuming that to be the case for now, as he had both motive and opportunity, there are two possible hypotheses. One, Henry killed his wife and this released some suppressed lust for killing so he went out looking for other women to kill.'

'One of whom just happened to be his alibi,' Ian pointed out.

The profiler ignored the interruption.

'The second option to consider is whether Henry killed his wife in a one-off fit of rage after thirty years of a marriage in which he felt trapped. Getting rid of Martha was his only escape and he snapped one day. The opportunity offered itself and that was it. He wouldn't be the first to lose it like that. If that's the case, then it looks like the other two women might have been killed in the fall-out from the first murder. Perhaps the woman who gave him his alibi changed her mind and told her friend. As a sad consequence, he killed them both to protect his identity.'

'What can we deduce about the killer, or killers, from the three victims and the way they were killed?' Rob asked.

'If we are looking for one killer, then we're dealing with an interesting character.' Gerard beamed, warming to his analysis. 'Is he sending us a clumsy sort of message with his different methods of despatching his victims?'

He raised an elegant hand and counted off each word on a separate finger as he spoke.

'Stabbing, strangling, suffocating. Is it his intention to avoid following a pattern because he's read somewhere that a pattern can give a serial killer away?'

'Seen it on the telly more like,' someone said.

'Indeed.' Gerard inclined his head.

'The victims were all women,' a female officer pointed out.

The profiler nodded. 'Yes they were, but that's

not much of a pattern. Is he deliberately avoiding a pattern, or is he experimenting with different ways of killing?'

'Or perhaps he's just using whatever comes to hand at the time, a knife, a piece of rope, a pillow?' Rob suggested.

There was a faint murmur of assent.

'That's a strong possibility,' Gerard agreed. 'The pillow would certainly suggest the third assault might not have been planned out in advance, but was rather an opportunistic, spur of the moment action.'

'That's a lot of speculation,' Rob said. 'Have you got anything specific for us?'

'This man is functional in his killing. He doesn't spend any longer than is necessary despatching his victims. He just wants to get rid of them. The experience of killing isn't his end.'

'It's the end for the victims,' someone muttered and a few other officers sniggered.

As the profiler's voice droned on, Ian's attention drifted. He had tried to imagine what it would be like for a man to be married for thirty years to a woman he didn't love. Henry must have loved his wife once, enough to want to spend the rest of his life with her, but it was hardly unusual for relationships to break down. What made the Martins' marriage different was that Martha's faith might have prevented them from divorcing. The statement made by their neighbour appeared to bear that out. If that was true, the marriage had become a life sentence for her husband. Ian focused his attention back on the profiler, who was still talking.

'All of which means a second killer may be responsible for the deaths of Jade and Candy, someone preying on –' he glanced at the female officer who had interrupted him aggressively earlier on, 'preying on vulnerable women.'

'Someone who's killed two women in a week,' Rob added quietly.

For a moment, no one spoke.

'Let's pursue a few more lines of enquiry,' Rob said. 'Ian, get yourself back to the club where the girls worked. Put pressure on the manager there. He must know something.'

This time no one made any light-hearted quips about Ian being given all the interesting tasks.

'You'd think they'd be closed, out of respect,' someone said.

'I don't think the girls there ever had much respect from anyone,' Ian replied.

CHAPTER 61

Ian didn't recognise any of the girls who were hanging around outside the club, leaning against the wall, their skirts halfway up their thighs, gossiping and smoking. He wondered if any of them had left young children at home, perhaps supervised by brothers and sisters not much older than their siblings. As he entered the club premises, he tried not to think about Joey and the bleak future stretching out in front of him. Some people came out of the care system to make a success of their lives. Joey had the same chance as any other disadvantaged child. He might be taken in by a loving and encouraging foster family. It was a horrible irony to speculate that his prospects might actually have improved now that his mother was out of his life. She wasn't likely to have been a positive influence on him.

He knew the way and went in without knocking. The fat manager was slouched behind his desk. He looked up when Ian entered and his pudgy fingers tightened around a tumbler of Scotch.

'What?' he snapped.

Lifting the glass, he downed the whisky in one noisy gulp. While Ian deliberated how to proceed, he realised the other man found his silence more intimidating than any rough words. As he watched, Jimmy's broad forehead began to shine with perspiration. The empty glass trembled in his hand.

'What?' he demanded again.

Ian guessed he didn't trust himself to say more without betraying that he was either drunk or terrified, or both. With a cold smile, Ian stepped forward and closed the door behind him.

'What was your relationship with Della?'

'What?'

'Della, the first of your girls who was killed, what was your relationship with her?'

Jimmy rose clumsily to his feet, swaying slightly. He thought better of it, and sat down again with a jolt. Pressing his lips together, he stared belligerently at Ian who stood silently waiting for an answer.

'What do you mean?'

Ian repeated the question for the third time.

'She was a dancer. She worked here. Blonde girl.'

'I know that. What was your relationship with her?'

Jimmy shrugged.

His small dark eyes lost their cowed expression and he straightened up, glaring across the room at Ian. The Scotch had hit him.

'I didn't have a relationship with her. If you want the truth, I probably couldn't have picked her out in a crowd, before all this happened.' He waved one hand in the air with a surprisingly graceful gesture. 'She was just one of the dancing girls. Same with the other one, Candy. Yvonne deals with the performers. Look at me!' He gesticulated angrily at his desk, cluttered with paperwork. 'I'm sitting here, up to my balls in bills, while they're out there having a good time.'

Ian did his best to push the manager to divulge information but the fat man resisted all attempts to rile him, insisting he had no dealings with Della or Candy, beyond paying them for the time they spent performing at the club.

'It's a bloody nuisance, all this. It's terribly sad,' he concluded, 'but if you want the truth, Inspector, by this time next week no one here's even going to remember their names. They're two a penny these tarts.'

Ian was disgusted at the way he dismissed the two dead girls, referring to them as if they were performing animals in a circus. But Jimmy was adamant he had barely spoken to the victims, and Ian was inclined to believe him. Ian asked to speak to Yvonne and Jimmy picked up the phone and summoned her.

'You can talk to her here,' he told Ian as he hung up.

Yvonne was a scrawny woman in her fifties. Her fine bone structure suggested she had once been good looking. Now wrinkled, with dark grey pouches under her eyes, she whined in protest at Jimmy for calling her away from her duties.

'There's a police officer here wants to talk to you.'

Yvonne turned and stared at Ian, sizing him up. Ian asked to speak to her alone and the manager clambered noisily to his feet.

'This is an outrage, a bloody outrage, asking me to leave my own office. You've got no right to do this, no right at all. Your chief is going to be hearing from me. I'll complain—'

'It won't take long,' Ian assured him. 'I would have thought you'd be only too pleased to help us with our investigation into who murdered two of your dancers. It can't be good for business. And it was your idea for me to speak to Yvonne in here,' he added with a smile.

'Three of the girls didn't show up this evening,' Yvonne chimed in. 'They're all getting the jitters.'

Jimmy spun round, swaying precariously on his legs, and squared up to Ian.

'You need to bloody do something about this. Catch the bugger, Inspector, lock him up. He's already killed two of my girls. Two of them dead.'

Ian let the man rant for a few minutes, listening to him carefully, but Jimmy gave nothing away. He just grew louder and less coherent.

'We'll get him, you can be sure of that, if you will just let us get on with our job,' Ian finally interrupted. 'Now, if you can stop obstructing my enquiries—'

'Don't you start threatening me. I know my rights. I've done nothing wrong. I do a good job here. I give the girls work. I keep them off the streets. You and I both know the type of girls we're dealing with here.'

'Sex workers, you mean?'

'Your words, Inspector, not mine.'

'But it's what you meant.'

'No, I said they're dancers.' He waved one hand up and down as though conducting an orchestra. 'Dancers, not prostitutes. I run a dance show here. People like to come and watch girls dance. There's nothing wrong with that. I run a respectable establishment. I'd bring my own mother here if she was still alive, God rest her soul.'

CHAPTER 62

It should never have happened. A lamp was supposed to stay on all night beside his bed. Not satisfied with that, he kept a light switched on in the corridor outside his room as back-up in case the bulb went in his room. But the bedside light had gone out and his door was closed, so it was pitch black when he opened his eyes. Fighting a growing panic, he pushed back the covers and slid his legs out of bed. Shuffling nervously forward, he felt his way across the carpet with his bare feet, running his hand along the side of the bed. From the end of the bed it wasn't far to the door, but he had to reach it without anything to hold on to. He could feel himself trembling as he edged forward, his hands stretched out in front of him. With an effort of will he reminded himself that he was safe in his own sanctuary in England.

It was years since he had escaped the night terrors of a heretical monastery where the monks had forbidden him to have a light in his cell. Night after night he had lain on his hard bed, unable to sleep. Sometimes he had been disturbed by dreadful screams. Now, in the dark, the memory of those long nights tormented him. At first he had been desperate to find out why the monks were crying out. When he had learned about the unspeakable horrors they practised, he had regretted ever learning the truth. It was more cruel than anything he could have imagined. He had stumbled on the truth when he had chanced on a group of monks burying a recruit. The novice had died very young, barely more than a child.

'What happened to him?'

'He is dead.'

'Yes, I can see that. How did he die?'

'God did not choose him to survive the initiation.'

'Only a few are chosen,' one of them added.

'What initiation? What did you do to him?'

'The chosen must leave behind all earthly desires.'

As he spoke, the monk made a gesture as though chopping off his genitals.

He opened the door of his bedroom. In the dazzling light he made out a blurred figure. He blinked, trying to distinguish her features as she bowed her head to him. A halo of light glowed around her fair hair and he could see she was very thin.

'Is everything all right, leader?'

'My light has gone out.'

She fell back in alarm. Sensing her panic, he was quick to reassure her.

'My bedside light, that is.'

'Oh, I thought you meant—'

'What?'

'Nothing.'

He understood her confusion. She thought he had been referring to his divine status.

'Who is responsible for leaving me in the dark?' he demanded, recovering from his terror.

'It was just the bulb –' she stammered. 'It couldn't be helped—'

'Who shut my door?'

'Your light was on when the door was shut.'

He sensed she was frightened and softened his voice. The gods demanded unquestioning devotion from the disciples. She had proved herself loving and obedient, willing to do and say anything he asked of her.

'Don't be afraid,' he said gently. 'While I am here, you need never be afraid. You are safe now, and the gods will watch over you for all eternity. All you have to do is keep the faith, and love me.'

'Yes, leader.'

'Look at me.'

She raised her head to reveal a very pale face with light blue eyes framed by white eyelashes. One of his favourites among the disciples, he had shared his divine love with her before.

372

'After you have fixed the light, you will stay with me,' he said. 'I don't want to be alone tonight.'

She lowered her head submissively.

He woke in the night to find her lying beside him.

'You have served me well. Now leave me.'

Her face lit up at his praise. Smiling, he watched her slip into her robe and scurry away. As the door closed behind her, he lay back on his pillows and looked around his room, dimly lit in the soft glow from his bedside lamp. In addition to a double bed, there was a wooden cabinet that housed the gods and the silver cup of salvation. Twice a day the gods were carried downstairs to witness disciples eating ambrosia and drinking from the silver cup. That was how the gods knew who lived under their protection.

He had brought the exquisite silver cup back to England from the ancient monastery where he had been virtually imprisoned, high in the Himalayas. His visit had come about by accident while he had been trekking in India. Losing sight of his companions, he had spent a day alone on the mountain, where he had been struck down with dysentery. For days he had wandered, lost, and increasingly sick. He would have died if he hadn't been discovered and rescued by a community of monks who nursed him back to health. Living high in the Himalayas, cut off from the rest of the world, the monks sought freedom from all earthly ties. Abandoning worldly possessions to pursue a life of asceticism, they flagellated one another until sinful impulses bled from their bodies, and revered the hallucinogenic plant extracts that took them to another level of existence. Having saved his life, they insisted that he stay with them. The eldest monk, who spoke with authority, declared that God had led the visitor to their monastery. Too weak to refuse their meagre hospitality, he had remained with them, sharing their diet of weeds and goats' milk. At night he slept on a slab of rock, with cold seeping into his bones.

Afraid of corruption from the outside world, the monks never ventured far outside the walls of the monastery. Before long, returning to England seemed as impossible as flying to a different planet. Only when he realised they intended to initiate him into their community was he terrified into action. The night before his castration ceremony he fled while the monks were sleeping. Passing a silver goblet on his way out, he seized it, intending to sell it when he could. Clambering down the mountain path was gruelling. Never obvious, at times the path disappeared completely. His bare feet were soon blistered and lacerated. He could no longer walk but crawled slowly on his hands and knees. Several times he was tempted to despair, but the gods appeared before him in a vision and led him safely down. That was when he understood that he had discovered the path of righteousness.

'You carry the cup of life,' they told him, and he knew he was saved.

After his experience on the mountain, he was ready to lead others to enlightenment. He had passed through death and seen the true light.

CHAPTER 63

It was past nine and Ian still wasn't home. He probably wouldn't be home for hours. Bev had showered earlier, and changed ready to spend the evening with him. Her black lacy lingerie was scratchy, her skintight jeans pinched her waist. With no one to see her, there was no point being uncomfortable. She ran upstairs and undressed. Ian's loss, she thought, stopping briefly to admire her naked body in the bedroom mirror: flat stomach, gently curving hips, the kind of breasts that women paid thousands for – most men would gladly sacrifice a few hours of work to spend an evening with her. In pyjamas and dressing gown, she went downstairs and sprawled on the sofa. There was an old Hollywood film on the television. At least she could watch whatever she wanted when Ian was out, small compensation for another night of solitude. By the time he came home, she was in bed and half asleep.

'Are you awake?' he whispered as he climbed in beside her.

She kept her eyes closed and didn't answer.

★ ★ ★

Ian fidgeted all night, muttering in his sleep. Disturbed by his restlessness, Bev was relieved when the morning finally came. How sad, she thought, to be pleased that she could return to the distraction of her day. As usual, Ian set off early, leaving her to clear away the breakfast things before she too left for work. Angrily she shoved crockery into the dishwasher, staring at the reality of her Happy Ever After, tied to a selfish insensitive husband. She wondered if every wife suffered similar regrets, or if she had just been unlucky. Ian had behaved very differently before they were married. How was she to know he would change? To cheer herself up she made a special effort to look smart when she went in to work that day and was pleasantly surprised when her boss complimented her on her appearance. It was a while since he had paid her any attention. Although he was a notorious flirt, lately he had only seemed interested in the younger girls.

When he suggested they go for a drink together after work, she agreed at once with a flush of pleasure. She wasn't sure if the invitation extended to all her colleagues, and hoped he was asking her alone. When that turned out to be the case she felt a tremor of excitement, and wondered what she was doing agreeing to accompany him. Still, it was reassuring to know she could still attract the attention of a good-looking man. She would never have guessed it from the way her husband treated her. Grant took her to a bar they knew close to the office.

'Remember when you first came to work for me?' he asked, gazing earnestly at her as he handed her a glass of white wine.

She remembered it very well. He hadn't been able to keep his eyes off her. Although she loved Ian, she couldn't help feeling flattered by Grant's interest. She smiled at him, and inclined her head without answering.

'You broke my heart when you married that policeman of yours,' he added with a rueful grin.

Bev grinned at his banter. She wondered how different her life might have been if she had married a man like Grant. With his chiselled features and infectious laughter, he appreciated women and enjoyed their company. Of course she would be fooling herself to think a man like Grant could ever make her happy. He was the kind of man who would be constantly running after other women. All the same it was fun flirting with him, allowing herself to forget fleetingly that she was married to a man who had no time for her.

'So how's married life treating you?'

Bev was tempted to unburden herself to him, but she held back. Ian was her husband. However much she complained about him to his face, she would never slag him off to a third party. Instead, she smiled and told Grant everything was fine.

He leaned forward.

'Are you sure you're happy?'

Bev began to feel annoyed. She hadn't come out with Grant to talk about her husband.

'My husband's very busy working on a very important murder investigation right now,' she began pompously, and faltered.

It sounded as though she was boasting about Ian's career. In any case, she probably wasn't supposed to talk about his work to anyone else. The conversation moved on and she relaxed. They stayed, chatting, for over an hour.

At last they prepared to leave, pulling on gloves and scarves against the chilly evening air.

'That was lovely,' she said, 'thank you.'

'We should do this again,' he replied, linking his arm through hers.

'That would be nice.'

Encouraged, he asked speculatively, 'You don't have to go home just yet, do you?'

Gratified but wary, she told him her husband would be waiting for her at home. It was a lie. Even though she had done nothing wrong, she couldn't help feeling guilty. She didn't fancy Grant, she told herself, it just made a pleasant change to enjoy the undivided attention of a man over a friendly drink. They both understood it was nothing more meaningful than a casual flirtation. Far from objecting, Ian would approve of her going out and having a good time. Even so, she decided not to tell him about her outing. With a faint stirring of dismay she realised he probably wouldn't be interested anyway. Right now, he didn't seem able to think about anything other than his wretched investigation.

Watching Grant walk over to his car, she was almost tempted to call after him and ask him what he had in mind. It would serve Ian right if she did have an affair with someone else. But the moment passed. She wasn't sure whether she was relieved or disappointed when Grant jumped into his car and drove away.

CHAPTER 64

Ian went into work early the next morning. There was no reason for him to be there, sitting at his desk at half past seven on a Wednesday morning, but he had to do something. Three women were dead and they didn't know who was responsible. They hadn't even managed to establish whether they had all been killed by the same person, although it was hard to believe the deaths were unconnected.

'Henry Martin's the key,' Rob said when they gathered in the Incident Room in Herne Bay to review the case. 'He's the link between Martha and Jade, and once we get to Jade, she leads directly to Candy.'

'But why would Henry want to kill the woman who was giving him an alibi for the time Martha was stabbed, and why then go and kill Candy who had nothing to do with Martha at all?' Ian countered.

'We're missing something and I'm buggered if I can see what it is. But it's staring us in the face,' Rob rambled on, voicing his frustration. They all knew they were going round in circles.

★ ★ ★

'Della – Jade, that is – gave him an alibi. She must have decided to retract, for some reason,' Ian said.

'Or she was demanding more money than he was prepared to give her?' Polly suggested.

'Yes,' Ian agreed. 'Having lied to give him an alibi, that would have put her in a position to blackmail him. She pushed it too far, he lost it, and decided to get rid of her.'

'So far so good, that all makes sense,' Rob said.

'Then Candy came along,' Ian went on, warming to his narrative. 'She was friends with Jade. They lived together. What if Jade had spilled the beans to Candy about her arrangement with Henry? Once Jade was out of the picture, Candy decided to take over, see how much she could screw out of Henry to buy *her* silence.'

'Taking over the blackmail Jade had started.'

'Exactly. Candy had no idea it was Henry who strangled Jade – or maybe she suspected him but went ahead anyway. With enough money at stake, she might have been prepared to take that risk.'

'Buying her way to a better life for her son,' Polly said.

Thinking of the little boy, Ian sighed. 'A better life for her son,' he repeated solemnly.

Everything pointed to Henry, but they had no evidence. A defence lawyer would list the different methods of killing and question whether one person had really murdered all three women. In any case, in the absence of any proof, the case against Henry was no more than speculation based on a credible motive. There was nothing to prove Jade had been lying in the first place, when she gave Henry his alibi. If Jade's account of spending time with Henry had been false, any chance of proving that had died with her.

'At least we've come up with a theory that makes sense,' Rob concluded, 'but that's all it is.'

Towards the end of the day, Ian picked up the phone and called his wife. There was no answer. With a sigh, he prepared to leave a message but couldn't think what to say. He felt guilty about having abandoned her at the weekend, guilty about going home late during the week, and generally guilty about being an inadequate husband. If he could turn the clock back, he would have taken her out shopping at the weekend and bought her a beautiful piece of jewellery. He knew she would appreciate that kind of love token. On Sunday evening he had thought she was beginning to change, but by Monday she had reverted to her usual hostility towards his work. It was easy for her, ensconced in an office, chatting to clients on the phone about potential employees she had recruited. She really had no idea what he had to endure on an almost daily basis. And now he wanted to talk to her, maybe even to apologise, she wasn't answering her phone. He guessed she was on her way home. He tried once more.

'Bev, it's me, I just wanted to say hope you're having a good day and see you later.'

He hung up, regretting having left such a lame message. He might as well not have bothered. Usually he nipped to the canteen for a quick bite when he was on a case. Today, he decided to go out. He needed to get away from the claustrophobic environment of the station. Hurrying past a couple of uniformed constables zipping up stab vests in the corridor, he went out into the cold fresh air. He drove along the front until he found a little café that served hot soup, baguettes and other sorts of rolls. It wasn't great food, but it would do. He hadn't realised how hungry he was until he tucked in to an egg and bacon baguette, washing it down with a mug of strong tea. As he ate alone, he wondered where Bev was and what she was doing for supper. Wiping his fingers, he tried her phone again, but she didn't answer. He felt a lot better after eating. The evening was bright and cold. Walking back to the car, he felt his characteristic optimism return. There was no point getting stressed about things. All married couples had their off days. The row with Bev would soon blow over. As for Henry, he hadn't struck Ian as particularly intelligent so he was bound to slip up soon. And when he did, Ian would be waiting.

'There's someone here to see you,' the desk sergeant told Ian when he arrived back at the station.

'Who is it?'

'He wouldn't say, just asked for you by name. He insisted he spoke to you, and no one else. He said it was urgent.'

'Why didn't you call me?'

'He only just this minute came in and I knew you wouldn't be gone long.' The desk sergeant leaned forward and lowered his voice confidentially. 'He's cuckoo, if you ask me. Still, you never know.'

'OK, I'll go and check it out now. I can't imagine it's anything important.'

Ian couldn't repress a flicker of hope as he strode along the corridor to the interview room where a potential witness was waiting. He crossed his fingers hoping this might be the lead they were waiting for, the missing piece of the jigsaw that would make everything slot into place.

CHAPTER 65

Ian recognised the dark haired young man straight away even though his head was lowered. Mark didn't stir when Ian entered the room, looking up only when he heard his name.

'You asked to see me?'

'Yes.' It was barely a whisper.

He raised his head. His face was very pale, his eyes bloodshot and red-rimmed. He was clearly still suffering from the loss of his mother. Ian felt sorry for him. The boy was barely eighteen but looked younger. At his age he should have been studying, partying, exploring the world. Instead he was slumped on a grey chair in a grey-walled room, his surroundings a metaphor for his colourless life. Ian did his best to inject some cheerful energy into his voice as he started to question the young man.

'You have something to tell me?'

Mark nodded. He looked terrified.

'It's OK, Mark. Whatever it is, you can tell me.'

'Yes. I want to. That's why I came. I wanted to see you, to tell you—'

Ian waited.

★   ★   ★

When Mark spoke again his voice was flat, as though it was an effort to force the words out at all.

'I know who killed my mother.'

Ian didn't say anything. Mark's hands writhed in his lap, long white fingers frenziedly twisting and intertwining.

'It was my father,' he said at last, in the same impassive tone.

'Are you telling me your father killed your mother?'

'Yes.'

'Are you certain? Could you swear to that in a court of law?'

The young man nodded his head.

'How do you know? Did you see him? Or did he tell you?'

Mark screwed up his face as though he was going to cry.

'I told you, he killed her,' he repeated, his voice rising in agitation.

'How do you know it was him? Mark, I don't want to press you, it's obviously very painful for you to talk about this, but we need to be certain.'

'I know he did it, because he tried to kill me too.'

The young man dropped his head in his hands and continued, his voice muffled by his hands.

'I wouldn't have said anything, I don't care what

he does to me, only he killed my mother. He has to be punished for that.'

'How do you know it was him?'

'I told you, he tried to kill me too. That's why I came here. So you can protect me. You have to stop him.'

The young man looked up at Ian, his eyes brimming with tears, his cheeks flushed.

'You don't believe me, do you? Do you really think I'd lie about something like this? He's my father. I could forgive him almost anything, but not this, not my mother.'

He was shaking now, and crying. Ian stood up.

'Mark, you don't need to worry. You're safe here. Now, I'm going to get you a cup of tea and then you can tell me exactly what happened.'

Mark sniffed loudly and wiped his nose on his sleeve. Rubbing his eyes with the back of his hand he mumbled an apology for breaking down. With a word to the uniformed constable who was standing outside the door, Ian went to fetch a mug of tea and a colleague.

Rob wasn't at the Herne Bay station but Ian found Polly in the Incident Room. She was taken aback when Ian told her what Mark had said.

'Poor kid.'

'He's eighteen.'

'I've got an eighteen-year-old brother and he's just a kid,' she repeated. 'He's only just out of school.'

Armed with a mug of tea, Ian returned to the interview room. Polly accompanied him, chattering excitedly, but he felt dazed. It hadn't really sunk in yet that the case was over. Henry was as good as convicted. No jury would disbelieve a son who accused his father of attempting to murder him. All that remained was to make sure Mark would stick to his story and prove a credible witness. Questioning him had to be handled with sensitivity and attention to detail. Meanwhile, the slightest slip could leave the way open for Henry's defence council to shoot Mark's statement to pieces, even if everyone knew he was telling the truth. Unless Henry confessed, the whole case would depend on Mark's statement. They had to get it right.

Mark took a few sips of sweet tea and wrinkled his nose as Ian explained the procedure for recording his statement.

'I was in the kitchen,' he said as soon as Ian had finished speaking. 'I was making myself some toast when he came up behind me.'

'He?'

'My father.'

He glanced at Polly then looked back at Ian.

'I heard him and looked round. He had this look in his eyes I'd never seen before, not with me anyway. I mean, he's always had a crazy temper – he used to yell at my mother all the time, over stupid things, like she'd put too much milk in his tea. I don't know how she put up with it for so long, but there was no talking to her about it. I tried, but she as good as told me to mind my own business. She kept up this pretence that nothing was wrong, but we both knew it wasn't true.'

'We both being . . .?' Ian prompted him.

'My mother and me. We knew it was only a matter of time before he'd kick off again. He was crazy, always yelling at her. It was horrible. I think I always knew he'd go too far one day. I tried to persuade her to leave him, but she wouldn't even talk about it.'

His voice shook. He fell silent and sat sipping his tea while tears slipped down his pallid cheeks. Ian remembered the neighbour accusing Henry of having a violent temper, and threatening to kill his wife. The net was closing in on Henry. After a moment, Ian leaned forward.

'What happened in the kitchen today?' he asked softly.

He thought of Candy's son, too young to understand the circumstances of his mother's death, and wasn't sure whether he felt more sorry for Joey or Mark. Two dead women. Two motherless sons. Henry had killed his wife. If they could pin the other two murders on him as well, the killing might stop.

'You have to tell us what happened,' he repeated, more firmly.

★   ★   ★

390

Mark took a deep breath, preparing to talk about his ordeal.

'He came up behind me and put his arm round my neck, here.'

He pointed to his throat, concealed beneath a black polo neck jumper.

'Did he hurt you?'

'Not really. But I was scared. He used to hit my mother—'

'Go on.'

'He said he'd had enough of me and the mess I made around the house. He was really angry because I'd left some stuff on the kitchen table.'

'Stuff?'

'A magazine,' he frowned with the effort of remembering, 'an empty crisp packet, my gloves – nothing much. A dirty plate and mug that I'd brought down from my room, stuff like that. He said he was sick of me leaving things lying around everywhere. And then he squeezed my neck really hard.'

He stared at Ian in silent appeal, his dark eyes wide with remembered terror.

'I thought he was going to kill me.'

He dropped his head in his hands. His shoulders shook with sobs. Ian gave him a moment then pressed him gently to continue. The boy looked up and nodded.

'You're doing really well,' Ian added, helplessly.

He wished he had left this for an officer trained

to question juveniles. But Mark was eighteen. Besides, he had asked to speak to Ian, and he was certainly talking. He might not have spoken so freely to anyone else.

'I punched backwards with my elbow, got him in the guts. I don't think I hurt him, but it winded him so he loosened his grip. Then I managed to pull away and turn round and I said something like, "Do you want to kill me?" and he said, "If that's what it takes to get rid of you, then yes. I did for your mother, so why not you? Don't you know what happens to anyone who gets in my way?" I was so confused, I can't remember exactly what happened next but I just ran out of the kitchen and saw his car keys on the hall table so I grabbed them and came straight here. I'm not insured to drive his new car, but I was too frightened to stop and think. I was afraid if I tried to get away on foot he'd come after me. I wasn't thinking straight. I was so scared.'

Ian reassured the distraught boy he had done the right thing. He was safe now.

'Just for the record, can you repeat what your father said to you about having killed your mother? I know it's difficult for you, but we have to be clear about this. Are you sure you remember what he said?'

'It's not something I'll ever forget. He said, "I did for your mother, so why not you?" That's what he said.'

Ian stood up.

'What happens now?' Mark asked.

'You stay here. I think you know where I'm going.'

For the first time, the boy gave a strained smile.

CHAPTER 66

Henry leaned against the door frame, crossed his arms and heaved an exaggerated sigh when he saw Ian and Polly outside.

'You lot just can't leave me alone, can you?'

Ian stepped forward so that his shoulder rested against the door.

'Henry Martin, I am arresting you on suspicion of murder—'

At first Henry looked startled. Then he shook his head and an irritated expression crossed his face.

'What the hell are you trying now? We've been through all this over and over again. You've already had me down the nick asking me all sorts of questions. You can't have forgotten already. You asked me every bloody question under the sun and you've still got nothing on me, so why don't you bugger off and start looking for her killer. She was my wife, remember. I'd like you to find out who did that to her. We were married for thirty-four years. That's not something you can just walk away from without a second thought. I want to know who killed her and you're not doing your job, mate. Now fuck off and leave me alone.'

Ian reached out and seized Henry by the arm. The other man put up no physical resistance, but continued with his tirade.

'You just can't let it rest, can you? I'm her husband, so it must be me. You've got it into your thick heads that I killed Martha, and you can't accept you got it wrong. And all the time you're wasting talking to me, instead of getting on with your job. It's unbelievable. I've told you everything I can, there's no point going over it all again.'

'We've received some new information.'

'What information?'

'A witness has come forward.'

'What witness? What are you talking about?'

'Come along, Mr Martin. Let's do this at the station.'

Still grumbling, Henry allowed Ian to lead him down the path to the waiting car.

'And you can fuck off and all,' he shouted to the next-door neighbour who was peering at them over her gate.

'It's about time you locked him up,' she called to Ian.

She stood watching them as they drove away.

Henry sat with his arms folded, refusing to answer any questions until his lawyer arrived.

'I know what you're doing,' he said. 'You think

you can bully me into agreeing to your trumped up story. You'll do anything to get a conviction, never mind if you're chasing after the wrong person.'

Ian waited patiently until everything was in place.

'There had better be a good reason for this harassment,' Henry said, when his grey-haired lawyer was at his side.

The solicitor looked bored. 'My client has already answered all your questions on a previous occasion, so unless you have any new information—'

'Oh, we have new information all right,' Ian answered promptly. 'And our information places you firmly back in the frame, Mr Martin.' He leaned back in his chair, smiling. 'We've got a witness who swears that you not only threatened to kill him, but you confessed to killing your wife. Read out what he said, Constable. Let's hear the exact words.'

While Polly leafed through her notebook, the solicitor whispered to Henry, then sat up and waved his hand in the air dismissively.

'My client's position is clear. He never so much as touched his wife, and your witness is lying.'

'The exact words please, Constable.'

Polly cleared her throat.

'This is a complete load of bollocks,' Henry snapped.

'Listen,' Ian repeated quietly, 'listen and then dismiss it if you can.'

'The witness states the suspect assaulted him. The witness said, "Do you want to kill me?" to which Henry Martin replied, "If that's what it takes to get rid of you, then yes. I did for your mother, so why not you?" The witness was clear those were the exact words his father used.'

The solicitor glanced anxiously at Henry who sat perfectly still, looking perplexed.

'I don't get it,' Henry muttered. 'I don't get it.' He turned to the lawyer. 'What does it mean?'

'It means,' Ian answered before the lawyer could respond, 'your son came to us after you attacked him, and told us what you confessed to him. He said he didn't care about you hurting him—'

'Hurting him?' Henry echoed.

'But he wants to see you punished for killing his mother. Try talking your way out of that!'

Alert now, the lawyer spoke swiftly as he requested a moment alone with his client. Henry had gone very pale.

'I never hurt my boy,' he muttered. 'I don't understand.' His eyes lit up suddenly. 'They're lying,' he cried out, grasping at the lawyer's sleeve. 'They're lying.'

He turned wild eyes to Ian. 'Don't think you can make this stick, you arsehole. You think you can trick me into confessing to something I didn't do. My boy never said any of those filthy lies. You've got no right – no right—'

'A moment alone with my client, please,' the lawyer insisted.

★   ★   ★

Out in the corridor, Ian sent for the statement Mark had signed while they were apprehending Henry. He smiled grimly at Polly.

'Poor kid,' she muttered once again, staring at the document Ian was holding. 'He's only just eighteen.'

'Pretty terrible at any age, discovering your dad killed your mother,' Ian said. 'Come on, then, they've had their moment.'

Any vestiges of sympathy he might have felt for Henry had vanished along with his doubts about the man's guilt. Henry had killed his wife and two more women. He would tell them the truth if they had to force it out of him.

'We know you killed your wife,' Ian began.

'Oh give it a rest, for fuck's sake,' Henry burst out, his aggravation getting the better of him.

The solicitor raised a restraining hand. A gold signet ring gleamed on his little finger. Without another word, Ian placed Mark's statement on the table in front of Henry.

Henry squinted down at the document. 'What the hell's this?'

'The suspect is looking at a signed statement from his son, Mark,' Ian announced for the benefit of the recording. He turned to Henry. 'Would you like to read it aloud?'

Henry's voice was wooden. 'I was in the kitchen making toast, when my father came in. He looked angry. He's always had a foul temper. He used to

398

shout at my mother all the time for little things, like if she put too much milk in his tea. She told me there was nothing wrong, but I knew it wasn't normal, the way he carried on. He was always yelling at her. Anyway, I was making the toast and he walked round behind me and put his arm round my neck . . .' Henry broke off and looked up with a baffled expression.

'Go on.'

As though in a daze, Henry resumed reading aloud. 'My father was complaining I'd left some stuff on the kitchen table. He said he was sick of me leaving stuff everywhere. And he squeezed my neck really hard. I think he wanted to kill me . . .'

Henry broke off. The paper shook in his hand. Gently he replaced it on the table. He looked stunned, as though unable to comprehend what he had just read.

'Shall I go on?' Ian asked.

Henry didn't answer so Ian picked up the statement and continued reading it aloud.

'I punched backwards with my elbow into his guts and winded him so he let me go. Then I said something like, "What are you doing? You could have killed me. Are you trying to kill me?" and he said, "If that's what it takes to get rid of you, then yes. I did for your mother, so why not you? Don't you know what happens to anyone who gets in my way?" I can't remember exactly what happened next but I just ran out of the house and came straight here.'

Ian put the statement down.

'He signed it, Henry. That's your son's statement. What have you got to say now?'

Henry shook his head, his face completely blank. After his earlier bluster he was oddly quiet.

'I don't believe a word of it,' he whispered at last.

'Mark signed it.'

'You leave my boy out of this. If I'm to go down, maybe it's no more than I deserve.' He dropped his head in his hands. 'Just leave the boy alone. He's been through more than enough already.'

'Are you ready to confess to murdering your wife? You can make this all a lot easier if you just tell us the truth.'

'Easier for you,' Henry muttered, without looking up.

After that, he refused to say any more. Even his brief couldn't persuade him to speak again.

CHAPTER 67

It was hard to believe they had caught the killer. By now everyone in Herne Bay and Margate police stations knew Henry was responsible for the murders of Martha, Jade and Candy. With a conviction assured, Rob decided to leave the next stage of the interrogation until the morning. There was no longer a sense of urgency in his orders as he strolled into the Incident Room in Herne Bay. At this stage of an investigation there was usually a sense of elation at discovering the identity of the killer and carrying out a successful arrest. On this occasion the atmosphere felt strangely flat, perhaps because they all knew there was still a lot of work to be done before the files were closed. No one suggested a celebratory drink, no one was even smiling, apart from the detective inspector.

'Come on, guys, we've got him!' he announced with forced exuberance.

An awkward silence greeted his announcement.

'Yay!' a constable called out lamely.

'A man killed his wife and two other women, and attacked his son,' someone else said.

'Oh for fuck's sake, this is supposed to be a

victory, not a bloody funeral wake,' Rob grumbled as he stomped out of the room, his good spirits dampened.

Back at Woolsmarsh and bored of paperwork, Ian escaped to the canteen for a break. His spirits sank when he saw Rob pause on the threshold and scan the room as though looking for someone. Rob caught sight of him and marched purposefully over to sit at his table. Ian nodded without speaking. He was entitled to a break.

'I've got some news for you,' Rob said.

'A confession?'

'What?'

'Has Henry confessed? That's the only news that would interest me right now. It's late and I'm knackered.'

He wondered whether to offer to buy Rob tea and a bun, only he couldn't be bothered to get up.

'This isn't to do with the case,' Rob said.

Ian frowned, puzzled, but Rob was smiling.

'Then what—?'

'This is about you, Ian.'

'Me?'

Rob nodded. 'Christ, you're a bit slow on the uptake. I wonder if you're really up to the task. What news have you been waiting for?'

Ian couldn't help grinning as he realised Rob was talking about his promotion. His colleague's smile signalled the news was good.

'Is it – am I –?' He couldn't get the words out.

'Congratulations, Detective Inspector! Of course it was a foregone conclusion, with your record, but well done anyway.'

'Jesus. I can't believe it. That's brilliant!'

Rob smiled back at him.

'Come along to my office when you're done here,' he said as he stood up, 'and then you'd better get off home and see how your wife feels about moving.'

'Moving?'

'Yes, they accepted your application up in Yorkshire right away. Can't say I blame them. They're lucky to get you, and it's a great opportunity for you to work in a different area, see a different part of the country. We'll tell the rest of the team tomorrow. Now you get off home and tell your wife you've been taken on up there. You should let her know first.'

Rob was right, of course. Ian would have to tell Bev. When a vacancy had come up in Yorkshire he had applied for it on impulse, desperate to get as far away from his in-laws as possible. But he hadn't mentioned it to his wife. He wasn't even sure how he felt about moving to Yorkshire himself. It would give him the chance to prove himself as an inspector, but while he was looking forward to the challenge, Bev would be moving solely for his sake. It had been her choice to buy an expensive house in Tunbridge Wells which they could barely afford on his sergeant's salary. That was one reason for all the additional hours overtime he worked, whenever he could. There were a lot of benefits to his promotion, if Bev could be persuaded to see it that way. With a sinking feeling in the pit of his stomach, he drove home. Usually he put his foot down. Tonight he crawled along letting every other car overtake him. The case was over, and he had his promotion. This should have been one of the best nights of his life. After all his hard work, instead of celebrating, he was dreading going home to confront his wife with the news. He played out the scene over and over in his mind, rehearsing different ways to tell her. Each imagined outcome ended with her shrieking at him.

'The north of England? Are you serious? You expect me to go and live in Yorkshire?'

He resolved not to mess around, but to come straight out with it. No sweet-talking, no sitting down with a bottle of wine – she would probably throw it at him anyway. He would simply tell her the news. Bev was his wife. She should be pleased for him. Psyching himself up, he went into the house and found her watching television. She glanced up and smiled. That was a good start. He noticed she was watching her favourite soap and decided not to interrupt her viewing. The news that their lives were about to radically change could wait while characters acted out fictitious lives on screen. Bev was happily watching them fighting, kissing, and shouting at one another. It was best not to disturb her. He wandered into the kitchen and opened a bottle of champagne, downed a glass, refilled it, knocked it back again and refilled it once more. It was an expensive sort of Dutch courage. He would have been just as happy with a beer.

'Drinking alone?' Bev asked, creeping up behind him and putting her arms round his waist. 'Ooh, champagne! What's this for?'

'Do I need an excuse to celebrate spending time with my beautiful wife?' he asked, cursing himself for his cowardice.

Bev kissed him behind his ear, and they drank champagne together. He felt pleasantly drunk, and hornier than he had been in a long time. It would be a shame to spoil the evening by sparking off a bitter row. Their future could wait for a while.

CHAPTER 68

Henry had been transferred to a cell in Woolsmarsh. Instead of ranting against his arrest he sat on his bunk staring straight ahead, refusing food. Admittedly, he was in a tricky situation, his son having accused him of murder, but teenage boys were notoriously unreliable. By now Ian expected Henry and his lawyer to have concocted a tale involving puberty, depression, alcohol, drugs, and teenage angst following his mother's recent violent death. It wouldn't have been difficult to fabricate an excuse that exonerated Henry while not being unduly judgemental of his son. Mark's betrayal seemed to have broken his father's spirit.

'There's something odd about his behaviour,' Ian insisted.

'You're telling me,' Rob agreed cheerfully. 'Unless you think it's normal to stab your wife, and then strangle and suffocate two prostitutes, and finish it all off by trying to strangle your own child. He'll plead insanity, and he'll get away with it, more's the pity.'

'That's not what I meant.'

'What *do* you mean then?'

Ian shrugged. He couldn't explain what was bugging him, but something didn't feel right.

'So how did your wife take the news?' Rob wanted to know.

'Oh, yeah, we got through two bottles of champagne last night,' Ian equivocated, smiling at the memory. It had been a good night.

'You haven't told her, have you?'

Ian gave a sheepish grin. 'It's not easy. Bev's – well, she likes it here. She likes her job and she likes being near her family.'

'You're her family now.' Rob smiled. 'I remember when I told my missus about my promotion. I was bricking it that she wouldn't want to move out of the area, but she was straight on the phone to her mother. 'You know that no-good bobby I married?' she said. 'Well, you can kiss my arse now because my husband's an inspector!' Honest to God, those were her very words.' He chuckled. 'And the funny part of it is, I had no idea until then that her mother had been dead against her marrying me. Rosy hid that well. Made me wonder what else she wasn't telling me.'

He winked before he wandered off. Ian had never seen him in such high spirits.

The custody sergeant dismissed Ian's qualms.

'Of course he's bloody odd. He goes around

killing people. That's not a normal way to behave, is it? Or have we been missing something about what you get up to in your spare time?'

'No, what I mean is, he's acting out of character.'

'Ah, that's because he knows he's nicked. They always quieten down once they know we know. Don't you worry, I've seen it all before. He'll soon give up on this not-eating lark, take it from me. He'll only make himself ill if he carries on like this. But he'll come to his senses soon enough. I've seen more prisoners refusing food than you've had hot dinners.'

The custody sergeant laughed, and Ian smiled. But the sergeant had missed the point. It wasn't the prisoner's refusal to eat that perturbed Ian, but the thought that they might have arrested the wrong man.

Even Polly wasn't sympathetic to Ian's misgivings and dismissed the idea that Mark might be lying.

'Why would he?'

Ian shrugged. 'Maybe he's the killer.'

'You don't really think he killed his own mother, for goodness sake. What kind of person would do that? In any case, he had an alibi, didn't he? You saw the girl the same as I did, and I called and spoke to her father afterwards.'

A terrible suspicion struck Ian. He assured himself Polly would have taken the time to corroborate Mark's alibi properly, yet the ambiguity of her remark bothered him. Just to be sure, he went back through the records and found her notes. Staring at the screen, he felt a sudden panic. His fingers shook as he logged out before going to find his colleague.

'Your report says you phoned Eve Thompson's parents.'

'Yes.'

Her smile faded when she saw his expression. 'You told me to check out her story about being with Mark when Martha was killed.'

'By phone? Didn't it occur to you to go round to the house and make sure the girl who gave Mark an alibi really was who she said she was?'

Polly shrugged. 'Why would she lie about it?'

'But you phoned. Didn't you think you should have gone round there and confirmed for yourself that it really was her?'

'I didn't think it was necessary. The phone number checked out. It was the Thompsons' landline and Mr Thompson's description of his daughter matched the girl we saw. If you read my report—'

'I read it. Was there any reason not to go round there?'

Ian could see realisation dawning on her face. Unable to meet his eye, she mumbled something about not wanting to cause trouble for the young couple.

'It's just that she's younger than him. Her parents might not know she's seeing an eighteen-year-old boy. I didn't want to get her in any trouble—'

'So you're happy to turn a blind eye to underage sex—'

'She's only just underage,' Polly broke in quickly. 'I checked. She's sixteen in a couple of months. But parents of girls that age don't like them seeing older boys. I should know,' she added sourly.

'Don't bring your personal issues in to work.'

'I'm not. It's not an issue, not any more. But it's not part of our job to grass up youngsters who are in love. You saw the way she looked at him. They were more than just friends. There was something much stronger going on between them, and she was nervous as hell about them being exposed. You could see that. She was shaking the whole time.'

'Oh Jesus, this isn't bloody Romeo and Juliet,' Ian broke out in exasperation. 'We have to be thorough. Look, I'm sure there's no harm done, but in future don't leave any loose ends. Not in a murder enquiry.'

Once Mark had provided his alibi, very little time had been spent investigating him. They had been so focused on pursuing Henry, they had accepted his son's story at face value. Polly had finally grasped the potential gravity of her blunder, but no one else had yet picked up on it. Ian didn't intend to tell Rob what had happened unless it proved necessary. For now, he was determined to establish the truth. If the girl who had given Mark an alibi had been lying, it might mean that two women had died on account of Polly's lapse of judgement. For the young constable's sake, he hoped it would prove inconsequential that she had allowed herself to be misled by romantic notions.

Ian drove to the address Mark's friend had given them without telling anyone where he was going. A tall thin ginger-haired man came to the door. Ian introduced himself and established he was talking to Mr Thompson, father of Eve.

'What's this about, Inspector? Has something happened to Eve? She's not in any trouble is she?'

'No. Your daughter isn't in any trouble, and we have no reason to suppose anything has happened to her.'

'Only we had a phone call a couple of weeks ago, asking if she lives here. They wouldn't say what it was about. But if there's anything wrong, we would like to know. She's only fifteen.'

Ian frowned. The girl who had come to the police station had claimed to be seventeen but had looked closer to fourteen. That might explain why she had been so scared. She must realise her eighteen-year-old companion could be convicted if the

411

police discovered he was having sex with an underage girl. If he was up to something nefarious, Ian hoped that seeing a young girl would prove to be Mark's worst transgression. Paedophilia was among the most despicable of crimes, but sex with a consenting fifteen-year-old girl was easier to stomach than matricide.

Eve was at school, so Ian asked if Mr Thompson had any photographs of his daughter.

'Of course. Come in. But can you please tell me what this is about?'

'Mr Thompson, all I can tell you is that your daughter may possibly be able to give us information that will help us in an enquiry.'

'Information? What kind of information? What enquiry?'

'I'm afraid I'm not at liberty to tell you that, but rest assured your daughter isn't in any kind of trouble with the police.'

Mr Thompson led him into a living room, and went off to look for his photographs. He returned to say he hadn't been able to find any recent pictures of his daughter.

'I'll call my wife. She'll know where to find them.'

He went off again and Ian heard him talking on the phone. He returned after a few minutes with a laptop.

'Here you are,' he said. 'My wife keeps all our

photos here. She's always saying she's going to print them out, but she never seems to get round to it.'

Ian found the folder with the most recent images and scanned through the slide show with growing concern.

'Which of these is the best likeness of Eve?' he asked at last.

'They all look like her.' Mr Thompson looked down and pointed. 'That's a good one of her.'

Ian stared unhappily at a thin blonde girl grinning at them from the screen. Apart from similar hair and eye colour, she didn't look anything like the girl who had accompanied Mark to the police station. With a hurried thank you to Mr Thompson, and an assurance that the police were unlikely to contact his family again, Ian took his leave.

'Do you really think he killed his own mother?' Polly asked when Ian told her.

'It's worse than that. If I'm right – and God knows I hope I'm not – but if I am, then he not only killed his mother, he tried to pin the murder on his father. My guess is he waited until he was eighteen so he could inherit the house and his mother's estate. Then he planned to get both his parents out of the way so everything went to him.' He paused, watching Polly's face as she registered the enormity of what he was telling her. 'It's the most evil murder I've ever come across,' he added.

'I should have gone round there.'

'Don't blame yourself. No one could have seen that one coming.'

'You saw it,' Polly muttered.

Ian gave her a sympathetic grimace. There was nothing he could say to make her feel better.

CHAPTER 69

They knocked several times before a window opened upstairs. Mark leaned out to see who was at the door.

'What do you want?'

Ian was careful not to say anything that might arouse the young man's suspicion.

'We need to ask you to confirm a few things about your father.'

'What about my father?'

'We have him securely behind bars but he's refusing to cooperate with us, and we need your help to clear up one or two small matters.'

Mark hesitated then disappeared. They waited but he didn't come to the door. Ian knocked again, then sent Polly round to the back of the house. Mark's refusal to admit them was futile given that they had seen he was in, but if he really was the killer he must be insane and unlikely to behave rationally. Ian knocked once more. Without waiting any longer for a response, he fished out his set of keys and attempted to let himself in. If he couldn't unlock the door, they would have to break in.

★   ★   ★

Having called for back-up Ian phoned Polly, but she didn't answer.

'What the hell is with this place?' he muttered uneasily as his key turned, with a sharp click.

It was like the *Marie Celeste*. First Mark disappeared, now Polly wasn't answering her phone. Trying not to make a sound, he stole into the house. The only natural light in the hall came from a small window halfway up the stairs. The darkness was hushed. Ian felt as though someone else was there, listening and watching, preparing to strike. He hesitated, holding his breath, straining to see or hear any indication of movement in the house. There was a muffled scratching in the walls, and a faint ticking of pipework. Then he heard a choking sound, as though someone had been running and was out of breath. Following the noise, he crept along the hallway. At the door to the kitchen he paused, momentarily dazzled by sunlight streaming in through a large square window. Squinting, he saw the back door was wide open. Beside it Polly was standing rigid, her eyes wide with terror. Mark was pressed up against her back, one hand clutching both her wrists in front of her, the other holding the point of a long-bladed kitchen knife beneath her chin, forcing her head back. Ian froze.

'Let her go, Mark,' he said, doing his best to keep his voice level. He sounded robotic. 'There's no need for you to be upset. We only want to ask you about your father. You know we have him locked up. He can't hurt you again. You don't need to be scared any more.'

'You're lying.'

Polly kicked out behind her. Mark tightened his hold on her.

'Mark, you're not in any trouble, but you will be if you hurt a police officer. She's got nothing to do with any of this. She just drove me here. I know you're frightened, but you need to calm down and think about what you're doing.'

Mark seemed too agitated to take in what Ian was saying. It was difficult to be sure with his dark eyes, but Ian thought his pupils were dilated. He was mumbling incoherently about salvation. Ian paused, momentarily lost in an all-consuming fear.

He had led Polly straight into the arms of a serial killer.

'Mark,' Ian tried again.

His throat was so dry he could hardly speak. He struggled to stop his voice shaking.

'Polly came here to help you. She's your friend. I'm the one who wanted to come here. It's down to me that we're here. Let her go and we'll leave. Let her go, Mark. Drop the knife and let her go.'

He stopped, aware that Polly was gagging, her head forced back so far she was struggling to breathe. Mark jerked his head towards the other side of the room.

'Get over there, now!'

Ian hurried to comply.

As soon as the table was between them, Mark began hauling Polly sideways across the kitchen towards the hall, keeping his eyes fixed on Ian all the time. Not looking where he was going, he stumbled. When Ian started forward, Mark jerked the knife so that it pressed harder against Polly's throat. She cried out in alarm. Ian drew back, his hands raised in a gesture of submission as he watched his colleague being dragged from the room. He waited until they were out of sight before racing silently after them. Peering into the hall, he stared at Mark's back framed in the open front door. A police car was waiting outside. Mark spun round, the knife still at Polly's throat. He glared at Ian.

'Send them away!' he shouted frenziedly, 'send them all away!'

It wasn't easy keeping his eyes fixed on Mark as two uniformed figures appeared in the open doorway. From their position behind Polly, they couldn't see the blade pressing against her throat.

'Put the knife down,' Ian called out loudly. 'Stop pressing it to the constable's throat.'

In his zeal, he had shouted too loudly. Aware that something was amiss, Mark tensed. He jerked the blade so the tip of it pierced her skin. Ian watched a thread of blood trickle down her neck, unbelievably dark against her skin. He took an involuntary step forward. As he did so, Mark shuffled backwards, dragging Polly with him.

'Get away from me!' Mark shrieked.

The two uniformed officers simultaneously lunged forward and seized Mark's arms, rendering him helpless. The knife dropped to the floor. It lay on the carpet rolling almost imperceptibly from side to side, reflected light winking from the shiny surface of its blade. Mark put up no resistance as he was handcuffed. Keeping up a constant babbling, he seemed oblivious to his capture.

'Is that a Hail Mary he's reciting?' one of the constables asked.

Ian shrugged. He couldn't speak. All that mattered was that Polly was safe. Her assurance that she was fine was the only time Mark seemed to take any notice of what was happening.

'Fine, fine, we're all fine,' he cried out in a curious singsong voice. 'Everything's fine, fine fine!'

'Shut it,' a uniformed constable snapped.

Mark lowered his head and resumed his mumbling.

'I told you to shut it,' the constable repeated.

'Leave it,' Ian said. 'He's a nut job.'

'Sorry, sir. All that gibbering was getting on my nerves. What the hell is he on?'

'God knows.'

★   ★   ★

419

Ian drove Polly back to the station while Mark was taken off in a van.

'Are you sure you're OK?' he asked several times.

'Stop going on about it, will you?' Her angry outburst startled him. 'For Christ's sake, you're worse than my bloody father. In fact, you sound just like him. I've already told you I'm fine. How many times do I need to say it? I mean, I was shaken, who wouldn't be? I was bloody petrified. I thought he was going to kill me—'

'So did I.'

He didn't admit out loud that if Polly had been killed, it would have been his fault. He wondered if she was angry with him for leading her into danger, but was too drained to summon the courage to ask her if she blamed him. Meanwhile, she hadn't stopped talking.

'But he didn't hurt me, did he? Not really. It's only a scratch, and now I'm fine, and it's all part of the bloody job, isn't it? So just shut up about it, will you?'

Under normal circumstances it would have been unacceptable for a constable to be so rude to a senior officer, but being threatened by a knife-wielding maniac was hardly an everyday occurrence. They drove the rest of the way back to Woolsmarsh in silence.

As Ian was about to get out of the car, Polly put her hand on his arm to stop him.

'Listen, I spoke out of turn back there—'

'It's perfectly understandable. You were in shock. As long as he didn't hurt you, that's all that matters. I'm not going to ask you again if you're OK, but I am going to recommend you speak to someone about what happened today.'

'I don't need to speak to anyone, I'm OK.'

'Yes, I daresay you are, but that's not my call to decide.'

'Well, thanks for not reprimanding me for speaking to you like that. It was uncalled for and I am sorry, really I am.'

Ian was the one who should have been apologising for almost getting her killed. Instead he said cravenly, 'Like you said, it's all part of the bloody job, isn't it? Now, you need to get that scratch seen to, and then you're taking the rest of the day off.'

It was slow going, questioning Mark about the murders. When he wasn't muttering to himself, his answers made no sense. There was no way he was going to stand trial as though he was sane.

'What are you talking about, Mark?' Ian pressed him, trying to understand his excited chatter. 'I'm sure it's very important, but I can't hear what you're saying.'

Mark stared Ian in the eye and spoke slowly and clearly.

'The unenlightened do not hear.'

'It's a waste of time trying to talk to him,' Rob said when they took a break. 'He's barking. We might as well leave it for the psychiatrists to try and fathom.'

Fascinated by Mark, Ian was keen to carry on. It was difficult enough to accept that he had killed his own mother in a fit of insane rage, but setting up his father to take the punishment for it was an act of calculated evil hard to credit.

'He seems to be on some kind of religious trip, sir, although he denies being a Catholic like his mother.'

Only when asked about his relationship with his parents did Mark make any attempt to respond to questions directly. Even then his answers didn't make much sense.

'Mark, if you hated your parents so much, why didn't you move out? You're eighteen. You didn't have to stay with them.'

Mark looked at Ian in surprise.

'I don't hate anyone,' he said mildly. 'Hatred is evil. Hatred leads to damnation.'

'You killed your mother and tried to get your father locked up for it. So I'm asking you again, why were you so full of hatred for those closest to you? What had they done to you?'

Mark shook his head. He looked serene.

'None of this has anything to do with hatred,' he repeated gently. 'Her death was an act of sacred love—'

He broke off abruptly and pressed his thin lips together until they disappeared altogether.

'What are you talking about? What kind of love would make you kill your own mother?'

Mark opened his mouth to speak and Ian leaned forward, keen to catch every word.

'Eternal salvation is mine,' Mark intoned softly. His eyes glazed over as he murmured to himself. 'Eternal salvation is mine.'

CHAPTER 70

Ian felt drained by the time he reached home that evening. Throwing his coat on the stand in the hall, he went into the living room and collapsed on the sofa, too tired even to sit up.

'We got him,' he announced. 'We caught the crazy bastard.'

Bev clapped her hands in the air, like a child.

'Tell me about it.'

'You don't want to know.'

'Of course I do. Why do you always shut me out like this?'

'It's not just you. No one could understand unless they do the job themselves.'

'I've never understood your obsession with dead bodies, that's true enough.'

He tried to explain that it wasn't the dead he investigated, but the living. Henry and Mark were the people who interested him, not Martha, once she was dead.

'But you got him, you arrested your killer. I want to know all about it,' she insisted.

'Oh, Christ, all right. If you really want to know,

we arrested a man for stabbing his mother to death and accusing his father of committing the murder, plus he killed two more women, one strangled, the other suffocated – one of them left a seven-year-old son with no parents – and this crazy bastard threatened to kill my constable during the course of the arrest. Are you happy now? Is that what you wanted to hear?'

Bev looked suitably shocked.

'Bloody hell. Did you say he killed his own mother?'

'Yes. Like I said, he's crazy. We couldn't get a word of sense out of him. Not surprising, when you consider what he did.'

'But how can you be sure it was him then? I mean, he must be insane—'

'What? What do you mean, how can we be sure it was him? What kind of a question is that?'

'I only meant, if the guy's insane, you can't necessarily believe everything he says so it might be – well, misleading. He could be making it up, fantasising. You know what I mean.'

Ian stood up and went into the kitchen without bothering to respond. This wasn't a press conference. He wasn't obliged to answer inane questions in his own home. If Bev thought she could do the job, she was free to join the force. He wouldn't stand in her way. Let her try putting up with the shit he had to deal with, day after day. Grabbing a bottle of beer, he returned to the living room and sank back on the sofa again.

'No dinner tonight?'

'I wasn't sure what time to expect you, so I thought we'd get a takeaway if you were home in time.'

'It's never long before she starts with her digs,' he muttered.

'Ian, you look shattered. Why don't I run you a bath and then I'll phone the Chinese? What do you fancy? Sweet and sour pork?'

And just like that, he was a happily married man once more. There was only his promotion to discuss and all would be well in the Peterson household. They would move to York and live happily ever after.

To his consternation, he began to shake. He couldn't help himself. Now it was all over, he was experiencing a physical reaction to the stress of the investigation. This had happened to him before, but only when he was alone. It never lasted long. He looked away, embarrassed, but Bev had noticed. She came and sat beside him and put her arms round him. Her sympathy only made him shake more violently.

'What is it, love? You're shivering. Are you sickening for something? Shall I call the doctor?'

He wanted to yell at her to stop asking questions, but his teeth were chattering.

'I'm fine,' he assured her, gritting his teeth so he could speak.

'You don't look fine.'

He remembered the demented killer chanting, 'Fine, fine, we're all fine, everything's fine, fine, fine!' and wished he had chosen a different word.

'It's all right,' he insisted. 'I'm just exhausted. And by the way, I got my promotion.'

He hadn't intended to share the news when he was too exhausted to argue with her. The words just slipped out of his mouth. She might not like it but she had to find out sooner or later, and he was too tired to care anymore. They might as well get it over with. If she stormed out of the house he would simply stagger up to bed and go to sleep.

'You mean you're going to be an inspector?'

'Yes, but the thing is, Bev—'

'So I can tell my parents?'

Ian recalled what Rob had said, and smiled.

'Yes, you can tell your parents, but we're going to have to move.'

'Move?'

She turned, phone in hand, waiting.

This was the moment to tell her about York. She was elated about his promotion, and concerned about his shivering. Her pride and her pity combined to put him in an unassailable position – and he bottled it. Again.

'We may have to move,' he hedged.

There would be hell to pay when she discovered he had sent off an application for the North Yorkshire post without consulting her first.

'Don't look so worried,' he reassured her. 'It won't be Siberia. It probably won't even be very far away.'

He wasn't sure why he was lying so shamelessly, but he couldn't stop himself.

'I'll just call my mum, and then I'll phone the Chinese. Why don't you go and have a long soak in the bath?'

He nodded, but didn't move.

'We're going to York,' he announced suddenly, surprising himself as well as her. 'It's York.'

Slowly she put the phone down. Her voice was oddly calm.

'York? But you just said—'

'York,' he repeated. 'We're going to York.'

'But York's hundreds of miles away,' she protested. 'We can't just go – what about the house?'

With a burst of energy he jumped up, pulled her towards him and kissed her, hard, on the mouth. When she tried to wriggle free he held on to her and whispered in her ear.

'There are lots of houses in York and I'm going to buy the biggest and best house in the whole city for my lovely gorgeous sexy wife. I'm going to whisk her away from her boring job, and her interfering family, and take her to live in a palace of a house in York. Because that's what detective inspectors do!'

428

He took a step away and punched the air with a triumphant cry. He had done it!

'Are you pissed?'

'Intoxicated by the thought of getting you away from here and having you all to myself.' Suddenly serious, he asked, 'we are going to make this work, aren't we?'

'Go and have a bath,' she replied. 'You stink. I want to phone my mother and tell her about your promotion!' She grinned and patted him fondly on the cheek. 'Detective Inspector Peterson!'

Grinning, he went upstairs, whistling.

CHAPTER 71

No one spoke while the leader's eyes were shut. They could see he was thinking. Patiently they waited until he sat up and looked slowly around the room. Each of the disciples trembled as his gaze rested on them in turn, penetrating their deepest desires and fears. He smiled sadly.

'We are beleaguered by lies and ignorance,' he said softly. 'Our enemies seek to destroy us. Take no notice. Prison walls cannot contain our souls. The day is coming when all nations of the earth will follow the gods. It may not be in our lifetimes, but we will never give up the one true cause. Assassin carried out his mission for all of us. For our sakes he is suffering.' He raised his voice. 'We will not forget his sacrifice.'

'We will not forget his sacrifice,' they repeated in unison.

'We will see him in paradise.'

'We will see him in paradise.'

The leader raised his hand for silence. He looked slowly around the room once more. His loving gaze rested on each of his disciples in turn. Calmed by his tender smile they fell silent. The leader lowered his head and they waited patiently. The gods willed it. The disciples accepted their good fortune and drank from the cup of life. One by one their shoulders drooped and their eyes glazed over as divine ecstasy flowed through their souls. Whatever happened to their brother in captivity, his soul would find eternal peace.

'Our brother's sacrifice transcends the cup of life,' the leader said. 'He will be granted everlasting joy.'

'Joy everlasting,' a disciple called out and a chorus of voices responded, 'Everlasting joy.'

The leader's expression grew solemn. 'Now Assassin has been taken from us, it is no longer safe for us to stay in this house.'

An anxious mutter of conversation fluttered around the assembled disciples. The leader resumed speaking and they fell silent.

'Assassin has proved himself worthy of our trust.'

Even so, the leader knew there could be no guarantee of another person's discretion. Assassin might unwittingly betray them. Their enemies were ignorant, but cunning. He stood up.

'We must vanish from this place without trace. Now hurry. The gods will not wait long. Go upstairs and pack your belongings. Bring everything here as quickly as you can.'

With an anxious glance at the gods who were watching silently, he dismissed his followers.

Losing Assassin's house was a disappointment. It would have given them twice as much room as their present refuge in Canterbury Road. Now they would have to start all over again and find another property large enough to house them all. But he wasn't worried. He knew the gods would lead them to a new sanctuary, just as they had guided him down the mountain. Each of his disciples had been sent to him for a purpose. All were single children of wealthy parents. The most recent follower was nearly eighteen. Already initiated into his bed, she was ripe to become a disciple. Her father was dead. Her mother lived in a remote farmhouse big enough for all of them. From there the community would grow. Although it was a setback, losing Assassin, others would take up the calling. No one was indispensable. All were but servants of the one true cause. Leading his disciples to salvation was all that mattered.

'Assassin will reap his reward in paradise,' he whispered to the waiting gods.

'Sacrifice cleanses,' they replied in the silence.

CHAPTER 72

Ian had the day off on Saturday. This time Bev insisted he really did stay at home. With the case resolved, he was only too happy to comply. For the best part of a month he had dedicated every waking moment to working, or thinking about work. It had been worthwhile in the end. They had obtained justice of a sort for Martha, Jade and Candy, and had ensured a demented psychopath couldn't kill again. Mark's madness seemed to have struck without warning. Once he had committed matricide there was no route back to sanity, no act more terrible than the one he had already committed.

Lying in bed, Ian considered Bev's accusation that he was obsessed with the dead. Maybe she was right, and he should have been more interested in Martha's history before she died, rather than in her murder. Beyond the cause of death, a corpse revealed few secrets if the killer left no trace of DNA at the scene. Perhaps if he had studied Martha's life he would have spotted a clue to her son's insanity and been able to save the other two victims. It was depressing to think that, if he had suspected Mark earlier, Jade might still be alive, and Joey might not have lost his mother. But it was destructive blaming himself for his shortcomings. At least they had caught Mark in the end. Rob had been very complimentary about Ian's role in uncovering the truth. If it hadn't been for Ian's sharpness, he said, they would most likely have continued pursuing Henry through the courts. Henry would probably have kept silent, reluctant to accuse his own son of murdering Martha. An innocent man might have been sentenced on the false evidence of an evil killer who would have remained at large, free and wealthy. It was impossible to speculate how many other lives might have been saved by Ian's perspicacity. He stretched out in bed, musing on this gratifying aspect of the case as he waited for Bev to bring him breakfast.

Propping himself up against his pillows he gazed hungrily at the tray she was holding: fried egg, crispy toast, fat sausages, beans and a hash brown, along with a steaming mug of coffee and a glass of orange juice.

'That smells damn good!' he grinned.

Placing the tray carefully on the bed, she sat down and twisted round to watch him eat.

'Go on, finish it,' she fussed. 'You need to look after yourself.'

'That's your job,' he smiled as he tucked in.

Her brow creased with faint exasperation at the mention of her job. She hadn't handed in her notice yet.

'What if it doesn't come off and I've already resigned?' she asked.

'It's going ahead all right. It's really happening. Even your mother's accepted we're moving away.'

'But why York?' she asked with a grimace.

He could tell she wasn't really angry.

He finished his breakfast and reached out to hold her hand. Fiddling with her wedding ring, he told her he had another surprise lined up.

'Oh no, not another surprise. I haven't recovered from this one yet.'

'You're going to like this one,' he promised her. 'This one's a very nice surprise.'

'Not another move then?'

'Well, in a way I suppose it is, but it's a temporary move. A very temporary move. I've booked us a holiday. It's a belated honeymoon, because we never had one after the wedding.'

'That's because we put all our money into the house,' she reminded him. That had been her decision, not his.

'Well, now we're having a honeymoon.'

'We can't afford it.'

'That doesn't matter.'

She stared at him, her neatly shaped eyebrows raised.

'We ought to wait, save up –' She fell silent as he shook his head vigorously.

★   ★   ★

He had no words to explain that life was too fragile to waste in waiting for better times that might never come. All that mattered was how they lived each day of their lives.

'You deserve the best honeymoon money can buy,' he said instead, and was rewarded with a smile.

With a surge of joy he knew that he loved his wife. A voice in his head warned him he couldn't keep buying his way into her favour, but he ignored it. Together they would make their marriage work.